T0044500

PRAISE FOR *NEW YORK TIMES* AND *USA TODAY* BESTSELLING AUTHOR ANNE FRASIER

"Frasier has perfected the art of making a reader's skin crawl."

—*Publishers Weekly*

"A master."

—*Star Tribune*

"Anne Frasier delivers thoroughly engrossing, completely riveting suspense."

—Lisa Gardner

"Frasier's writing is fast and furious."

—Jayne Ann Krentz

PRAISE FOR *FOUND OBJECT*

"I LOVED this book! The character development, the plot, the story building—everything was perfect. The story was never short of surprises, and the author kept springing them up at every turn. It is one of the BEST books I've read this year!"

—Goodreads review

"I COULD.NOT.PUT.IT.DOWN! GEEZ! The hits and twists just DID NOT STOP! One right after the other. By the end, I was completely worn out and totally in love with the character of Jupiter and her story. SO hoping for a series with this character. Anne Frasier is a master at tying so many different things together and making it all believable. GREAT atmosphere! I wish I could give more than five stars. I cannot recommend this author enough!"

—Goodreads review

"Anne Frasier did an amazing job of establishing the characters in *Found Object*. Jupiter is witty, Ian is mysterious but loving, and I can picture Marie Nova in all of her glory. She described each scene amazingly, and I felt like I was there in several instances."

—Goodreads review

"A fast-paced book with a satisfying ending. This is the first of Frasier's works that I have read, but it won't be the last."

—Goodreads review

"*Found Object* is an absolutely fantastic read, and I am immediately heading over to fill my Kindle with more of Anne Frasier's books!"

—Goodreads review

"I found this book intriguing, and I finished it the same day I started it, and the ending had me with my mouth dropped open. I will certainly be reading more from this author."

—Goodreads review

"Anne Frasier is new to me, and she is now on my to-be-read list for her other and future books."

—Goodreads review

"Twisted and unpredictable, the story is a wild ride of whodunit and secrets."

—Goodreads review

"Totally gripping, really enjoyed this book, totally recommend."

—Goodreads review

"I'm a huge fan of anything Anne Frasier writes, and this one did not disappoint. Twists and turns that I didn't see coming! This book had me hooked from page 1 to the 'you won't see [it] coming' end!"

—Goodreads review

PRAISE FOR *TELL ME*

"Outstanding! Perfect follow-up to *Find Me*. Equally unputdownable! Good suspense, nice bond developing between Reni and Daniel, plot twists, some expected, some not. One of my favorite things about these two books is the detail in each scene. Perfect, as was the ending. Loved it. I would welcome more Inland Empire series books, but even if there aren't any, these two are perfect as is."

—Amazon reader

"Great read! What a whirlwind of a story! I have to say, Anne Frasier makes you feel things. Her description of Reni's reactions to trauma are amazing. It makes you understand some of the damage that is done to people by the ones we love. I enjoyed the character development and am looking forward to the next installment. Highly recommend."

—Amazon reader

"This two-book series was a fantastic read. As a person who grew up and lived in the areas she based the book on, her descriptions were very accurate. As I read these books, I could envision every area she described. Well-written books. I like books that keep me captivated and have surprise endings. Worth reading again to glean even more clues. Highly recommend. Also, I love how she came to write these two books."

—Amazon reader

"I loved the twists and turns."

—Amazon reader

"Excellent read, Anne doesn't disappoint. Such good characters and suspense. Just when you think it's wrapped up, the floor falls out and you are dropping."

—Amazon reader

"Gripping and suspenseful! I really enjoy this series because you are glued [to it] from page one! The plot is masterfully written and woven together until the end when we find out the truth! Really, these days, I bet this fictional story is closer to truth than ever before!"

—Amazon reader

"Great read! Another great dark story with surprise twists from Anne Frasier. The first book was a bit darker and with a few more shocking twists, but this one has a modern-day topic that makes you think of what could cause people to do extreme things. I love seeing the loose ends tied up. I loved seeing Daniel and Reni work together once again."

—Amazon reader

"Worth the wait! The continuation from *Find Me* was seamless. I've waited over a year to read this book and was not disappointed. I especially love the twists and turns of the storyline. Also that questions were answered without a cliff-hanger ending."

—Amazon reader

PRAISE FOR *FIND ME*

An Amazon Charts number 1 bestseller.

Number 26 Amazon bestseller of 2020.

"An exquisitely crafted thriller. Frasier has outdone herself with this shocker."

—*Publishers Weekly* (starred review)

"For thriller fans who appreciate intricate and unconventional plots, with shocking twists."

—*Library Journal*

PRAISE FOR *THE BODY READER*

Winner of the International Thriller Writers 2017 Thriller Award for Best Paperback Original.

"Absorbing."

—*Publishers Weekly*

"This is an electrifying murder mystery—one of the best of the year."

—Mysterious Reviews

"I see the name Anne Frasier on a book and I know I am in for a treat . . . I thought it was a very unique premise and coupled with the good characters, made for an almost nonstop read for me. I highly recommend this."

—Pure Textuality

"*The Body Reader* earned its five stars, a rarity for me, even for books I like. Kudos to Anne Frasier."

—The Wyrdd and the Bazaar

"A must-read for mystery suspense fans."

—*Babbling About Books*

PRAISE FOR *PLAY DEAD*

"This is a truly creepy and thrilling book. Frasier's skill at exposing the dark emotions and motivations of individuals gives it a gripping edge."

—RT Book Reviews

"*Play Dead* is a compelling and memorable police procedural, made even better by the way the characters interact with one another. Anne Frasier will be appreciated by fans who like Kay Hooper, Iris Johansen, and Lisa Gardner."

—*Blether: The Book Review Site*

"A nicely constructed combination of mystery and thriller. Frasier is a talented writer whose forte is probing into the psyches of her characters, and she produces a fast-paced novel with a finale containing many surprises."

—*I Love a Mystery*

"Has all the essentials of an edge-of-your-seat story. There is suspense, believable characters, an interesting setting, and just the right amount of details to keep the reader's eyes always moving forward . . . I recommend *Play Dead* as a great addition to any mystery library."

—*Roundtable Reviews*

PRAISE FOR *PRETTY DEAD*

"Besides being beautifully written and tightly plotted, this book was that sort of great read you need on a regular basis to restore your faith in a genre."

—Lynn Viehl, *Paperback Writer* (Book of the Month)

"By far the best of the three books. I couldn't put my Kindle down till I'd read every last page."

—NetGalley

PRAISE FOR *HUSH*

"This is by far and away the best serial-killer story I've read in a long time . . . strong characters, with a truly twisted bad guy."

—Jayne Ann Krentz

"I couldn't put it down. Engrossing . . . scary . . . I loved it."

—Linda Howard

"A deeply engrossing read, *Hush* delivers a creepy villain, a chilling plot, and two remarkable investigators whose personal struggles are only equaled by their compelling need to stop a madman before he kills again. Warning: don't read this book if you are home alone."

—Lisa Gardner

"A wealth of procedural detail, a heart-thumping finale, and two scarred but indelible protagonists make this a first-rate read."

—*Publishers Weekly*

"Anne Frasier has crafted a taut and suspenseful thriller."

—Kay Hooper

"Well-realized characters and taut, suspenseful plotting."

—*Minneapolis Star Tribune*

PRAISE FOR *SLEEP TIGHT*

"Guaranteed to keep you awake at night."

—Lisa Jackson

"There'll be no sleeping after reading this one. Laced with forensic detail and psychological twists."

—Andrea Kane

"Gripping and intense . . . Along with a fine plot, Frasier delivers her characters as whole people, each trying to cope in the face of violence and jealousies."

—*Minneapolis Star Tribune*

"Enthralling. There's a lot more to this clever intrigue than graphic police procedures. Indeed, one of Frasier's many strengths is her ability to create characters and relationships that are as compelling as the mystery itself. Will linger with the reader after the killer is caught."

—*Publishers Weekly*

PRAISE FOR *THE ORCHARD*

"Eerie and atmospheric, this is an indie movie in print. You'll read and read to see where it is going, although it's clear early on that the future is not going to be kind to anyone involved. Weir's story is more proof that only love can break your heart."

—*Library Journal*

"A gripping account of divided loyalties, the real cost of farming, and the shattered people on the front lines. Not since Jane Smiley's *A Thousand Acres* has there been so enrapturing a family drama percolating out from the back forty."

—*Maclean's*

"This poignant memoir of love, labor, and dangerous pesticides reveals the terrible true price."

—*O, The Oprah Magazine* (Fall Book Pick)

"Equal parts moving love story and environmental warning."

—*Entertainment Weekly* (B+)

"While reading this extraordinarily moving memoir, I kept remembering the last two lines of Muriel Rukeyser's poem 'Käthe Kollwitz' ('What would happen if one woman told the truth about her life? / The world would split open'), for Weir proffers a worldview that is at once eloquent, sincere, and searing."

—*Library Journal* (Librarians' Best Books of 2011)

"She tells her story with grace, unflinching honesty, and compassion all the while establishing a sense of place and time with a master storyteller's perspective so engaging you forget it is a memoir."

—Calvin Crosby, Books Inc. (Berkeley, CA)

"One of my favorite reads of 2011, *The Orchard* is easily mistakable as a novel for its engaging, page-turning flow and its seemingly imaginative plot."

—Susan McBeth, founder and owner of Adventures by the Book, San Diego, CA

"Moving and surprising."

—The Next Chapter (Fall 2011 Top 20 Best Books)

"Searing . . . the past is artfully juxtaposed with the present in this finely wrought work. Its haunting passages will linger long after the last page is turned."

—*Boston Globe* (Pick of the Week)

"If a writing instructor wanted an excellent example of voice in a piece of writing, this would be a five-star choice!"

—*San Diego Union-Tribune* (Recommended Read)

"This book produced a string of emotions that had my hand flying up to my mouth time and again, and not only made me realize, 'This woman can write!' but also made me appreciate the importance of this book, and how it reaches far beyond Weir's own story."

—Linda Grana, Diesel, a Bookstore

"*The Orchard* is a lovely book in all the ways that really matter, one of those rare and wonderful memoirs in which people you've never met become your friends."

—Nicholas Sparks

"A hypnotic tale of place, people, and of midwestern family roots that run deep, stubbornly hidden, and equally menacing."

—Jamie Ford, *New York Times* bestselling author of *Hotel on the Corner of Bitter and Sweet*

THE
NIGHT
I DIED

THE
NIGHT
I DIED

ANNE FRASIER

This is a work of fiction. Names, characters, organizations, places, events, and incidents are either products of the author's imagination or are used fictitiously. Otherwise, any resemblance to actual persons, living or dead, is purely coincidental.

Text copyright © 2023 by Theresa Weir
All rights reserved.

No part of this book may be reproduced, or stored in a retrieval system, or transmitted in any form or by any means, electronic, mechanical, photocopying, recording, or otherwise, without express written permission of the publisher.

Published by Thomas & Mercer, Seattle

www.apub.com

Amazon, the Amazon logo, and Thomas & Mercer are trademarks of Amazon.com, Inc., or its affiliates.

ISBN-13: 9781542036429 (paperback)
ISBN-13: 9781542036436 (digital)

Cover design by Damon Freeman

Cover image: © E.J. Miles / Arcangel

Printed in the United States of America

THE
NIGHT
I DIED

1

Private investigator Olivia Welles had died five times so far in her life.
The first happened on a dark night in Kansas when she was a kid. The
others took place on the operating table over the years. Five deaths were
nothing, really. And, at her current age of thirty-eight, she figured she
might have a few more left in her. Could she break the record? Doubtful.
She'd found a man in the UK who'd died thirty-two times. *Thirty-two*.
That research led her down a rabbit hole of actors and actresses who'd
met their makers on-screen.

Shelley Winters, twenty times.

Julianne Moore, seventeen.

Sigourney Weaver, twelve.

Dying was no big deal in either real or pretend life.

Olivia's assistant, Ezra Tobias Rafael III, had died twice, both of
those from a heroin overdose. He tried to claim a third, the time he got
a Skittle stuck in his throat and dropped straight to his knees, unable
to breathe. But she'd pointed out that his heart hadn't stopped beating
before she'd performed the Heimlich maneuver. *Almost* dying didn't
count. It was all about flatlining. And being *pronounced* dead? That gave
a person some serious dead cred.

She hurried down the steps of her bungalow, a rolled mat tucked
under her arm. Venice Beach and morning yoga awaited a few miles
away. When Ezra found the class and signed her up, they'd both laughed

about how California the idea of beach yoga was, yet she was surprisingly looking forward to it. She needed a mental break. The past year hadn't been an easy one. Both her father and her black Lab had died within months of each other. She wasn't sure which hurt the most. It should have been her father, but if she were honest, it was her sweet Lab and companion of nine years. She'd named him Cecil Hotel after working a case there and finding him in a trash container, just a puppy. Many people didn't understand the bone-deep level of grief that came with the loss of a pet of any kind. The bond, the years, that friend living your various lives right alongside you. Then gone.

Her phone rang.

She should let it go to voicemail. This was her time, her day, but years in the detective business made ignoring a call a hard thing to do. She pulled out her phone and checked the screen.

Finney County Jail, Kansas

Her stomach dropped.

It wasn't unusual for her to get calls from jails and prisons, but this was the first time she'd gotten one from Kansas. Uncomfortable with the idea of talking to a potential client on the sidewalk, she turned and strode back to the house, dreading the discovery of the name of the person on the other end while also having a good idea who it was.

"Hello?" Olivia said.

No response. She kept walking.

Olivia and Kansas had a history. Which was especially odd since she could recall nothing of the time she'd lived there as a child. Didn't matter. Kansas was an undeniable part of her. She felt branded by it—some strange place she couldn't recall. While her first memories were of California, there had always been something inside that felt incomplete, the pull of a darker, unknown land and an unknown history and legacy.

Something more of the earth, deep, that harkened back to her ancestors, of whom she knew little about.

Kansas held the allure of an unremembered loss. Her inability to recall any of it made it even more mysterious, almost mythical. A life she'd heard about, read about, but one that didn't seem real. If not for her damaged and repaired body, along with yet another surgery scheduled, she'd have no proof the car-train collision had ever really happened. Just a story. But it *had* happened, and it had destroyed her father, who'd been the town coroner at the time. How horrible to have gone to the site to find his own family there. It was the thing nightmares were made of. Her mother had lived a week. Sometimes Olivia wondered if that had made it worse. Maybe it would have been better if she'd died immediately.

"You're lucky you don't remember any of it, peanut," her father used to say. "It's a blessing."

In the today world of Venice, California, she unlocked the door, turned off the alarm, and dropped her yoga mat. In the privacy and quiet of her home, she said hello again, and this time someone replied. A soft female voice.

"Olivia? Is this Olivia Welles?"

"Yes. Can I help you?"

"This is Bonnie. Bonnie Ray."

Another stomach plunge.

Kansas was known for a lot of things. The Dust Bowl. Vast wheat and sunflower fields. *The Wizard of Oz*. But it was also known for various horrifying murders.

You had the Truman Capote *In Cold Blood* killings, and those weren't even the worst in Kansas history. There were the Bloody Benders, a family that had owned an inn and murdered tourists. And you had BTK (Bind, Torture, Kill). Now there was Bonnie Ray-Murphy and the Murphy children. The death tally was up to three, the most recent having happened just last week. The main suspect was the mother, the woman calling from jail.

"My mom always talks about how smart you are whenever you're in the news," Bonnie said. "I seen the stuff about how you proved that woman innocent when everybody thought she done it, thought she killed that guy."

It was easy to guess the motive behind the call. Bonnie's sister had been Olivia's best friend, and they'd all three been in that wreck together. It was probably hard to find much support when the whole world thought you were guilty of killing your own children.

"You have to help me," Bonnie pleaded. "Please. I can't afford to pay you much, and I'm not smart like you. I didn't even graduate from high school."

Pregnant and married at seventeen, if Olivia remembered right.

Olivia had a box of yellowed newspaper clippings about the wreck that she'd saved over the years. Because her father hadn't talked about it, she'd had to look beyond him for information and read what she could find where she could find it. That was probably where her interest in detective work began. Digging up anything and everything on the event. Old archived articles and newer ones whenever some journalist decided to write about it again. And it was impossible to forget it when Bonnie Ray's children kept dying. That tended to keep someone in the news.

Olivia had no personal memory of Bonnie, but she knew she'd been there that day, and she knew Bonnie and Bonnie's mother had walked away from the wreck. Bonnie had only been four or five, and a dog had finally found her in a nearby wheat field.

Olivia glanced at the mat she'd dropped on the floor. She thought about how she'd been looking forward to beach yoga. She thought about how her father hadn't wanted her to return to Kansas. She wanted to respect his wishes. She thought about how he was gone now.

Kansas.

Three of Bonnie Ray's children were dead. It shouted Munchausen syndrome. People tended to think of Munchausen as a parent who injured or poisoned a child to get attention, but they also killed for the same reasons. Sympathy and money. Bonnie had gotten off for the other children. Not enough evidence, but now a third made it seem especially damning. It was hard for Olivia to wrap her head around the murder of innocent children, no matter the case. The murder of several just made her brain refuse to go there completely.

"This is going to sound harsh, but I don't take cases I don't believe in," Olivia said. "I don't take cases where I'm not on my client's side from the beginning."

Bonnie was quiet for so long Olivia thought maybe she'd disconnected. She imagined her sitting or standing near one of the jail phones and gently putting the receiver back in the cradle. But then her voice returned, timid, sad, wistful, and reflective.

"Do you ever think you're a ghost?" she asked.

"Ghost?"

"Yeah. Like we both should've died that day. There's no reason we survived. And you did die. That's what I heard."

How often had Olivia contemplated the very thing Bonnie was talking about? That this life wasn't real? She tried not to think about it. When her thoughts went there, she'd redirect, think of something else. Was she in a coma? Was this her coma world? Had the wreck happened days ago? Months ago? Years ago? She'd known a few people who'd awakened after being in a coma for a few days, and they said they'd lived a whole life in there while they were gone.

Bonnie was still talking. "And instead we're just living a life that shouldn't exist. Like we're in the wrong world now. And you know what else?" Her voice dropped to a whisper, and Olivia imagined her cupping her hand near the phone.

"They haven't told me anything. Could you come and just tell me if my youngest, my baby, is still alive? Her name's Calliope. Calliope

Ava Murphy," Bonnie said. "Ava, after my mom. Nobody will tell me if she's alive or dead." She started crying, and the sound was the most heartbreaking thing Olivia had ever heard. Her pain, the pain of losing her children, was real whether she'd done it or not. Olivia imagined Bonnie begging for information and everyone ignoring her, thinking she didn't deserve to know.

The woman was a monster, Olivia told herself. And yet . . . It seemed morbid to want to return to Finney. But she'd always, in the back of her mind, thought of going there, seeing if any of it felt familiar.

So far she'd had a total of twenty-two surgeries. She'd hoped she was done, but then the headaches started. With this upcoming surgery, she'd been told her chances of surviving weren't good. She tried to tell herself that under anesthesia she'd just go to sleep and never wake up. Didn't seem that bad. Without the operation, she'd definitely die. Kansas seemed like a good way to avoid dying a little while longer. A way to put it off and make that visit before her last and final death.

"Please come," Bonnie whispered in one final attempt to sway Olivia. "I'm a good person, a good mother. I don't think I could have killed my own child. I need help, and nobody here is helping me. Please. I'm begging you. One ghost to another."

2

Grandma Darby used to say people love you till they don't. Bonnie never fully understood what her grandmother had meant by that until she got older, until she learned about it firsthand.

Right now, in the early morning, so early the birds were still singing their specific morning songs and dew was still heavy on the grass, Bonnie Ray-Murphy sat at the kitchen table in the farmhouse she shared with her husband. He was the town marshal, and she was proud of him. *Bloom where you're planted.* They both believed that, and he proved people could stay in their hometown and still make something of themselves.

For Bonnie, mornings were the hardest. She'd learned that too well from past tragedies and loss. Going to sleep, dreaming of happier days, waking up to find the children gone. Living that reality over and over again.

Bonnie's baby, little Calliope, was nursing at her breast. A window was open, the curtain billowing in a comforting way, and Bonnie could feel the sweet breeze on her hot skin. A perfect June day. Or should have been. Could have been.

From off in the far distance came a sound she also found comforting. A tractor was moving back and forth across a field. Occasionally, that soft early-morning breeze would bring the hint of freshly cut alfalfa inside. Alfalfa that would be loaded onto semis and hauled to areas of the country that couldn't grow what they could grow here in Kansas. Kansas was special.

The table in front of her was loaded with all the goodies brought by kind, supportive, and concerned neighbors. Cakes and breads and plates of cookies. The refrigerator was filled with more casseroles than a family could eat in a month. Proof they'd loved her yesterday.

The baby quit nursing, and Bonnie noticed with vague surprise that the child was sleeping now, mouth open, milk running down her cheek, hair wet from sweat, cheeks flushed. So innocent, so unaware of all the bad in the world, the reason for the table of food.

With a soft cotton cloth, like a good mom, Bonnie wiped the milk from the infant's cheek. Then she buttoned her shirt, got to her feet, and took the sleeping child upstairs.

Time was irrelevant, as it always became during these sad days. She was unsure how long she stayed upstairs, trying to find solace in the familiar, looking for answers within her own mind, staring at the wall, staring out the window that needed to be washed, staring at the baby in her crib. At some point, she went back downstairs.

She glanced at the food again, most of it homemade. The thought of eating any of it made her feel queasy. She spotted a few packaged cookies.

Henry would like those. But then she remembered Henry was dead.

Yesterday and the day before, neighbors had come with tears in their eyes, hugging her. But even before they'd scurried back to their parked trucks and cars, she'd seen the suspicious glances they'd shot at one another.

Henry was number three.

How did a mother lose three children and not have something to do with it? Of course they were suspicious. Of course they talked about her behind her back. They'd done so for years, but they were the only community she had, and she still drew strength from them. Her family had quite the history, and some people who might have always thought she was guilty of killing her own children defended her with words like *After all she's gone through* and *That kind of thing scars a person for life* or *She could never be normal after that.*

She was four, almost five, when the first bad thing happened. That seemed too young to remember the tragedy in such detail, but she still had vivid dreams of being inside the car and feeling the impact of the train hitting them. The deafening screams and shriek of metal, the car shoved sideways down the track, sparks flying until the vehicle began to roll and tumble, finally landing upside down in a field. It was amazing anybody had lived, because most people didn't survive car-train collisions. That's what she'd been told.

When the movement and the screaming stopped, she had become aware of the pain from her seat restraints. And the continuous blare of the train horn. Later someone said it got stuck somehow during the impact, creating that one deafening note that filled the world, a single headlight from the broken train engine shining into the car, illuminating the interior.

She was hanging upside down in her car seat. It might have been the seat that saved her. That was something else people said. She was more protected than the others.

Bonnie had unfastened the latch and dropped straight down to the car's ceiling. Her sister and Olivia were above her, arms dangling, blood dripping, faces and bodies smashed.

But how could she remember that? How was it so vivid? Had she overheard adult conversations?

She'd crawled out the shattered window, cutting her arms and legs on broken glass. The train horn, the light, someone in the field walking away. Her mother. It was her mother, wasn't it?

Bonnie had followed her across the field.

She'd heard the story and theories of how she ended up in the middle of a wheat field so many times that she was sure it was a borrowed memory, not hers.

What she did know was that she'd been missing for forty hours. A dog found her, licked her face, whined and whimpered, sat down, whimpered more, and the search team came running. They said her mother had walked away and just kept walking because her brain was messed up, either from shock or the blow it took. When Papa discovered her safe at home, her hands and feet were blue and ice-cold, and she was shaking so hard she'd broken a front tooth that, to this day, was still chipped.

When they found Bonnie, she had a medallion on her cheek. It was one of the necklaces the girls had bought at the state fair. A cheap souvenir from a vending machine, the jewelry gold-plated. That year the fair had used an image of Dorothy and Toto from *The Wizard of Oz* for all the signs and advertising.

Bonnie was red and blistered from the sun, but under the token, her skin had been burned so deep from the searing metal that it left a round scar. She called it her real souvenir.

When she was still little, she'd imagined Dorothy and Toto living somewhere under her cheek, under her skin. She'd liked to think of them there.

Back then, Bonnie had heard the sound of the moving wheat above her head, kind of a shushing noise, as if the world was telling her to be quiet and stay hidden. She'd watched the curved strands for so long she went sun blind. Even in her adult life, whenever the wheat fields moved a certain way and the wind drew a gentle pattern in the grain, a path that could lead to or from, just like the yellow brick road, Bonnie could easily find that day in her mind.

After being rescued, she couldn't see anything for a long time. It was called solar keratitis. She eventually recovered, although her night vision was bad. But with deeper understanding, she realized the crash had made her into a special kind of human who saw things in a way most people didn't. She understood that the opposite of tragedy was joy. The opposite of light was dark. The opposite of life was death. Death was not the enemy, not a bad thing. It could be good. It could be your friend.

Of the five in the car, three survived. Her mother; her sister's best friend, Olivia Welles; and herself.

And now Bonnie's sweet little boy had been found . . . How long ago had that been? Days? Hours? Yesterday? Last night?

Unlike thirty years ago, news traveled faster today. Once Henry had been reported missing—Had she reported it or had her husband? Her mother?—a search was launched, and Bonnie had remained near the scanner for several days. She'd hardly slept, wasn't sure if she showered, couldn't eat any of the food brought to them, although her husband, Conrad, forced himself to eat, running off to vomit after. And all the while, the squawk of the scanner played like a soundtrack in the background.

She knew the codes and knew when they'd found someone.

After that (Last night? This morning? Yesterday?), her phone began blowing up with texts. The messages came from a bunch of women in a craft group called Old Wives Tales, even though most of the members were in their thirties. Bonnie hadn't actively participated in the group for a long time. She'd thought of just quietly leaving, but instead, a year or two ago, she'd changed her profile name so nobody realized she was even in the group anymore. No idea why she did that. She did a lot of things she didn't understand.

Once the messages started coming in, Bonnie had to look. One of the women was married to another policeman in town. She posted all the details about the dead boy in the thread.

It only took one person to get the word out. An hour later, Bonnie could practically feel the information flying between cell phones.

A child had been found in an old well.

Of course it was Bonnie's child. No other child was missing. And yet she hoped it was some other poor child.

The women in the group started talking about her. About how she probably did it. Some of them were the very people who'd brought food.

Always figured she'd killed her own kids.

Oh, I know! The way she would act whenever it came up.

And then it suddenly went silent. Someone must have realized Bonnie could read the thread and had alerted the others. She imagined them freaking out, sending side texts to one another.

Her phone rang, and she answered.

It was her mother, poor thing. Of course her mother would have heard the news. Bonnie felt especially bad about that. So many deaths in their family already. Sometimes it felt like she was wading in dead bodies.

Her mother asked about Calliope. "Where is the baby? Is she there with you?"

"I have to go."

"Wait!"

Bonnie ended the call.

She could hear sirens. Not a memory but real time. Why turn them on at all? It made her wonder if they were trying to give her a chance to run. Or maybe it was an announcement to the community.

We've got her this time! It's something we should have done years ago.

She *could* run. Just race out the door and jump in the car. But that would be silly, especially when she'd always known this day was coming. Really, it was a relief.

She could also get the gun from upstairs, just end it all, stop the pain, stop the public shaming. But she wouldn't do that either. The baby was up there. She couldn't go back up there.

Instead, she slipped on the shoes she'd left near the door. Serviceable tennis shoes, stained with mud from the nearby field. Maybe that had happened when she'd gone to look for little missing Henry? Or had she led him out there? Had she taken him to the open well?

She bent over and tied her shoes. When she straightened, a wave of dizziness hit her, and she had to grab at the wall. Once the world righted itself, she made her way outside, the screen door slamming behind her.

It might have been a sound she was hearing for the last time.

She sat down on the porch, her feet on a bowed wooden step.

The land was so level here. Hardly a tree. Not another house. Just fields and fields for miles and miles. The only things to break the horizon were grain elevators in the town several miles away. They looked like robots, something alive, watching over all of them, moving them to their will. The huge space between her and them was both frightening and comforting.

Three police cars were heading her direction.

They passed the one single tree in the vastness of her vision, slowed for the railroad tracks, *those* railroad tracks.

The accident hadn't happened nearby, but she thought of the tracks like an umbilical cord, something carrying blood all the way to their property while the grain elevators watched and waited and seemed pleased by all they surveyed.

The police cars were on the gravel road now, traveling too fast. The racing tires created clouds of dust even though it had rained two days ago. Even though her shoes were muddy. The town of Finney only had two squad cars; at least one must have been the county sheriff.

They turned down the dirt lane and completed the half-mile stretch, fanning out in the grass, pulling to such abrupt stops they all lurched. Doors flew open, men and women got out. Her husband, Conrad, was there, and she could feel his discomfort. He hitched his pants and belt and started moving straight for her.

"Where's the baby?" he shouted. "Where's Calliope?"

The baby.

She pressed her hand tightly to her mouth to hide what she was afraid might be a smile. She didn't even glance toward the house. She got to her feet and began walking toward her husband's squad car. Someone put handcuffs on her. Oh, that was Darlene.

"Hi, Darlene."

The female cop said nothing.

Bonnie had suspected her husband of having an affair with Darlene. But then again, he liked 'em younger.

Darlene walked Bonnie to the nearest squad car and put her inside, pushing her head down. Once the door was shut, Bonnie looked out the window.

So much drama.

Her husband was gone, maybe in the house.

Now that she was locked up, the cops, four in all, stood in the front yard, as if they were waiting for something. News, bad news.

Finally, her husband stepped out the door.

Despite Darlene, he was a good man. He'd been a good husband. Not one she'd rate five stars, but a solid four.

As she watched through the dusty window of the squad car, she saw all the officers turn and begin moving toward the house, almost like something planned, choreographed, from the way they each had one hand on their gun and the way they had the same long stride, legs moving them forward even though the house was the last place they wanted to go.

She thought about the upstairs nursery, about how the morning breeze had lifted the thin white curtain, making it billow in a sweet hello or goodbye.

Now her husband was outside, holding a bundle in his arms. Baby Calliope. He was sobbing and shouting. Was he happy to find her alive and well? Or sad to find her dead, like the other children?

Mothers protected children, but Bonnie couldn't seem to protect hers. How did a person do that? Keep them safe?

Wrap them up? Lock them up? Just make them stop? Stop growing? Breathing? Being?

It was so hard to say. Bonnie didn't understand how that worked, but the words of Grandma Darby came back, with a different and more current spin.

Children are alive till they aren't. Just the way it is.

3

Thirty hours after Bonnie Ray-Murphy's phone call, Olivia was heading for the airport.

One thing most decent private investigators had in common was curiosity. It was almost mandatory if a person wanted to stay in the business. Even without her own Kansas history, Olivia would have been intrigued by the case.

She had a lot of ideas, a lot of possible hidden reasons behind the call, the biggest being Bonnie's mental state. Olivia wasn't a psychiatrist, and she certainly couldn't diagnose anybody, but she planned to talk to Bonnie and get a read on her. Could be she was guilty. But the other thing that Olivia hadn't really contemplated until the call—what if she was innocent?

Ezra hadn't been happy to hear Olivia's plans. But he wasn't so annoyed that he'd refused to give her a ride to the airport. Right now, they were on the 90 heading for the 405. It was a less congested but indirect route. If they didn't hit any snags, she should make her flight.

"Thought you were gonna chill for a couple of weeks, hang out on the beach, maybe meet someone special," he said.

"Like a dog?" Ezra had wanted Olivia to replace her old Lab immediately. Olivia needed more time.

"I mean like a man. Or woman. But a dog. Yeah, that's good too. I sent you links to some cute rescues."

"I won't be gone long, and I can relax when I get back."

"I know nothin' about Kansas. I don't even know where it is. Like maybe near other states I know nothing about. It's somewhere in the middle, right?"

"Yeah."

"I'm going to keep sending you links to dogs."

"That's fine." But she wasn't weakening. The grief of losing Cecil had lasted months now, and she was beginning to think it might go on for years. And maybe Ezra knew that and thought a new dog would help.

Ezra was a good kid. *Kid.* He wasn't a kid. He'd soon be twenty, but still a kid in her book. Emotionally, he was immature. But handsome and he knew it. That alone could get a person in trouble.

"I want you in the office from nine to four every day, even if I'm not going to be there."

"You don't have to babysit me."

"Oh, I do. For now. I trust you, but not one hundred percent. Not yet. But we'll get there."

His mother was in prison for killing her boyfriend. Low-income single mom, someone who had easily slipped through the cracks. Olivia had taken Ezra's mother's case because it was one of those horrendous domestic-abuse situations. Her boyfriend had been using Ezra to deliver drugs, and she blew up when she found out. She'd killed him, but it wasn't technically self-defense.

Her initial story was that someone else had done it, and she wanted Olivia to find that person. Olivia had been skeptical, and it quickly became apparent the woman was lying. Once she was incarcerated, she asked Olivia to find her son. And she did find him. Methed out in a homeless encampment in Skid Row, one of the worst areas of LA.

That had been three years ago, and during that time he'd gotten his GED, met a stable girl, was taking night classes, and found he had real talent for organization and research. He'd been working for Olivia for the past year, and lately he'd been talking about becoming a detective himself.

She'd plucked him from some very dire stuff, and his mother believed he wouldn't be alive if Olivia hadn't gotten him out of there. Olivia wasn't sure about that, but she was confident he'd be in a much worse place today if she hadn't intervened.

Even she sometimes marveled at how it had played out. She'd walked into the drug den, stepped over sleeping and passed-out bodies to reach Ezra. She'd grabbed him by the ear, tugged him to his feet, said something about his mama being in prison for him, and then pulled him out of that place while twenty druggies watched, some laughing, some clapping, some not even noticing. In truth, she'd wished she could help them all, but there was a limit to what she could do.

Ezra pulled up to the loading and unloading zone. They both got out and circled to the back of the car. He lifted her suitcase from the trunk, put it on the ground, and she extended the handle with a satisfying click. Then he passed the locked black hard-shell gun case to her. She'd need to declare it at the check-in counter. "You really think you'll need this?"

"Hopefully not." It did seem like too much, and it wasn't her style. But . . . Kansas. The word itself felt threatening.

When it seemed like he might hug her, she almost panicked. After a moment they both laughed, then he told her goodbye, ran around the car, and blasted away.

He was one of those people who could hurt you. She understood that. If he tripped up, stumbled back, if he returned to being that other Ezra, the one she'd found in Skid Row. He was clean now, but if he relapsed, he'd do whatever he could to get his fix. She'd dealt with addicts, and she knew that the people they cared about were not a priority when it came to getting whatever they needed to stay high. She didn't like leaving him on his own even for a few days. She made a mental note to keep in touch with him daily, maybe even surprise him with annoying FaceTime calls. She wished he could stay at her house when she was gone, but she didn't trust him enough. Not yet.

She couldn't imagine being a mother. So much worry even in the best of circumstances. That's why it was especially impossible to comprehend mothers who killed. Did some do it just to stop the pain of motherhood?

Taking the alternate route meant they'd arrived later than anticipated. Inside the airport, the flight display screen indicated her plane would be boarding soon. She got in line and checked her luggage, then placed her weapon case on the counter and declared it. The process always attracted unwanted attention.

Passengers on both sides of her were staring. People in line were staring. A guy clutching a book was staring. And not just any book. A hardcover. It used to be over half the people traveling had a book in their hand. Nowadays it was unusual to see someone with a real paper book.

She'd noticed him moments earlier because, until the interruption, he'd been so engrossed in the pages in front of him that he'd seemed totally unaware of his surroundings. Which had made her wonder *what* he was reading. His luggage looked like something from the forties, as well as the brown leather briefcase he was carrying. He had long dark hair, slightly curly, and he was sporting one of those shirts with the straight tail and some embroidery. Like something you might find in a place like Cuba or Florida. Beige cargo pants and leather sandals completed the ensemble. Now she could see the hardcover title and she was more intrigued. *In Cold Blood* by Truman Capote, a story she'd been thinking about since the call from prison, and a book she'd uploaded to her Kindle last night. The tale was based on the real-life Clutter family murders that took place in Holcomb, Kansas, not all that far from Finney, her destination.

Journalist or wannabe journalist, she guessed. The clothing and the luggage seemed to borrow from several famous people. Hemingway, Truman Capote, Hunter Thompson.

She continued her interaction with the counter agent, and when she glanced up again, she saw the guy was holding the book open with both hands, as if not wanting to lose his place while he looked at Olivia with a hard-to-pin-down expression.

Did she know him from somewhere? It was always surprising how small LA really was. She seemed to be constantly seeing some of the same people in various places, almost as if they were characters assigned to move through her particular scene. Or maybe he'd seen the Discovery Channel thing. She couldn't even bring herself to think of *that* title in the silence of her own head.

The agent handed the ID back to her, along with her luggage-claim stickers. "Gate 14B, Terminal 8."

Olivia thanked her and headed through the maze that was LAX. Unfortunately, she'd allowed her TSA PreCheck status to lapse. That meant she had to go through the regular security line. Something stressful for everybody, but especially stressful for her.

She removed her belt, black leather jacket, and black boots. Her watch too, leaving her in faded jeans, an old black T-shirt that was beginning to reach the end of its life span, and white socks. She knew they'd make her go through the detector regardless of what she told them, and a doctor's letter wasn't enough anymore.

As expected, she set off the alert.

She was ushered to the side, where a blonde woman in a blue uniform told her to stand on the worn footprints on the floor and hold out both arms. The agent passed a wand under Olivia's arms, then down her legs.

"I have a metal plate in my head."

Olivia didn't like to talk about it, didn't like to think about it, certainly didn't like to explain to people how it had happened, but the reminders were always there, regardless. The chill of the blasting air conditioner in a car. The biting wind on the beach, her face and the side of her head suddenly cold to the touch.

As a kid, she'd gotten a buzz out of entertaining classmates by putting magnetic letters on her face. There had always been some question as to whether her plate contained enough of the right kind of metal to achieve such a feat. Some said she just had sticky skin. Hadn't really mattered to her, because either way she'd accomplished the task.

Her first-grade teacher hadn't been happy about the letter thing and had called her dad. He thought it was funny, especially when he found out what she'd spelled. S-H-I-T.

The woman continued to move the wand, down Olivia's body now. More alerts.

Because the plate was such a big deal, Olivia tended to forget she had metal in other places.

"You're going to have to step into a room for a full inspection."

Olivia had once thought about legally changing her name, the idea being that she'd yearned to start over and didn't want people to know who she was. She'd wanted the questions to stop. *How did it feel to die? How did it feel to be one of the only survivors of a lethal crash? How did it feel to lose your best friend? How did it feel to lose your mother in the wreck? How did it feel to get hit by a train?*

But then she'd realized most people weren't even interested in her story. Nobody had cared much beyond those first few years when it was on the news. People died in train-car collisions. It was just another kind of tragedy, and it didn't really interest anybody beyond the little town in Kansas where it happened. Yet here she was, being interrogated in the way she didn't like to be interrogated. Under literally bright lights, but also by the extreme scrutiny of strangers. *Where was she going? Why was she going?* All presented as casual conversation that was not casual in any way.

"How do you end up with so much metal in you?" the woman asked.

"I was in a car accident."

It was what she always said. Mentioning the train took it to a whole other, invasive level.

"That had to be tough."

"I was a kid. I don't remember it."

"I guess that's good."

"Guess so."

The agent was holding Olivia's driver's license. She looked from it to Olivia a few times.

Olivia felt insecure about her face. People stared, and she worried there was something wrong with it that she couldn't see or that her mind just blocked out. Or something people were too polite to mention. And it wasn't just adults who stared. Kids did too.

Doctors had assured her that the facial reconstruction she'd had over the years had resulted in a good job. Not perfectly symmetrical, but no face was, and perfection itself would look odd. They'd even done a good job with the scars, which were only noticeable in certain light that illuminated her from the side. But she swore people could tell. They knew she was different. Somehow, they knew.

"I'm always changing my hair," Olivia said. Right now it was a deep red. She'd cut it short in preparation for her surgery. She wasn't sure if they'd shave her entire head, but this would make it easier for them and for her to transition, if need be.

"It's not that," the agent said. "I can tell it's you, but you look older in person. Usually it's the other way around. I mean a *lot* older, and it was only taken two years ago. Honestly, I'm not sure red goes that well with your pale complexion. I used to be a stylist, and I think the dark brown was working for you." She passed the ID back.

Olivia stuck it in the pocket of her jeans. "Been a tough two years." The past year, with her father dying and her not being there to tell him goodbye, not even knowing until he was gone, along with her poor dog requiring so much care . . . The roller coaster of Cecil's good days and bad, of deciding it was time, of changing her mind. Over and over, day in and day out, until the hour to let her best friend go arrived. It had taken a toll.

"Love your tattoo," the agent said, redirecting her comments to something she might have hoped was more positive.

Olivia lifted her arm and looked, as if she'd never seen the large octopus tattoo before. It was purple and black and covered her arm from shoulder to elbow. She'd always loved octopuses.

She suddenly realized they weren't done with her. Her gun case was in the room, closed, in the middle of a long table. Another agent, a guy, stood nearby, looking as if he wanted to get this over with as much as Olivia did.

"We were able to pull your luggage," the female agent explained. "We inspected your suitcase, but this is locked, as it should be."

"I declared and checked it," Olivia said.

"I'm going to need the key."

She dug out her keys and stepped forward to unlock the hard-shell case.

"Stay back," the woman said.

Olivia handed her the key chain with her business logo. A silhouette of a woman with a gun, under it a movie-style font that said *Have Gun, Will Travel.* It had been kind of a joke that had long ago gone sour.

Her case contained more than just weapons. It held surveillance equipment, including her binoculars and telephoto lens. She'd considered not bringing them, but in the end she'd just grabbed everything and anything she might want or need at a crime scene. She wasn't even sure why she'd brought the surveillance stuff since she didn't plan on being in Kansas long. But the two handguns got the biggest reaction from the agent. A Glock 19 and her little Smith & Wesson M&P Bodyguard 380.

"You in trouble? Running from somebody?"

"No."

She felt vulnerable. Not because of the guns, but because her secrets had been exposed in front of the agent and all those people out there, some who were watching through the window. She didn't like to be reminded of how she'd been put back together with metal parts and metal screws and plastic and even cadavers. She didn't like to think about the metal plate in her head that held her brain in place. She still had nightmares about the thing falling out and having to crawl around on the floor searching for it.

"A female with two guns is either running away or toward something."

Olivia looked at the weapons. "It's a little much, I can see that now. I packed quickly and couldn't decide." She really liked her Bodyguard 380, but the Glock had a better balance and feel. More accurate too.

"So you just brought them both." She shook her head. "Kinda like me and shoes."

"That's basically it. I'm a private detective. I'm the person on the key chain. That's my logo. 'Have gun, will travel.'"

The other agent smirked a little, probably because anybody could call themselves a private detective. Olivia really wished there was some kind of license a person needed to actually hang a shingle, but there wasn't. California had a special permit a person could get. It took work, and she'd earned her certification, but many didn't bother, because it was hard and expensive.

The agent closed and snapped the case shut, locked it, handed the key back. "You're free to go." Then she stared some more, but this stare was different from the earlier one.

"Wait!" Her expression bloomed, changing from deadpan to interested. "You were on that show. What was it?" Finger snap. "*Private Dick Chick!*"

Agreeing to that Discovery Channel thing—what had she been thinking? Olivia liked to believe she was beyond being swayed by flattery and money, but the producers had come at her with both, and she'd caved. Six episodes that aired two years ago and that she hadn't been able to watch even though colleagues had assured her they hadn't been *that* bad.

The first title suggestion had been *Chick with a Gun*. Olivia protested, and the title became *Chick Dick*. She complained about that, made some other suggestions, and it became *Private Dick Chick*. She asked if they could go back to *Chick with a Gun*, but by that time the team had moved on while also applauding the removal of the word *gun*.

Why hadn't she insisted upon title approval? She kept telling herself nobody was going to watch something that sounded so lowbrow, and she'd been told it had drawn a small audience. She hadn't asked what "small" was.

Way to remain under the radar, Welles.

Olivia started to apologize for the existence of such a horrendous title when the agent broke in.

"I loved that show! Loved it! I was home with the flu and watched all six episodes. I was sad when it was over. I sure hope you're going to make another season."

"No, probably not."

She felt the woman wanted to say more, maybe even apologize, but, thankfully, TSA agents had to stick to the script.

4

Some people didn't like to fly because it meant relinquishing control while in the sky. Olivia actually liked to fly for that very reason. Zero control, nothing was expected of her, and there was absolutely nothing she could do about the flight. She considered it her extreme version of unplugging.

This particular airline was newish, trying to fill a lack of nonstop flights to smaller cities. It was the only one she'd been able to find that would land her within driving distance of Finney. Once they were in the air, the pilot announced the flight would take three hours.

Over the years, she'd traveled quite a bit for her job, her skill garnering her the attention of people who could afford to fly her in and put her up for weeks and months at a time. But she'd never really visited the Midwest, unless Chicago counted. On the way, as they got closer to the airport located in Garden City, Kansas, traveling at a lower altitude, clouds above them, she marveled at how vast and unbroken and just plain bleak and barren it looked from above. Would it be worse on the ground?

Garden City Regional Airport was small, which meant a quick landing. No circling, no waiting for their turn at the runway. Once the wheels were on solid ground, the pilot announced the time and temperature and told people to leave their seat belts fastened. That resulted in a flurry of subtle and not-so-subtle metal-against-metal sounds of belts being unfastened. As they taxied to their gate, Olivia checked her phone. She had two messages from Ezra. Both were links to dogs.

She also had a voicemail from her doctor.

I got to the office today and found out you cancelled your surgery. I don't think I need to tell you how important it is that you get this done sooner rather than later. I want you to call the office and reschedule. I'll try to work you in as close to the original date as possible, but I can't promise.

Olivia might call and tell them not to rebook.

They disembarked.

She spotted the guy with the copy of *In Cold Blood*. With a jolt of surprise, she realized he'd been on her flight. As the crowd around the luggage carousel grew, she noted that his beige pants were frayed at the hems. He seemed a little nervous, kept looking at his watch and checking his phone. She hoped he wasn't there to write a piece on the Murphy killings.

She'd bet he was.

The conveyor belt began to move, and luggage began to appear. In Cold Blood grabbed a leather suitcase, checked the tag, and vanished into the crowd. She waited, and waited some more. Fifteen minutes passed. Then the conveyor belt and ceiling lights were shut off by some mysterious and unknown hand. There was no sign of her bags.

Off in one corner, looking nondescript and like something nobody was supposed to find or notice, she discovered a lonely looking door with a sign that said LOST LUGGAGE. She knocked. After a few minutes, a woman poked her head out. Olivia held up her claim tickets. The woman took them, vanished, returned. "Your luggage was flagged in LA and put in another area of the cargo hold. We just found it."

At least it had arrived.

Out of habit, she thanked the person even though she didn't feel thankful, then followed the signs to the only car-rental counter in the airport. She had to ring a bell, and a guy showed up. She gave him her name and reservation number.

He hunched over his computer screen. "We just rented your car, but you're lucky. We have one vehicle left and it's a sweet one. Cadillac convertible."

"I paid a deposit," she said. "I specifically made reservations for a compact car."

"I understand, but we don't actually hold vehicles."

She pulled out the information she'd printed at home and put it on the counter. "But I have a reservation."

The clerk didn't even look at it. "It's all in the fine print. We don't hold specific cars. And we still have a vehicle for you. Just not a compact. Your flight was late, plane landed, you didn't show up to pick up your car. We rented it to someone else. That's how it works."

He turned to a pegboard on the wall, grabbed a set of keys, and returned, dropping them on the counter. A key chain with two keys, no fob. "The Cadillac is sweet. I promise, you'll love it. I mean, you're lucky. It's vintage and usually costs a lot to rent, but you're getting it for the same price as the compact. It's a deal. Well, except for gas." He made a sad face.

"I doubt I'll love it." So much for the *private* in private detective. A Cadillac convertible did not say stealth. She hoped the room she'd booked was still there when she arrived.

"Are there any other car rentals in town?"

"There used to be, but we're the only one left. This airport isn't that popular."

Elbows on the counter, he leaned close and talked out of the side of his mouth. "I shouldn't tell you this, but we've been having trouble with the compact car. Electrical issues. I tried to talk the other person out of renting it, but he didn't want a Cadillac."

"I'm not falling for that excuse."

He shrugged. "Okay. No falling, but whatever."

She slid her credit card across the counter, and he slipped it through the reader, printed out the paperwork, and passed it all to her. After returning her card to her wallet, she headed for the exit and the rental lot.

There were two cars. A white compact, most likely *her* car, and a ruby-red convertible with metallic paint that sparkled in the sun. The compact's door was open, and she spotted her book-reading nemesis bent over, head inside the vehicle. Sticking out from a back pocket, caught under his shirt, was what looked like a map, the kind you got at the car-rental counter.

She marched over to him.

"Did you just rent this?"

He untucked his head, turned, and looked at her. Now that he was so near, she was startled by how blue his eyes were. He might have been younger than she originally thought. Early thirties, maybe?

"Yeah. At the counter," he said.

He was wearing a black cap that said *Hard Times*. Ah, so that was who he worked for. *Hard Times* was a newish online-only paper that had started a few years ago. They were known for long-form reads.

"This is my car," she said.

He looked confused. "Uh, no. It's mine. For now at least."

"It's mine. I rented it. I don't want to drive a convertible." There was no reason to be mad at him though. It wasn't his fault that he was able to walk up to the counter and rent her car. "I think the convertible might be more your style."

He glanced at the car she was talking about. It looked like a boat docked next to his. "That does seem kinda sweet. Well, other than the cost of gas." He removed his cap and tossed it to her. She caught it, just a reflex, because now she was holding some stranger's cap in her hands. She was torn between dropping it and throwing it back at him.

He must have noticed. "It's new. I haven't sweat in it. Keep it. I have more." Now he was practically reading her mind. "I say put the top down on the Caddy and enjoy the ride." He seemed to consider another option. "Where you headed?"

"Finney."

"Me too. I can give you a ride."

"I want to have my own car. Are you going there for work?"

"Yeah. I'm doing a piece on the Murphy murders. Heard of them?"

"I have." He was fishing for more information; she wasn't giving up any.

"I guess most people have, after the most recent homicide."

"Not sure it's being classified as a homicide yet. Last I heard, they were waiting on an autopsy report."

"Right. But we *know*. Everybody knows."

"A journalist shouldn't jump to conclusions."

"Ouch. Okay." He got in his car, really *her* car, slammed the door, put on his seat belt, started the engine, and lowered the window. "Sure you don't want to share a ride? I can show you my credentials if you're worried about getting in a vehicle with me."

"I don't need to see them, because I'm not going with you." She might have been a fan of relinquishing control in the air, but she wanted total control when her feet were on the ground. She certainly didn't want to be at the mercy of some Hemingway-Capote-Thompson enthusiast.

"My name's Will LaFever."

She smiled a little because this was the point where she should be sharing her name. So many people, no matter the circumstances, would have felt compelled to share that kind of information in the moment. It was one of the reasons psychopaths could convince innocent people to do things that led to harm or death.

Instead of giving her name to a stranger for absolutely no reason, she said, "Have a nice drive."

"You too." He slipped on a pair of sunglasses, put up the window, reversed, then drove off.

Once he was gone, it was just Olivia and her monster of a sparkling rental car.

She couldn't remember when she'd last used a key to unlock a car. It seemed so archaic. The two keys weren't even the same cut. She realized one was for the trunk. She unlocked it and found a space as big as some small New York City apartments. It could hold a couple of bodies with ease. She put her bags inside, being more careful with her weapon case, closed the trunk, and five minutes later she was heading down the highway, toward Finney. According to her map app, the route would take about an hour and a half.

She was surprised to find it didn't take her long to adjust to driving such a large vehicle. The leather seats were almost too comfortable—she had to fight the urge to pull over and take a nap—and the radio worked. It was already tuned to a Wichita station playing folk-rock, and once she reached the two-lane, she relaxed into the drive and the car. She started to think the kid at the counter and even the guy who'd taken her compact had been right. It *was* a sweet ride.

But a convertible said something very specific about a person. That the driver was, at the very least, young at heart, possibly more interested in having fun than working. Nobody would describe her that way. Maybe the car would end up being the best disguise yet.

Ezra had confessed to not knowing where Kansas was. She, on the other hand, almost didn't need directions, because she'd pored over maps of the area her whole remembered life, so much that it was burned into her brain. She found the state and the area where she'd lived those first years of her life both fascinating and repelling. She was like somebody watching a horror movie between their fingers.

She might have studied Kansas, but nothing had really prepared her for just how flat and vast it was. Nothing to break the horizon other than an occasional field of giant white wind turbines, their blades moving in slow, lazy circles. She felt overwhelmed by the openness, yet also captivated by it, the yellow lines painted on the blacktop flashing under her, very few cars on the road, so few it almost seemed she had the world to herself except for the occasional school bus, reminding her that people actually lived and raised families in the forsaken place.

She'd worked with somebody who'd gotten a job for the Kansas Bureau of Investigation in Wichita. They'd lost touch, but she wondered how Coco liked living in this desolation, although, it occurred to her, Wichita might seem like any other city.

As she was driving, she came upon signs announcing the next town. More often than not, she'd get there to find an abandoned gas station, a few empty houses, and a cemetery in the distance. She glanced at her gas gauge. Half a tank, but who knew how fast her guzzler was drinking fuel. She should have stopped at a station outside Garden City. She was imagining herself broken down along the highway, walking to the nearest town, when she caught sight of what looked like a vehicle pulled over beside the road. That would be her soon.

She smelled something toxic, then spotted heavy black smoke.

The broken-down car was on fire.

She slowed, keeping her distance while pulling off the road behind the vehicle. A somehow familiar suitcase sat by itself next to the highway. And then she realized the burning car was a white compact. *The* white compact. Her rental. The suitcase, the affected old leather one from LAX. Beside it, the briefcase and a backpack.

Her heart beat faster. Where was LaFever? In the car? Now she imagined herself trying to put out the fire with a fire extinguisher of unknown source. He would be sitting behind the wheel, a charred corpse with white teeth, wearing a *Hard Times* cap.

She pulled out her phone and called 911. As she was talking to the operator, she caught sight of the journalist in a nearby field, one of the giant white wind turbines turning slowly behind him. He had his own phone to his face, talking and gesturing.

The 911 operator informed Olivia that she was the third caller, and that help was on the way. Olivia ended the call as she continued to watch LaFever and his madly waving arms.

At one point he appeared to be taking photos. Then he tucked his phone away and began walking awkwardly across the field of knee-deep alfalfa, stepping over planted rows. When he reached the road, he headed straight for her car.

5

An hour earlier

The journalism world was cutthroat, and nobody seemed to care about quality or fact-checking anymore. It was just about getting a story out, even if it wasn't well written or well told or accurate. Will LaFever was sick of working his butt off on a lead only to have some hack break the story before him, leaving his months of writing and research wasted.

Once the story broke, nobody was interested in a similar report, even if the article was better. So he'd decided to plant himself in the middle of his next piece, thus circumventing any chance of it being something already done. Kind of a self-directed memoir, where he put himself in an interesting situation and wrote about it.

When he saw the news about the woman in Kansas who'd killed her kids, he'd decided this was the one he'd been waiting for. And he'd always found the process of Truman Capote's *In Cold Blood* fascinating, so he planned to tie that in too.

Even though Olivia Welles hadn't shared her name with him, he'd recognized her at the check-in line in LA from her show. He wasn't really interested in diverting focus to her story, but she might give his some extra zing. An interesting subplot. And he was understandably curious about why she was going to Finney too. She was a detective, a good one, from what he understood. Maybe somebody had hired her.

Maybe she was just going for moral support. Maybe she still had ties to the place where she'd survived that train wreck.

As he was driving away from the airport in what was supposed to have been her car, he came up with a plan that fit his idea of being figuratively behind the wheel of his own narrative. He stopped at a nearby gas station.

At the pump, he kept one eye on the road, watching for that Cadillac, as he filled the red plastic container he'd purchased inside, accidentally splashing gas on one foot and the hem of his pants. Hopefully she was still behind him, and, thankfully, there was only one decent way to Finney. With his container full, he put it in the trunk, switched out his footwear, and hit the road.

Kansas was big and flat, and a person could see for miles. He hated it, hated the feeling it gave him, like there was no point in being alive. It made him aware of the planet Earth and the solar system, all things he really didn't like to think about too much. He was more of a narrow-streets, coffee-shop kind of guy.

When he thought he spotted her shiny red Caddy far in the distance in his rearview mirror, it was time to act.

He pulled to the side of the road, grabbed his belongings, and placed them where he hoped would be far enough away. Then he opened the hood and poured gasoline over the engine, a little worried it would catch on fire right then and there. It didn't.

He struck a match from the box he'd also purchased at the station. He tossed the match at the gaping hood, missed, did it again.

With a loud *whoosh*, the gasoline ignited so fast he felt a flash of heat. It singed the hair on his forearm. He jumped back, then grabbed the gas can and ran, heading toward a nearby field of alfalfa and giant white turbines.

Now that he was nearer to one of the monsters, he could see it was a lot bigger than he'd thought. More like a skyscraper, the base so big a person could live in there. He missed tall buildings, but he didn't like the turbines. Far from the flaming car, he stuck the plastic gas container under a bunch of plants and kicked some dirt over it. With the container hidden, he pulled out his phone with no plans to call anybody.

Pretending he didn't see Olivia Welles pulling to a stop in a cloud of dust, he shouted into his phone and gestured big gestures so she could see him from the road and think he was actually talking to someone. Then he realized he hadn't taken any photos. He remedied that, turning to get the white giants looming above him, then Welles behind the Caddy's wheel, and finally his burning car from every angle. Then he headed for the Cadillac and Olivia Welles.

This story was going to be better than he'd anticipated.

6

Olivia and the guy who'd introduced himself as Will LaFever stood in the middle of the highway. Even though they were upwind from the burning car, the air was heavy, making it feel like she might be breathing toxic water rather than toxic air. She wasn't sure if the heaviness was caused by the burning car or the nearby fields, fields that seemed to be cloaked in haze and humidity even though there wasn't a cloud in the sky.

She suddenly had an overwhelming sense of déjà vu.

She'd always told her dad she didn't remember anything about the night of the accident, but that might've been a lie. At some point in her post-Kansas childhood, she'd begun having a recurring dream. Oddly enough, it was the one and only dream she ever remembered. And like recurring dreams, it was hard to know how often she had it. Was it a few times a year? Or every night? She was only aware of having the dream at all when something woke her, pulled her out of it. Whenever that happened, she'd lie in bed and try to replay its events in her head, hoping to spot something new, something she'd never seen before. But the dream was always the same. Mostly sound and sensations. A high-pitched screech of metal against metal. A train horn. A single blinding light from the train engine. That was always followed by screaming, and then wonderful and horrible silence.

But now that she was standing next to a field in Kansas, she recalled something new from the dream. That earthy, loamy, rich smell of damp soil.

She'd been told she and her friend Mazie Ray had still been belted in the back seat, rescued as they hung upside down, unconscious. Or dead. In the dream she was always aware of her dangling arms and legs, hanging straight down. Aware of the thick red blood dripping from her fingertips and plopping against the ceiling of the car. *Plop, plop, plop,* like a clock or a heartbeat.

Something was dripping now. Even though she and LaFever were at least fifty feet away from the inferno, the heat brought her back to the present. It was a moment before she realized the sound was melting paint hitting the ground. She could hear sirens in the distance and the *whoop, whoop* of police cars. The wind was picking up, and she hoped they could easily put out the fire.

"I don't know what happened," LaFever said. "I think maybe a gas line busted. Guess you were lucky it wasn't you."

"Guess so."

Fire trucks and police arrived. Road crews set up barricades and began directing what little traffic there was. With everything under control and thinking she'd get out of the way while LaFever talked to one of the officers, Olivia headed back to her car. She drank some water, checked her phone, and was surprised to find she had a couple of bars. A few emails, no new texts. She called Ezra.

He answered right away.

"Just wanted to update you," she said. "I'm still thirty minutes from the motel."

"Everything okay? I noticed you weren't moving." He'd been tracking her with an app.

She shared what was going on. "Also, I'd like you to find out what you can about someone named Will LaFever. He might be from California. I'm going to guess he's thirty to thirty-five. White guy. Works for *Hard Times*, that trendy online paper. Do a background check on him and see if he has a history of arson."

"So you think he set fire to his own car?"

"It's highly suspect, I will say that. He smelled like gasoline, and he was able to rescue all his belongings. And by *rescue*, maybe he got them out before he set fire to the car. Could all be legit, but when I pulled up, he was taking photos of himself in front of the burning vehicle."

"I would have done that. Never miss an opportunity to go viral."

"That could be all there is to it." The rental agent had mentioned the car having an electrical problem. She hadn't believed him at the time, given the circumstances, but maybe it was true. She told Ezra goodbye. As soon as she ended the call, he sent her a text. Another dog.

It was a miniature Aussie. It was cute, she had to admit. Three years old, house-trained, walked well on-leash, didn't like children. Perfect match, Ezra would say. She didn't know why people thought she wasn't a fan of kids just because she'd never had any of her own.

She had to applaud his tenacity.

He knew she was suffering, and it was sweet of him to think a dog might help. And it might, but she just couldn't. Not yet.

She sent a smiling icon in reply, then restarted Google Maps, waited for it to figure out where she was, and turned the ignition key. When she looked up, LaFever was walking down the side of the road, black backpack on, carrying his suitcase and briefcase, heading in the direction of Finney.

Her brain continued to gather and file information about him. Around six feet tall, one hundred and seventy-five pounds, minimum. Walked at a normal gait, unlike herself. When she was full-on walking, she had a tight knee that impacted the smoothness of motion, something she'd hoped the yoga would help.

She drove forward, pulled up beside him, and lowered the passenger window, mildly surprised to find the car didn't have crank windows.

He slowed his pace but continued walking. She coasted along next to him.

"Shouldn't you wait for the rental company?" she asked.

"They can't be here for a few hours, so I said to hell with that. I'm leaving. They can't bring me a new vehicle until someone returns one. Then two agents have to drive here in two vehicles. And as flaky as that place is . . . I could be waiting here for days."

"Come on. I'll give you a ride." It would be good to keep an eye on him. Figure out what he was up to, and if he'd been desperate enough to set his rental car on fire.

He stopped.

She stopped.

"You sure?" He was still wearing dark sunglasses. His shirt had breast pockets. One of those pockets had a pen sticking out, the other a case for his glasses.

"It's twenty miles to the next town. And if it's anything like the ones we've seen so far, there's a good chance it'll be abandoned."

"The whole state looks abandoned. Why would anybody want to live here?"

"I think that's kind of the appeal, right? Get away from people."

"Far away."

He opened the back door and tossed his two leather cases inside. "Can we put the top down?"

"If we can figure out how to do it."

It wasn't that hard.

They unlatched a few things. Then, with a push of a button, the top slowly folded and retracted. Once it was all the way into a recessed area behind the back seat, they tugged a section of vinyl over it, snapped it down, and that was it. Then they were headed down the road, the charred car and the wind turbines in the rearview mirror.

He hadn't been lying about having more than one cap. He pulled a second one from the backpack he'd placed at his feet and slapped it on his head like a pro.

How freaking weird was this?

She suddenly noticed he was no longer wearing his sandals. He'd changed to loafers. Had he done that before or after he set the car on fire? He'd been in the field when she'd first spotted him.

"Where you staying in Finney?" she shouted over the noise of the wind.

"Blue Moon Motel."

She groaned to herself. No surprise that he had a reservation at her motel. When she'd looked up lodging, it was the only place in town.

Olivia kept her eyes on the road, both hands on the wheel. With the wind sometimes tossing the car to the side, she was thankful to actually have something heavier than the compact Will had been driving. At one point she slowed the car, craning her neck as they passed through another empty town. "Look at that water tower. It's like the body and hat on the Tin Man."

"Good eye. They totally used that design." He rummaged in the backpack again, retrieved a notebook, flipped it open, and scribbled on a page. He also pulled out his phone and dictated in it, beginning with date and time. When he was done, he tucked his pen back in his breast pocket and said, "I like to use both digital and analog."

"Same here."

They stopped at a gas station that was somehow open even though it gave no hint of life. It had one ancient and rusty pump and felt more like a movie set than a legit business.

She'd visited the Mojave Desert a few times. People often said it was barren and desolate, but this was some of the most barren landscape she'd ever seen. She wondered if the people who managed to live here thought differently about it. Maybe the sunsets were spectacular. Sometimes, when the ground under your feet seemed unappealing, there was nothing left to do but look up and enjoy what was above your head.

LaFever took a photo of her standing next to the car, filling the tank. His shirt was snapping in the strong wind, but he seemed to be enjoying himself, acting like he was on a vacation rather than being upset that he might have narrowly escaped death in a burning inferno.

After she was done at the pump, she followed the hand-painted restroom sign to the side of the cement-block building. She opened the door, recoiled, let it slam closed, and marched back to the car. She'd stop at a rest area. They got in the Cadillac, LaFever jumping in without opening the door. It wasn't all that graceful.

The only rest area she spotted was equally as sad as the gas station, just a concrete picnic table surrounded by windblown trash.

"You're going to have to turn your back," she told Will. "Look over there."

"It's all the same. What am I supposed to be looking at?"

"Anything. I have to pee."

Once he understood her mission, he turned toward the distance, talking with his back to her as she squatted behind the car. "I don't know if I've ever been able to see this far except in a plane."

She pulled up her jeans and latched her belt. "You need to get out of the city more."

"I like cities."

"High crime."

"I don't mind."

"Pollution."

"I'll bet it's not so great here when they're applying nasty chemicals to those fields."

"Yeah, maybe you *should* stick to cities."

They took off again.

"This is like *Thelma and Louise*," he said.

She tried to think of another convertible movie. "Maybe more like *Fear and Loathing*."

"Oh yeah. Good call."

"Seemed obvious."

"Remiss of me."

"So you're reading *In Cold Blood* for research?"

"Brushing up on it. It's a shame that kind of reporting isn't possible today. We don't have the luxury of time like they did back then, when things moved slower, but yeah. I have to admit I'd like to write something like that. A nonfiction book from a more personal angle."

"Didn't it take him something like ten years?"

"Six."

"Wow. Some people live a few lives in that amount of time."

"Yeah."

"I read Harper Lee helped him write it."

"I don't believe that. She was his research assistant, and she gave him notes on his work, but I don't think she wrote any of it."

"Do you have a title idea yet?"

"*Bad Blood?*"

"Maybe too derivative."

"Everything's derivative today. People want derivative."

"You're probably right. I don't know anything about the publishing business."

"And what are you going for? I mean, I'm guessing because of the recent events, and I happen to know who you are. And I know you're a private detective. So I'm guessing you are maybe taking the case. But for who? Which side?"

"I'm not at liberty to say why I'm going," she said. "It's confidential, but yes, it has to do with the case."

"Well, maybe we could team up. You can be my Harper Lee. We could work together. Share notes."

"I prefer to work alone, and I don't plan to be in town very long. Just a few days." And if he'd set fire to his own car, as far-fetched and unfounded as that idea might be, what would his end game be? *This. Right here.* Riding in the car with her. Which also meant his hitchhiking had all been a pretense. Some reporters only cared about getting the story and not about who they stepped on to get it. Those kind could be devious. If he was up to no good, it wouldn't be a bad idea to keep an eye on him.

"Well, just an idea. If *I* come across anything interesting, I'll be sure to share it with you."

After that, they drove in silence. She followed the yellow lines on the road, and thirty minutes later they reached the small town of Finney.

Olivia had learned that Finney's current population was less than two thousand, which had shrunk drastically over the years; it was possibly destined to become a ghost town like the others she'd seen on the way there. But it was also a curiosity, and that might have kept it barely kicking, not because of her personal tragedy, but maybe because it was located not all that far from the events of *In Cold Blood* and Holcomb, Kansas, which gave it another layer of interest and creepiness no matter who you were—a stranger contemplating the historical event or someone who'd actually experienced it.

If Ezra had been interested, she would have told him Kansas and the corner where Finney was located was east of Colorado and south of Nebraska and north of Oklahoma and west of Missouri. A better description might have been flat terrain, treeless and lonely fields that stretched for what seemed like hundreds of miles. Prairie land that had experienced its own form of upheaval, from those early settlers who'd broken it with the sharp bite of plow blades, earth ripped deep, exposing the slabs of soil to wind that, unknown to them at the time, would carry it from one ocean to the other, even as far away as Mexico.

The Dust Bowl didn't just happen. It was a result of overtilling and drought, which resulted in an agricultural disaster a person could still feel today. Back then, wind had carried dirt and dust that blacked out the sun. Many who witnessed the darkness thought the world was coming to an end and had killed themselves in fear.

They arrived at the motel.

It was just what a person might think. One story, pale brick, rooms with six orange doors facing the parking lot. A matching six on the other side. She pulled under the carport next to the office, and they both went inside.

The desk clerk, a teenage girl with long dark hair, thought they were together, and giggled when Olivia said they weren't. Olivia realized they were both still wearing the caps. She pulled hers off with an exasperated movement and turned to Will. "Could this be more cliché?"

"I'll bet I've seen this very scene in many movies."

"Like ten. Or twenty."

"Was Sandra Bullock in one of them?"

"Oh you're right. And Ryan Gosling."

"Reynolds. Ryan Reynolds."

"*The Proposal?* Was that it?"

Their conversation alone seemed designed to prove they weren't together, thus disproving they weren't together.

"Yeah, but usually they check into the hotel only to find there's only one room."

The desk clerk, who until this point had acted as if she'd heard nothing, glanced up. "There's only one room."

Silence.

"Just kidding." She laughed and put two keys on the counter. Room three and room eleven. "They aren't even next to each other."

"Thank God," Olivia said.

"I will say you were lucky to get a room at all. Mazie Ray Days is coming up."

"Mazie Ray Days?" The very idea of having what sounded like a festival in honor of her dead friend was both horrifying . . . and horrifying. Olivia considered canceling her reservation, getting back in the Caddy, and heading for the airport. And rescheduling her surgery. Sometimes when a string of badness happened, it was best to cut your losses, admit you were in the wrong place at the wrong time. And yet here she was, a place she'd wanted to visit for ages. And she didn't want to leave without seeing Bonnie.

"Starts with a parade, then games and a crowning of the queen," the girl behind the counter said. "Free pie and ice cream. I love the pie and ice cream. The town council thought maybe it should be skipped this year on account of the new death in the family, but people have been working so hard on floats and food, and the carnival was already paid for in advance. And even the grandmother didn't want it to end. I guess she's the one who started it to begin with, so I kind of get it." She shrugged and tried to look sad.

Ava Ray, Bonnie and Mazie's mother. Olivia wondered if she was the person supplying the pies since she had a local baking business. Olivia wasn't a big fan of pie.

They both took their keys.

To LaFever, Olivia said, "Good luck."

"Thanks for the ride, Harper."

She ignored the Harper thing and went off to find her room. It wasn't hard when there were only twelve in the whole place. She was able to park in front of her orange door, which she propped open with a rock while she unloaded, and locked up with the chain once she was inside and had the two matching lamps turned on.

The room was a time capsule, even down to the diamond-shaped plastic key placard with the motel name on it. She touched the painting above the bed. It was a real oil, not a print. She looked behind the frame and could see lighter wall color, as if the uncovered part had darkened over the years, maybe even going back to the days when people smoked inside. There was a mustard-colored landline phone next to the bed that had to be from the eighties. It all looked real, nothing done by design. She loved it; it also gave her the creeps.

She hoped the mattress wasn't as old as everything else. She'd lift the top sheet and check it out later. Or maybe she wouldn't. Maybe she didn't want to know, because if it was nasty, what else could she do? Although the back seat of the Cadillac might be wide enough to stretch out in. That thought reminded her about the top.

She went outside and put it back up. Not as easy as down, but not bad. LaFever should have done it, she thought, but she was just glad he was gone and glad he was on the opposite side of the building. Maybe she wouldn't even run into him again.

Back in her room, she unpacked some of her things, putting toiletries in the bathroom. She decided to forgo examining the mattress and instead lay down on the orange bedspread and closed her eyes. She was falling asleep when her mobile phone let out a polite alert. She checked the screen. Ezra.

She answered.

"I got some info on your guy," he said. "Let's make sure this is him. Sending a pic."

She got another alert and checked her text messages to find a photo of LaFever. He was smiling, wearing a white dress shirt and dark tie. It was possibly a press photo. "That's him."

"I'll start with the easy stuff. An internet search makes him look pretty boring. Went to college on a swimming scholarship, but a diving accident his first year ended that. I think he probably got hooked on pain meds—just a guess, but I know that shit when I see it. Kind of vanished for a while. Background check turned up a few arrests, nothing major. Public intoxication and fighting. The interesting part is that his real name isn't LaFever. He legally changed it a few years ago. Used to be William Blake Bellamy."

"Oh interesting. Related to Augustus Bellamy?"

"His son."

"Any history of arson?"

"Not that I could find."

"It was just a weak theory. I think I'm on the wrong track there."

"Don't know, boss. If you think he's shady, he's probably shady."

Once they disconnected, she pulled out her laptop and searched for *Hard Times*. She found a couple of articles LaFever had written, skimmed them.

He was decent, but not amazing. She felt a little bad for him. It had to be hard to be the son of one of the biggest fiction novelists in the country. Dad had even won a Pulitzer. Going into sports might have been Will's attempt to do something just the opposite. When that failed, he found himself once again in his father's shadow. And now he might have been attempting to either make up for that or outshine him.

She felt a little annoyed with herself for focusing so much of her attention on LaFever, although maybe that had been intentional. A handy distraction.

She was in Kansas.

She was in Finney.

The first place where she'd died.

She searched for the most recent news of Bonnie Ray-Murphy and came upon a photo of her husband, the town marshal. He was standing in front of their house, cradling a blanket that contained a baby, the infant not visible in the picture. But the headline was a relief: Murphy Baby Found Alive.

Well, that was easy.

When she visited Bonnie tomorrow, she'd at least have something positive to share.

7

Olivia woke up, confused at first to find herself in a strange environment. That confusion was quickly replaced by recognition of her motel room.

It had been about an hour since she'd talked to Ezra. It would be dark soon, and she wanted to explore her immediate surroundings before that happened. Maybe find something to eat if anything was open. She'd spotted a gas station on the way into town, so she could always resort to snacks. But she had one place she particularly wanted to visit tonight, a place that was nearby, with an address she knew by heart.

The motel was next to the junction of two highways on the outskirts of town. When she stepped from her room, she could see Main Street stretching a few blocks into the distance, the shapes of various brick buildings lining a mostly empty street. There were only three other cars at the motel, at least on her side. A sidewalk led deeper into town, and she decided a walk would do her good. She checked the weather app on her phone and saw the temperature was seventy-five with high humidity. Sunset in an hour.

Once she reached the business district, she realized most storefronts were empty. The glass had a telling dingy brown tint that coated her finger with a single test swipe. There were faded CLOSED signs in windows and weeds in the cracks of the walk.

She passed a bank that seemed to still be in business, along with a café called the Machine Shed, its hours posted on the door. They closed at two in the afternoon. Definitely geared to farmers who got up early and were looking for a hearty breakfast and lunch.

She passed a hair salon and insurance company, both closed for the day. Also an antique shop with a mannequin wearing a vintage black dress.

She'd heard the saying about a town being so small they rolled up the streets at night. That's how this felt. The next block, what seemed to be the final stretch of downtown, had more life to it. She spotted a small park with shade trees. Another cozy street with houses, mostly bungalows that looked inviting. She wondered what it would have felt like to live here. With a jolt, she reminded herself that she *had* lived here.

Nothing seemed familiar.

Nothing.

She found the street she was looking for, then the address. It would have been a hard building to miss, no matter what. The coroner's office and morgue. It was also the place she and her parents had lived.

Back then, it hadn't been unusual for small towns to combine the jobs of coroner and mortician, or for the morgue to be connected to a home. Now that she was standing in front of the sprawling three-story dark-brick building, she guessed it might have started out as just a house before expanding. It took up two lots, with a curved drive and an overhang in front of double doors. Abandoned now, many of the windows covered in plywood, a wrought-iron fence with a padlocked chain holding the two sides of the gate closed, discouraging access. She tried to imagine herself as a child playing on the grounds, now deep with weeds, but she couldn't.

It was so quiet. A few birds were singing, and she could hear the occasional sound of cars far, far away. That was all. She closed her eyes and took a deep breath.

"Kinda spooky, right?"

She jumped and turned to see Will LaFever leaning against the trunk of a tree. It was unlike her to let someone sneak up on her, and she blamed it on the house and her distraction. He was sucking on a straw stuck through a covered drink. He strolled closer to stand beside her in front of the gate. "I'd love to see inside that place."

She would too.

"I saw you heading this way and thought you might want some company."

He'd taken a shower. She could smell the single-serve bar of Ivory soap he'd used. He'd also ditched the cap, and his hair was damp and slightly curly. Another Hemingway shirt had replaced the previous. Looked like the same cargo pants, plus his signature cologne—gasoline.

The sandals were back.

Interesting.

"I'll see if I can find out who owns it," he said. "Maybe somebody can give us a tour." He seemed to be watching her closely. Waiting for a reaction. He probably knew she used to live there.

Why had he sought her out? Why was he watching her? Why had he creeped up so creepily? "You aren't one of those people who can't stand to be alone, are you?" she asked.

"I can be alone," he said with what sounded like resentment in his voice. "But I'm a people person. You kinda have to be, in this business." Like a suddenly distracted baby, he said, "Oh hey. You hungry? The only joint open was a place called Dairy Dream, and they were getting ready to close. Grill was turned off, but I was able to grab a couple of milkshakes. They hadn't cleaned the machine yet." He held out a tall, narrow drink that matched his blue-and-white paper cup, this one also with a lid and straw. "Got one for you. It's called a Tornado." He laughed. "Everything on the menu was that corny. *The Wizard of Oz* references were painful, but this doesn't taste too bad. Kind of a mint-and-chocolate combination. I guess the mint is supposed to represent grass and the chocolate dirt. Who knows?"

"Thanks." She appreciated his thoughtfulness and felt a little guilty over her suspicions. But he might have been trying to soften her up. He was holding his container high. She raised hers, they bopped shakes, said "Cheers," and drank.

He was right. It wasn't bad. In fact, it was delicious. She was wondering if any place made such a thing near her home in California, when a girl on a tricycle appeared out of nowhere, flying around the corner, not looking up, making revving sounds. Colorful playing cards were attached to the spokes of her bike with clothespins, adding a flutter to the mouth-revving. She was barefoot, pigtails, wearing a white disposable diaper and nothing else.

One, Olivia was surprised kids still put cards in their spokes. Two, wasn't the child too old for diapers?

A woman showed up behind her, out of breath, grabbing the bike handlebars. "You aren't supposed to ride so far from the house. There's a kid killer loose."

Oof. So that was how mothers kept their offspring in line here.

Will looked surprised too, then stuck the straw in his mouth as if trying to hide a laugh. That turned into a down-the-wrong-pipe cough.

The woman wheeled the child around. Will got his coughing under control. Mother and child headed back in the direction they'd come. On the way, the girl paused in front of Olivia and stared up at her. And kept staring. Finally she pulled her finger from her mouth and pointed at Olivia. "You got funny face."

Olivia gasped.

Leave it to a child to blurt out the truth about Olivia's disfigurement. After dropping that emotional bomb, the kid took off, the mother following, pausing briefly to glance over her shoulder, make a face, and say, "Sorry."

Olivia realized with dismay that she was shaking. Her head began to pound in a way that signaled a possible severe headache. She had to calm down. She focused on her breathing.

Will pointed to his own face and drew an imaginary line from his forehead to his jaw. "You have a pillow crease."

Her heart was still racing, and she was beginning to sweat. She was aware of the sound of the bike tires, the cards in the spokes, the feel of the freezing drink in her hand, an urge to run. She didn't understand what he was trying to tell her.

"A pillow crease. On your face."

Oh hell. Right. "Is this going to be in your book?"

"Maybe. Not a big deal, right? Standing in front of the mortuary where you used to live and some little munchkin comes barreling around the corner, almost running into you. Looks up, horrified by your face." So he did know the full extent of who she was. Of course he did.

"And who are you in this scenario?"

"Just an observer."

"I think you're the Wizard. Who, as we know, was really a scam artist."

"Way to spoil the plot for me. Just kidding. I've seen it a million times. Well, not a million but at least ten."

He didn't appear to be mad. She had to give him credit for that. She rubbed her face, feeling the crease he was talking about. Her heart rate slowed. Hopefully she could avoid one of her debilitating headaches. She began walking away, toward the park. "Thanks again for the drink."

Instead of taking the hint that she wanted to be by herself, he fell into step beside her, chattering.

"Must be weird for you to see this place again."

In the park, she spotted a picnic table and sat down on the top, her feet on the seat, something she'd always done. These were those little habits she wondered if she'd also done in the before time, before she'd lost her memory and started over. Or were these behaviors part of the newer her?

He sat down beside her, not close, several feet away, leaned forward, elbows on his knees, hands clasped.

She caught a strong whiff of him. A reminder of her earlier suspicion. "You might want to wash your sandals," she said.

"Why?"

"They still smell like gasoline."

"I don't know what you're talking about."

"Really?"

"I stopped for gas. The pump didn't work right."

"The car should have had a full tank."

"You stopped for gas."

"I was driving a boat that gets bad mileage."

"I got you a shake."

"Thanks. I can pay for it."

"I don't want you to pay me."

"Why do you smell like gasoline?"

"I have no idea. What are you trying to say?"

"Just saying you smell weird."

"I've been told that before. Maybe a skunk sprayed me when I was out in that field. Listen, I think I've handled the day pretty well, all things considered. I could have been killed."

"That's true." She suddenly realized it was hard to see his face, hard to read his expression. "It's getting dark." She jumped off the table and began walking quickly back toward the motel.

"You scared of the dark?"

She didn't answer. Although she couldn't remember the events of that night, she felt strongly that her best friend and her mother would still be alive today if it hadn't been dark. Bad things happened in the dark.

8

Bonnie Ray-Murphy was clearly and profoundly broken. That was evident to Olivia as soon as the woman started talking. And yet there was an unexpected pureness and innocence about her that managed to take Olivia by surprise. The contrast between that innocence and possible maternal filicide was especially unsettling, and it reset all preconceived ideas Olivia had about her. Maybe they both *were* ghosts caught between two worlds. Maybe Bonnie was just part of Olivia's coma dream. An idea she'd found disturbing before this moment suddenly took on a cloak of comfort.

Olivia hated visiting people when they were behind bars. It was bleak and depressing, and she never knew what to expect as far as setup. She was surprised to find that the jail had a visitation booth. Right now she was sitting on a stool that was secured to the cement floor. In her left hand she held a phone receiver to her ear as she looked at the suspect through the plexiglass separating them.

"You are so cute," Bonnie said, all smiles and enthusiasm. "And cool. Nobody around here is very cool. Is that your real hair color?" She was alone in her own booth, and no one was supposed to be able to overhear their conversation. "I thought about cutting my hair that short, but I always chicken out. I think I'd feel naked."

Even through the phone line, Bonnie Ray's voice was soft, almost ethereal, and her movements kind of dreamy, floaty. Olivia felt oddly transfixed.

She was pretty—beautiful, really—with pale skin, a few freckles across her nose, straight dark hair parted in the center. No bangs, big eyes, and full lips. If anyone had wanted to cast her in the role of an innocent angel, she would more than fit the part. Olivia knew she was in her thirties and, according to online research, that she'd gotten her GED after getting married.

"The color isn't real." Olivia touched her short hair, remembering how the TSA agent hadn't liked the shade on her.

"I love it."

"Thanks."

The feeling Olivia had gotten during that phone call in California, the need to protect her, was more intense here in her presence. No wonder she'd gotten off when her other two children had died.

"You ever know a person who just copies you?" Bonnie asked in what seemed like a severe diversion.

"What do you mean?" Olivia asked.

"Like they imitate the people they're talking to. Voice, actions, personality."

"Oh, you might be talking about personality mirroring. People sometimes employ that technique in relationships." There was also something called narcissistic mirroring, at times done to win someone over. Or if they had no personality of their own. So you might meet someone and think you met the person of your dreams because that person was so much like you. And you basically fell for yourself.

"You're so smart."

"Do you know someone doing that?" Was this her roundabout way to say she suspected someone else of harming her children?

"I don't know why I was thinking about that. Bored, I guess."

Another weird thing to say. Olivia would expect her mind to be completely focused on her child. Yet she was careful to temper all these impressions of Bonnie with caution and care. She believed raw and true evil did exist in the world, and she could be looking at it right now. Evil was full of tricks and could take on any guise. Evil would be especially comfortable living in the skin of someone who looked like an angel and practically radiated purity and innocence.

The only flaw on the woman's face was a red circle on her cheek, almost like someone, a child, might draw a perfectly round circle of rouge. With a start, Olivia realized what it was. A scar from the souvenir necklace Bonnie had been wearing when she was found in the field. Olivia had paid little attention to the story because it seemed more myth than anything real, but they said the token had burned the side of the girl's face.

Olivia's own necklace had vanished, but she reached into her T-shirt, felt for the gold chain, and pulled out the round token she'd purchased online, lifting it so Bonnie could see.

Kansas State Fair.

The design was a winding path, the yellow brick road, and a girl with pigtails holding a dog.

"Oh, we're twins!" Bonnie said, her eyes brightening with a momentary flash of happiness. "I remember when all three of us bought one. Do you remember that?"

"No, I don't." But in that moment, Olivia knew she'd help her. Probably not prove her innocent, but make sure she had the proper evaluation, if she hadn't yet, so she could at least get a fair sentence. Find out if anybody had gotten her that help, and if not, why not.

"What about my baby? I asked them for a breast pump, and they said I didn't need to do that anymore. Then I really started worrying, thinking she was dead. If they don't want my milk, she must be dead. Is she dead?"

Olivia could see why they were reluctant to let her know. If she'd truly killed her own children, many would say she didn't deserve to know how her youngest was doing.

"I heard she's fine."

Bonnie let out a relieved sigh. "Thank God."

"I'll see about getting you a pump. If the milk is going to the baby, someone will have to monitor you, and I doubt they have the staff for that. Honestly, you might be better off letting yourself dry up." Anything coming from her and going to her remaining child would be extremely suspect.

Bonnie began crying again. "Maybe I *am* a bad mother."

Olivia had no words of comfort to offer her. Even if the deaths had been accidents, which seemed unlikely given the number of them, she was certainly not a good mother.

"I can see you think the same thing."

"I won't say something just to try to make you feel better," Olivia said. "I don't do that."

"I get it." She nodded, pressed her lips together, got herself under control. "I just kind of wanted to see you. Somebody from the old days, when things were still good. I can't believe you came."

Olivia couldn't really believe it either.

"One more thing. One more favor. I'm worried about Dorothy."

"Dorothy?" Good Lord. Did she have *another* kid? People multiplied like rabbits here.

"Our dog. My husband never liked her. Can you check on her for me?"

A dog. Olivia's heart dropped. "I can do that." It would give her an excuse to go to their house. "Did you name her Dorothy because Toto was too obvious?"

"What? No, I just liked the name."

Right.

"Oh, I almost forgot. A reporter called here and asked to meet with me for an interview. He left a message sayin' he was a friend of yours." She held up a piece of paper that had been torn from a tablet. Somebody must have written down the information and given it to Bonnie. The piece of paper had LaFever's name, a phone number, and

Olivia's name with the word *friend* beside his, along with an arrow pointing from Will's name to hers.

He hadn't wasted any time. If he'd had a car, he probably would have beaten her to the jail.

"I don't know anything about him," Olivia said, "but I'm pretty sure whoever is representing you will advise against talking to the press."

"Someone was appointed to me. I met him the other day, but he was mean, and I didn't like him. He hasn't been back since."

"Okay, well, I can't give you advice, but I would not talk to LaFever if I were you."

"I thought it might be a good idea. To tell my side of the story." Her face clouded over. "If I have a side," she added with vague confusion.

"I have to go now. I'll check back, but in the meantime, I'll find out what I can about the dog."

"Thank you." She stared at Olivia for too long. "I heard about all your surgeries, and I thought your face would be scary. Like Frankenstein, or at least a lot of scars."

Olivia thought about how she'd freaked out last night when the kid had pointed at her. "I have scars," she said, "but they aren't hard to cover up."

"You look normal. Better than normal. Makes me think of pictures I've seen of you and your mom."

Instead of her words being comforting, they sent a chill through Olivia. Few people, maybe no people, knew how insecure Olivia was about her face. She didn't talk about it to anybody, not even to her father when he was still alive. Only a few minutes together, and it was like Bonnie had tapped into Olivia's biggest insecurity and knew exactly what she needed and wanted to hear.

Bonnie scooted closer to the glass. "Can I ask you one more thing?"

"Sure."

"Kansas has the death penalty, you know. And I was wondering . . . What does it feel like to die?"

Olivia sucked in a breath.

"Is there a light like some people say? Or is it dark? Empty? I sure hope there's a light." Her eyes filled with tears.

Even though she'd died several times, Olivia had no idea what it felt like, no memory of any of it. People, her dad for one, had just told her about it. "There is a light," she said softly. "It's like being hugged."

"Oh." Bonnie's shoulders relaxed. She smiled. "I'm so glad."

Olivia told her goodbye and hung up the phone with a clatter. She got to her feet and walked toward the heavy locked door, where she pushed the buzzer, indicating she was ready to leave. All the while, she could feel Bonnie still sitting in the booth, watching her.

The day was early yet. She had to find out about the dog, and she wanted to visit some dead people. Hopefully they wouldn't stare at her.

9

Prairie View Cemetery was located on the outskirts of Finney. It had an impressive stone archway at one end that was big enough to drive a car through. Only problem was it led to a cornfield, giving one the impression that stepping through it might deliver you to another world, another dimension.

The vastness of the grounds drove home how much the population had shrunk over the years. Olivia knew that to be typical of many rural places, but to actually see the previous population density with her own eyes really underscored how much the town had died. The exodus and the allure of cities were reversing some now, but that wasn't evident in Finney.

Right now she was walking down a row of tombstones, hunting for names. With the use of the website Find a Grave, she had a rough idea where to search for the burial plots she wanted to see. As she walked, she felt closer to pioneer history and closer to the soil and the way the richness of it provided for the world. A person could feel the homesteading spirit in this place where there were no skyscrapers. At a distance that could have been miles away or not that far—it was so hard to tell—she saw barns and grain elevators, black silhouettes against a sky that was turning pink. This in-between world didn't feel firmly connected to the rest of the United States, even though it was surrounded by land on all sides.

Like everything in the town, the cemetery was flat, the very flatness making it unique and remarkable. There were a few trees, like the one she'd parked the Cadillac under, but beneath her feet was mostly dry prairie grass. The wind had been increasing throughout the day. Right now it took her breath away if she turned in the wrong direction. It also carried a not-so-pleasant odor. Maybe from the pig farm she'd passed earlier.

Some grave markers were more elaborate than others, indications of poverty and wealth. It was sad to see the years when Spanish flu had wiped out many residents. The dates of death were similar, and there were a lot of small graves.

Mazie Ray's was easy to find because it was a popular one to visit. People had honored the plot with big and small tokens; flowers, alive and dead; solar lights; toys of various types, most of them things a girl might have liked at certain periods of her life. Creepy dolls that might not have been creepy way back when they were first left there. Now rain and weather and seasons had given them more of a horror-movie feel than anything comforting. Nearby—and something Olivia hadn't expected but should have—were the graves of the two older Murphy children that had died. And there was a spot already marked for Henry, though the ground hadn't been disturbed yet.

Once she was done taking photos of the Ray and Murphy graves, she moved to another area with some large and amazing statuary, mostly giant angels, plus a few mausoleums. Surprising, considering Finney wasn't a wealthy town. She found the Welles name on a family stone that loomed over a grouping of individual flat marble markers that would be easy to mow over.

And she found her mother's grave.

Florence Welles.

Cremation was becoming more the norm now, but thirty years ago, it was not as accepted, especially in the Midwest. Her mother had been buried in an old family plot that had belonged to Olivia's father. There were a lot of names she didn't recognize, some dating back a century. She wasn't even sure where her father had ended up. Cremated, she supposed.

He'd remarried when Olivia was in college. At that time, his wife, Maureen, already had a couple of kids, but a year after the wedding they had another child. Olivia tried to be part of her father's new family, but it had always been stressful work, and there had never been any encounters that hadn't felt awkward even though her dad's wife tried to make Olivia feel welcome. But Maureen had tried *too* hard, and it had been excruciatingly obvious. Everybody wore fake smiles and laughed loudly at Olivia's jokes. The bad theater of it made Olivia even more aware that she was an outsider. So she'd stepped away. Let them have their cozy life without her uncomfortable visits.

The main reason she'd come to Kansas was to see if she could shake loose some tucked-away memories. So far, there was nothing, and that was okay. This was more like something she just needed to do. She didn't know what it felt like to remember early childhood. Her father had been her memory for her. And like he'd always said: "You can't miss what you don't remember."

With a start she realized it was getting dark. How had that happened? When she looked to the west, the sight was so spectacular she forgot everything else for a few minutes. The sky was breathtaking, maybe one of the most amazing things she'd ever seen. More intense than the sun setting into the Pacific Ocean. This was deep red, with black silhouettes that once again reminded her of *The Wizard of Oz*. It was easy to see where so many of those ideas came from if a person just stood out in the middle of this strange world. It was all there. This bleak, wonderful place, both magical and repelling.

Darkness had come more quickly than she'd expected, and she hadn't checked on the dog yet. Would have to do that tomorrow. And she still needed to visit the train tracks, *the* train tracks, but she'd put that off for now.

She returned to the motel, and by the time she got there, it was pitch-black. Will was sitting on the sidewalk, his back to the motel wall. He seemed to be waiting for her, because before she even pulled to a complete stop, he got to his feet. As she unlocked the door, words were pouring from him, as if he'd been saving them up, waiting to unload.

"There's my replacement rental." He pointed to a silver sedan parked near the end of the parking area, on her side of the building, not his. "Some shitty base model with seventy-five thousand miles on it."

"I totally get that they wouldn't want to send you a new one."

"Oh. Man. Yeah." He thought a moment, then jumped in with some news. "I tracked down the mortuary information," he told her. "It was sold to some company for a dollar years ago, but I've been unable to find out more about it. Nobody to contact about getting inside. There seem to be people in town who want it torn down. Anyway, I think we should go in."

"Break in?"

"Not break in. Just maybe walk around the place and stumble inside."

"I'm going to act like I didn't hear that." She turned her back to him and said, "I'll see you later." Inside her room, she plopped down on the bed, head on a pillow, feet crossed at the ankles, and called Ezra to check in on him. It was two hours earlier in California.

He answered, and he sounded coherent. She didn't have anything much to share, but she pretended she did just to engage him in conversation and ease her mind. As they were talking, he sent her a photo of another foster dog, this one a cute Pomeranian. The charm in his trying to push a new dog on her was wearing thin and losing its charm.

"See what you can find on Conrad Murphy," she said. "He's the town marshal and Bonnie Ray-Murphy's husband."

"Will do, boss."

"Don't call me that."

"Oh, I forgot. Will do, Olivia."

10

Back when Olivia was a homicide detective for the LAPD, she put in a lot of all-nighters because very often there was a danger and urgency to catching the killer, who was usually still at-large. For the most part, that urgency of working Homicide didn't exist with private investigative work. She got more sleep. She liked to sleep. She got grumpy when she didn't sleep. Or grumpier.

She was engaged in that very activity, sleeping, when a light knock sounded on her motel door. At first she thought the knock might have been part of her recurring dream, but it happened again. She put on pants, a habit she'd acquired as a detective. Jump into your clothes as your feet hit the floor. A peek through the peephole revealed, and not at all to her surprise, Will LaFever. He must have heard her movement inside the room, because he waved and smiled.

She checked the clock next to the bed. Three a.m. With a sigh, she slid the gold chain and opened the door.

"I know you said you weren't interested in pooling resources and working together, but I was hoping we could at least share phone numbers. I just realized I don't have your number, and I'd like to be able to call somebody nearby in case I get thrown in jail."

Breaking and entering must have been on his agenda.

"Yep, I'm going in the mortuary." He nodded, seeing she'd put it together. "Just wanted to let you know in case I vanish. I'm kidding about vanishing. Well, not completely."

"What about cameras? I'll bet they have security cameras."

"I doubt it. It's a building they're talking about condemning. I don't think anybody cares." He had a black bandanna around his neck that he pulled up over his nose. At first she thought it was part of his breaking-and-entering attire, but then she realized it was probably due to the blowing dirt that had moved in that evening. The wind didn't even rest at night. In fact, it seemed to get worse.

"I'm just going to be in and out. Fifteen minutes, tops."

She could see he was passively hoping she'd come without actually asking her to come. "I'm not a bail bondsman. I'm not going to be of any help if you get arrested," she said. "You know that, right?"

"If I get arrested, you can put the top down on the Caddy, park under the window, and I'll somehow remove the jail bars and jump out. Then we drive into the moonset." He fiddled with his mask. "In all honesty, it would just be nice to have a friend in town. I don't know if you've dealt with many people here, but they aren't friendly. At all. Buncha flying monkeys, if you ask me."

"It's because you're a journalist."

"I don't know. People weren't friendly at the jail. At the gas station I tried to make small talk and people just grunted. I didn't know it would be so hard. Nobody wants to talk to me."

"My advice is to blend. Which of course is advice I'm having trouble following with my rental car. Wear jeans and a T-shirt," she suggested. "Don't wear your newspaper logo. Pick up something from the gas station, maybe a John Deere cap. A lot of people aren't going to talk to you if you seem too unlike them. That's just the way it is. But this shouldn't be anything you don't already know."

It occurred to her that he was working the same angle he'd worked on her before. If he wasn't acting, she got the idea he wasn't a potential threat but rather someone who needed babysitting.

"Give me a minute." She'd at least ride along, keep an eye on him, even if she didn't go inside. Although she had to admit the idea of being able to sneak into her childhood home was extremely tempting.

She grabbed her bag, then paused over her gun case. In the end she decided to leave it. She made a mental note to buy some sort of face covering, but once she was outside, Will handed her a bandanna, a pink one.

"Sorry, that was the only remaining color they had at the Pump and Go. I know you don't seem like a pink person."

"What do I seem like?"

"Black. Gray."

"I can do pink. I have no problem with pink."

"Good. Guess we're learning things about each other." He laughed at that.

What she was learning about him was that he liked to make small jokes, nothing a person would laugh out loud over, then chuckle to himself. Kind of like a laugh track, she guessed, so the other person would understand it was a joke.

They left.

As she rode in the passenger seat of Will's rental car, she was surprised to find the streets cloaked in fog. Everything looked different at night, in the dark. She didn't like that, had never liked that. Right now the traffic light at the Main Street intersection had an eerie halo around it. But then, with a start of surprise, she noticed the streetlight bulbs seemed especially weak, like someone had put a sepia filter over Finney. It seemed rather progressive for such a small town to employ night-sky muted bulbs. No, they weren't that at all. The glass was covered with a layer of brown soot.

The fog was dirt.

Did someone have to clean all the light bulbs in town? If so, how often? Because at this rate, they would be useless soon.

The swinging metal street sign attached to a pole let out a high-pitched squeal that seemed to be coming from another dimension and not from anything as mundane as a sign. The dust reached through the car, seeped through the vents, and fell on her bare arms. She could feel grit on her skin. The dirt, the poor air quality, added to the eeriness, the whole scene disorienting. And now that she was fully aware, she began to wonder if her throat felt a little raw. Yes, she was sure of it. She pulled out the pink bandanna and tied it at the back of her neck, bringing the thickest part over her nose and mouth.

There were all the sad and horrifying tales of Dust Bowl madness, a mental anguish that took hold of pioneers during days and weeks of being trapped by blowing dirt. They'd stuffed the cracks of their cabins with fabric, but still the dirt had come, creeping in around windows, settling on blankets and faces while they slept, choking infants who suckled breasts, their little mouths ringed in dirt because it was everywhere.

Some of those mothers lost all reason. In their need to escape, they'd chosen death for both themselves and their children. Olivia wondered if Bonnie Ray had suffered any of the same feelings out here. If so, she'd not joined her children in the hereafter, if she believed in such things or believed she was sending them to a better place than this.

"I know you were born here," Will said, "but I gotta tell you, this town is creepy. It's like being in the middle of an open sea with a bunch of dubious and potentially dangerous strangers. Then you have your own dark story of the train wreck. It's a lot."

"I agree. And on top of that, you don't like being alone, right?"

"Okay, it's true. I've been thinking about that since you first mentioned it. I like to talk. I like to have somebody listen." He did that laugh again, then stopped the car on the street, in front of the mortuary. Right in front of it. Couldn't get more in front of it.

"Go around back, or down an alley, or under that tree over there." She pointed. He should have realized you don't park in front of the building you are planning to enter illegally.

He squinted through the windshield that was getting dirtier by the minute. He seemed to be pondering her instructions, not seeming to get that he should be in stealth mode. Stealth was second nature to her.

"You're really bad at this," she said.

He put the car in gear. "I guess that should be a positive indication of my character."

She thought again about the gas on his shoes.

He pulled around the corner, under the tree, away from the street-light, the tree itself adding another layer of cover. The dirt helped too. He cut the engine and handed her a black stocking cap. "In case you change your mind about coming in."

She put on the cap and tugged it down. "I know you set your car on fire."

"What are you talking about?"

He was such a terrible actor. "I know you did it."

"Oh, man. Did they call you or something? The car-rental place?"

"No. And I might or might not say anything. Just depends on whether you pull more stupid stuff. Which is ridiculous to say because look where we are."

He made a sound of protest but didn't say she was wrong. "You coming? You know you want to." Without waiting for a reply, he got out, grabbed his backpack, and slung it over one shoulder. Then, without even bothering to crouch, he walked toward the building like he owned the place.

"Oh, for shit's sake." She pulled the keys from the ignition, quietly closed the car door behind her, and crouch-ran after him.

The back of the lot was surrounded by a chain-link fence, but most of the fence had been torn down or had just collapsed. It served to mark the property boundary but didn't provide any real barrier. Once inside the perimeter, they moved toward the three-story building. A sprawling black silhouette with a giant brick chimney in back, probably connected to a crematorium.

"Keep a low profile," she whispered.

He hunched a little. "This is like the best first date ever."

"Are you kidding me? It's not a date."

"Wishful thinking."

"I'm practically old enough to be your mother."

"I looked you up. I'm six years younger, which means you'd have to have had me when you were six, which would be even creepier than this town."

His immaturity made him seem younger.

"This isn't a date, and we aren't partners." He'd already proven himself to be untrustworthy. He would manipulate to get the story he wanted. She suspected his flirting was because he hoped she could get him an interview with Bonnie. Without at least one interview and hopefully many more, he didn't have a strong story. Truman Capote interviewed hundreds of people for *In Cold Blood*, including both killers. It was what made the book so compelling. Capote had even become friendly with them, and when the killers were hung, they'd requested Capote be there.

Will pulled a penlight from his pack, and they both crept along the building, remaining under cover of its even darker shadow, until they came upon a door that wasn't closed completely.

Someone had been there before them. Maybe a lot of someones over the years. It seemed like the kind of place kids would have dared one another to go. Or a place urban and rural explorers broke into. Lots of YouTube channels featured just that kind of criminal activity, presenting it as if they were doing something good and informative. Like historians. But with no one caring or looking out for them, abandoned buildings became easy targets. They were vulnerable to all who wanted to exploit them. Olivia called those people criminals, yet she wouldn't pretend what she and Will were doing was in any way less illegal.

Will shoved the door with his shoulder. The sagging, warped wood scraped and shuddered against the threshold until the opening was big enough for them to squeeze through.

Olivia closed the door behind her.

"I found the layout online," Will said. "You might remember it, but the living area is up there."

She didn't remember, but she didn't mention that she had a copy of the blueprints on her laptop and had pored over them throughout the years. She knew where every room was.

"Morgue and mortuary that way." Will shot the beam to the left, using it as a pointer.

She pulled out her phone and turned on the flashlight app. Both of them keeping their beams low, they walked up a wide set of stairs to the second floor. A long hallway led to a living room, kitchen, and bedrooms.

Because of the condition of the back door, Olivia had been prepared for vandalism, but she hadn't been prepared for the extent of it. It looked like someone had taken a sledgehammer to the place, breaking out large areas of drywall just for the fun of it. On a more practical level of destruction, fixtures and floorboards were gone, trim was missing, as if someone had come through to scrap everything that might be sellable. That explained the fence in back. Scavengers had torn it down and pulled their trucks up close so they could load their loot.

There was also evidence of preteen activity. She guessed preteen because the walls had been spray-painted with poorly depicted genitals of all sorts, along with a lot of curse words, some small but some several feet tall.

They were careful where they stepped, moving through debris.

The three bedrooms were in the same shape as the hallway and living room. Bed frames were still there, pitiful and revolting, with sagging mattresses that had been shredded and strewn about the room by humans and animals.

Terrible.

It was hard to understand why so many felt the need to destroy. Olivia had studied human behavior, but this was one area she'd never been able to classify or figure out the motive for, other than that a large number of people seemed to like to annihilate.

She knew when they found her room because some children's books were still on a shelf. Apparently, the vandals weren't readers, only writers. Drawers of a dresser were wide open, barely hanging on, a pitiful pair of kid's underwear caught on the edge of one. The nearby closet had empty hangers and a pile of clothing on the floor.

If she'd been hoping to find a room that might stir some memories, this certainly wasn't it. The only thing it stirred was disgust and bafflement.

"I've never understood the joy people get out of doing this," she said. "I also don't get how they let this house go to hell to begin with. They have a Mazie Ray Days parade to commemorate the people who died, and yet this beautiful building has been allowed to fall into irreparable condition."

"In my research I came across some obscure posts somewhere," Will said. "About how some people here think the town is haunted or cursed. Maybe this house is part of that fear. Maybe some people are afraid to tear it down, and afraid to build it up, so they just left it alone and hoped it would leave them alone."

"Nonsense." She might be wary of the dark, but she had no belief in hauntings or ghosts, despite what Bonnie had suggested. Living in a coma world was a totally different thing.

They went back down to the first floor, then cautiously took a set of stairs to the mortuary. Olivia was surprised to see it wasn't quite as ransacked as the living area. "Maybe they were afraid to come down here," she said.

"I wonder."

There were no windows in this subterranean area, which was meant for nobody's eyes but the professionals tending the bodies. Now, due to that lack of windows, the two intruders cast their beams of light more freely, illuminating layers of cobwebs. Olivia saw dust particles drifting and adjusted her bandanna. Will handed his flashlight to her long enough to adjust his own mask. Then he took back the light and shone it along a wall, stopping on an arched doorway that was filled in with bricks now, many of them practically teetering, the grout crumbling, evidence of the work being done in haste or by an inexperienced hand.

Olivia pictured the blueprints in her mind. "There's a room behind that wall."

She'd hardly finished the sentence when Will reached out and dislodged a few bricks. That was all it took for the entire barrier to spill to the floor like a small avalanche. They jumped back, waited for the dust to settle. Since he had the better light, Will stepped over the pile of fallen debris first and Olivia followed until they stood in the secret room.

He directed his beam of light at shelves filled with dust-coated embalming fluid. "I think we've found where the goblins go."

She made a small sound of dismay. "This must be why it was sealed. This needs to be carted to a hazardous-waste facility," she said, fully realizing they'd created an even more serious hazard by opening what felt like a sarcophagus. "Before it starts leaking. Before kids get into it. It's not safe."

"I have no idea how a person disposes of embalming fluid. I'm gonna guess you can't just throw it in the trash. I'm not even sure a hazardous-waste facility will take it."

"Is this going in your book?"

"Oh definitely."

They moved around the room and came to a quick stop in front of two gurneys positioned side by side, not in the center of the room, but close. In a place of importance, a secret shrine to the past. Her past.

Both gurneys had unexpected articles of clothing. Two frilly blue dresses with deep-brown stains—evidence of blood that had turned dark with age. Along with the dresses were matching pairs of red shoes, also blood spattered.

"Not sure what we're looking at here," Will said.

"I know what this is," Olivia said quietly.

Finally something she at least understood, something that pulled up a memory from a story she'd heard in her remembered life. They were looking at the clothes and shoes she and Mazie had been wearing the night of the tragedy. The two of them, Olivia and Mazie, had gone to the state fair to compete in a tap-dancing competition. Olivia hadn't realized they must have worn their dresses home.

Had her father put up the bricks? Had he meant to leave this room as a time capsule to what had happened here? A time capsule to his grief? And if so, had he thought about this room over the years?

She'd never been told the story of that night by her dad. He'd never shared it. Ever. What information she'd gleaned she'd gotten from articles and a couple of documentaries. Their tale hadn't gotten the attention a murder would have. It was something that had come and gone pretty quickly, so there had never been a lot to be found. But many times she'd thought about how horrible that night must have been for her father. Just thinking about it even now made her want to sob.

To arrive at the scene of a gruesome and horrendous accident only to find that his own wife and child were involved. Olivia had always understood the reason behind his need to move away and close the door to his past, their past. He'd been a stoic man, and she didn't recall ever seeing him cry. But he must have. Silently, quietly, privately.

His wife—Olivia's mother—had been rushed to a hospital in Garden City. The two friends, Mazie and Olivia, had been pronounced dead at the scene. *By her father.*

That was the first of many times Olivia had died.

It was hard to think of the event in terms of herself. Easier to think of it as something that had happened to *the girls. The best friends.* Not *we.* The girls both ended up here, at the morgue.

The story had never felt so close and real to Olivia as it did right now, standing in front of the gurney where her body had rested, presumed and pronounced dead.

This was where she'd come back to life. Right here. She'd heard and read about that too. And until now, it had always felt like someone else's story, not hers. It still felt like someone else's story because this, being here, evoked no memory. A person would think that was a good thing, unless you were the one who couldn't remember.

On one of the gurneys was a necklace that was identical to the one Bonnie had been wearing in jail the other day, and the same mass-produced one Olivia had found on eBay a few years back.

She kept her flashlight on it. She stared hard, as if trying to hypnotize and transfix herself. This one was either Mazie's or the other girl's—hers, Olivia's.

As she stared at the cheap trinket, she was vaguely aware of Will walking around the room, flashlight in one hand, taking photos with the other.

And then she couldn't help it.

She picked up the necklace. She rubbed her thumb across the design, wiping away dust.

That night long ago, at the same time the dead friends were being transported from the crash scene to Finney, searchers were trying to find Mrs. Ray and Bonnie, who weren't at the scene of the accident. The idea of alien abductions had been popular back then, and some had been eager to attribute it to that. Even today, when the occasional article on UFOs popped up, someone was likely to mention the Finney abduction, completely ignoring the eyewitness accounts of what had really happened. She guessed a train hitting a car and killing some of the occupants wasn't enough for them.

There was speculation as to whether her father, in his frantic despair, had just missed Olivia's faint heartbeat, but she went with the popular theory that she'd really died and that the ride to the morgue had shaken her enough to restart her heart. And that's when her father had found her there, barely alive, and rushed her to the hospital himself.

Her heart was pounding for real right now. At the same time, she felt the blood in her veins turn to ice. Her hands and feet went cold, and a stab of excruciating pain shot through her head.

She stifled a gasp.

She stuffed the necklace into the pocket of her jeans, stepped over the pile of bricks, and ran through the outer room and up the stairs to the first floor. Will might have shouted after her; she wasn't sure. Her heart was hammering, and she knew she was going to either pass out or throw up. Maybe both.

She spotted the door and made a beeline for it, aware of the awkwardness of her movements. The stumbling, her breathing coming short and fast. She ripped the bandanna off her face, burst through the broken back door, and stumbled into the parking lot, falling to her hands and knees, throwing up, and finally rolling to her back, one hand over her face. The pain in her head was blinding. She breathed quick and shallow, hoping it would subside quickly.

As she was lying there, a spotlight suddenly illuminated her, and a disembodied voice spoke through a muffled police radio.

Despite feeling as if a knife were stabbing into her head, she forced herself to sit up. She put a hand to her face to shield her eyes.

A squad car.

The driver got out and strode toward her. A guy, hands on his belt, the spotlight on both of them now. Thankfully, the pain in her head wasn't as intense as it had been inside. She could see and hear. And kind of think.

"This is private property," he said, stopping a few yards away. "What are you doing here? And it's a little late to be out."

"I didn't realize there was a curfew in town."

"You been drinking?"

"Sometimes I get sick after flying. It's vertigo."

He was dressed in beige from head to toe, a shiny badge with the town name of Finney on it, the logo attached to his shirt lapel. No hat, possibly left in the car. He was someone who worked out a lot, his arms and chest straining the fabric of his crisp shirt, his neck unusually large.

He gave her a good hard stare, then nodded as if to confirm his own thoughts. "You're the private investigator. I heard you were in town."

It seemed they'd recognized each other about the same time. She saw the name on his badge and with a jolt realized this was Bonnie Ray's husband, Marshal Murphy. That made sense. She wondered if Bonnie had ironed that particular shirt. And if so, what would he do now, with his wife in jail? Was there a dry cleaner in such a small town? Maybe he'd take his things to Dodge City.

She got to her feet, reminding herself he'd lost three children, one recently, so she'd cut him some slack. She was surprised he hadn't taken time off. Her next thought was to hope Will didn't come blasting out the door. She spoke loudly so he'd hear some of the conversation and stay hidden.

"I'm visiting for a few days," she said. "I'm from Finney, and I actually used to live in the mortuary. Well, in the house part. I'm sorry. I was just curious."

"You out here alone?"

The question suggested it was hard to believe a woman would do such a thing.

"Yeah. It's just me."

They heard a rustling sound. Olivia turned toward the building, fully expecting Will to appear. A cat ran across the parking lot.

They both let out their breath.

"Okay, seeing as how you used to live here and your history with the town, I'm going to let it slide. But don't try it again, and don't try anything else or I might have to arrest you."

"I appreciate it." Good thing Ezra was doing a deep dive into this guy. Bonnie might be her number one suspect, but the husband needed to be investigated.

"Oh, and, Marshal?"

He turned.

"I'm wondering if you have any information on the dog. Dorothy."

"What about it?"

"Bonnie asked me to check on her."

"You've talked to Bonnie?"

"That's why I came."

"So you're working for her?"

"Not really. I'm more here as an observer and someone who wants to make sure the right person is prosecuted."

"Stay away from Bonnie. I mean it. She's getting out on bail soon, and I don't want to see you around our place."

"She's going to be running around free?"

"The baby will be safe with Bonnie's mother, Ava. And Bonnie will be wearing a tracker."

Olivia wasn't surprised to hear Bonnie was getting out, at least temporarily until trial, and maybe that had been Bonnie's fear. That she'd have access to her single remaining child.

"Do you think she did it? You must have some opinion on that." Not that Olivia expected a truthful answer, but she wasn't one to sidestep what was right there in front of everybody. She was hoping he might at least be surprised into defending her, which would make him seem less guilty in Olivia's opinion.

His shoulders sagged, and the tough-cop demeanor fell away. "You've talked to Bonnie. So you know how fragile she is. I don't know if she did it, but everything points to her guilt." He let out a sob and spun away, started walking back toward the car, then seemed to have another thought, stopped, and turned to look at Olivia.

"Oh, and I'm not worried about a damn dog. I lost three children, so don't talk to me about a dog. I took it to a shelter. The little bitch bites, so I hope it's been put down. Now get in your car and get the hell out of here before I change my mind and arrest you for trespassing."

"Have a nice rest of your night," Olivia said. Her own code for *screw you.*

She strode to Will's car, got behind the wheel, stuck the key in the ignition, and drove away, hoping Will had enough sense to stay hidden until the cop left.

The cop left.

But he followed Olivia to the motel, parking on the street and watching until she went inside her room. She sent Will a text to let him know she'd driven his car back.

Good thing the town was small. Thirty minutes later there was a light rap at her door. When she opened it, Will was standing there with two small containers of Häagen-Dazs ice cream, the kind a person could find in a gas station. Holding them stacked in one hand, he slipped inside and closed the door behind him.

"That was wild." He lifted the containers higher. "I got these yesterday. Want one? Double chocolate or vanilla peanut butter."

She took the vanilla peanut butter.

He pulled plastic spoons from his shirt pocket.

"You seem to really like ice cream, or is that the only thing they had there?"

"I love ice cream. When I was a kid, they thought I had a dairy intolerance. Didn't eat dairy until I got to college, where I found out I could tolerate it just fine. Maybe I outgrew it. Maybe I never had it."

He sat in the chair near the floor-to-ceiling window. Curtains were closed. Olivia sat cross-legged on the bed, and they ate their ice cream and discussed what had happened. He suddenly pointed to her and said, "What the hell?"

She looked down and realized she was wearing the necklace.

"You took something? That's not cool."

She fingered the medallion in much the same way Bonnie had in jail yesterday. It was warm from her skin. "I shouldn't have. I don't know why I did it. Well, I do know why. I'm pretty sure the necklace is mine, but that doesn't mean I can take it."

"I guess that is kind of a gray area."

"I don't think so." And yet she couldn't muster any regret. Instead, she felt a sense of comfort having it around her neck. Like she'd found part of herself she'd been missing all her remembered life.

11

Olivia pulled the car across the gravel lot, parking under the shade of a single sad tree. So far, she'd been to two shelters. It was now afternoon, and she was at a third. She'd started near Finney, then expanded the field in her search for Dorothy. This shelter was a full thirty miles away. Maybe Murphy had intentionally dumped the pup at a shelter far from home, but Olivia was beginning to wonder if he'd lied about taking the dog to a shelter at all. It did seem odd if he hated her so much. A man with a gun and a lot of land. And no doubt a good shovel.

"I'm trying to find a dog," she said once she was inside. "A specific dog."

The kid behind the counter was a young guy who seemed uncomfortable dealing with people.

"It belongs to an acquaintance and was turned in without her approval," Olivia added.

"What's it look like?"

She had no idea. "Maybe a big dog. Maybe an aggressive breed. Her name is Dorothy."

"We get a lot of Totos," he told her. "I kinda remember one with a tag that might have said Dorothy. Not sure. We don't euthanize many animals here, but that one was turned in as a biter and went straight to the death-kennel area. Oh, not supposed to call it that," he said more to himself than Olivia. "Today's the day they're euthanized, so I think that one is probably already gone, but we have more dogs here. Ones that don't bite."

She hoped he was wrong about her being dead. She was already having trouble being there, knowing dogs were being euthanized, having had her own sweet Cecil Hotel put down not that long ago. Although it had been months now, it might as well have been two days. Such a hard thing for pet lovers to do.

A family with two excited kids came in.

"We're here to get our puppy!" the girl shouted.

"Go ahead and go into the second building," the kennel worker told Olivia. "If she's still alive, that's where she'll be. And the only dog there." He pointed. "Out that door."

It was a grim walk.

It smelled like dog excrement and disinfectant. Concrete floor with small chain-link kennels on both sides, a narrow walkway in the center. All appeared empty, like he'd said, which could only mean one thing. If it had been Dorothy, Bonnie's Dorothy, the dog was gone. And it sounded as if she'd just missed saving her, which made it all the more awful.

Feeling close to tears, and Olivia prided herself on her self-control, she tried to reason that it might not have been *the* Dorothy. And the only person who could confirm where the dog had been taken was Murphy. She could try to contact him, but she had the feeling he wouldn't tell her.

A movement caught her eye. In the corner.

No, couldn't be. But it was. A dog. Cowering in the back of the last pen was a tiny brown dog with long matted hair. Breed? Maybe some kind of miniature terrier.

She walked slowly up to the pen and crouched down, making herself smaller, not looking the dog in the eye. She didn't want to frighten her more than she already was.

The dog whimpered a little, took a few steps closer, barked, ran off, barked again, returned to the corner.

Olivia unlatched the gate and stepped inside, closing the gate behind her. She settled herself cross-legged on the concrete, put her back to the dog, and just sat there awhile.

At one point, she spoke the dog's name.

As if a switch had been flipped, the animal came running, jumped into Olivia's lap, and licked her face, her tail wagging so fast it was a blur.

Olivia tried to hold her, but she squirmed, whimpered, and wiggled so furiously it was hard to even pet her. "You can't possibly be the terrifying Dorothy, can you?" This was ridiculous. "Well, whoever you are, you aren't staying here on death row."

She found a frayed leash and looped it around the pup's neck. Then together they walked down the center of the building and back to the main entrance.

"Yeah, that's the one I'm talking about," the worker said when he saw them.

"What do I owe you?"

"We have to do a background check on you and get her updated on her shots. All that stuff first."

No way was Olivia leaving without the dog. Some part of her recognized that she was letting her emotions override everything, but she didn't care. "I'm taking her today."

"I'm gonna have to call my supervisor."

Olivia dug in her bag and pulled out a business card and put it on the counter. "Here's my number. Have them call me."

"Okay. But hey, you have to leave the dog. I'm serious."

"Just call me. And send an invoice to that email address." Even if they knew she wanted the dog, mistakes might be made.

"You're stealing the dog," the kid said.

"I'm taking care of it. Like a foster," she said. "Think of it that way."

That seemed to make him feel better. "Okay. That makes sense." But then he gave it more thought. "We have a three-strikes thing here," he said. "If a dog bites three times, they have to be put down. Those are the rules. That dog was turned over to us as a three-biter. Some counties only allow one bite, so we're actually pretty lenient."

Olivia lifted the dog up and looked her in the eyes. She smelled terrible. If this was *the* Dorothy, she was going to guess Murphy lied about the biting. "Do you know anything about her? Like age?"

"When they're turned over for bad behavior, it's our policy to not ask. We try to keep our distance, physically and emotionally. That's why I can't remember her name for sure."

"Where's the collar?"

"What collar?"

"The one with the tag."

"Thrown out. We don't keep them."

Before he could take any drastic measures, whatever those might be, maybe call Murphy, she gave the leash back and left with the dog tucked under her arm. Outside, she paused long enough to take a selfie of her and Dorothy, posed in front of the red Cadillac. She sent it to Ezra.

His reply was to call. "Please tell me that filthy cutie is yours."

"No, but she is cute, isn't she?"

She opened the car door and put the dog inside. Dorothy jumped across the console and sat on the passenger seat. Riding in first class. "I've got to find a pet store or grocery store to stock up."

"Send me a pin."

She dropped a pin of her location. "I'm heading back to Finney, so if you see anything near my route, that would be great."

"Looks like there's a farm supply store on the way. I've never been in one, but I'll bet they have dog food."

"Thanks. I'm sure they do." She got in the car and headed back toward Finney, keeping Ezra on the phone. "I know it hasn't been long, but did you find anything on Conrad Murphy?"

"Just boring stuff. I'll bet everybody is boring there. And yet, they kill. Boring killers. Okay, now I'm wondering if most killers are boring. I'll bet Jeffrey Dahmer was really boring. What do you think, boss?"

"I need to find out if Murphy was seeing anybody." A lot of times love triangles could cause someone to kill a child. Maybe the first two were accidents but the third wasn't. Or maybe they were all murders.

"I'll work on it."

"That might be something hard to find from California." Could be a job for Will, since he seemed so eager to be involved. They talked a little more, then she ended the call. Ten minutes later she was pulling up to the farm store Ezra had told her about. They allowed dogs, so she took Dorothy inside.

When she was done shopping, Dorothy had been petted by two children and one woman. She'd snarled at one large man. And, at the checkout, she rang up a total of over three hundred dollars in supplies, including harness, collar, leash, bed, bowls, food, shampoo, and a pink wire kennel.

Borrowing scissors from the nice girl behind the counter, Olivia cut off price tags, put the collar on Dorothy, and snapped on a pink leash. Then they were off.

On the way to the motel, she called Will.

"I have a job for you if you want it," she said.

"I never thought you'd ask. I'm at your service."

"See if you can find out if Conrad Murphy, Bonnie Murphy's husband, was having an affair or involved with anybody else. In my experience, an outside relationship can put pressure on an old one. People kill their children to start over with a new person. Check Bonnie's background in that arena too. See if you can sniff out any gossip. Maybe she was seeing somebody."

"Oh, this is going to be fun. Where are you now?"

"Heading back to the motel with my new friend. You can meet her when I get there. I want to see how she reacts to you. She's a little young for you though."

At the motel, Will was waiting. She didn't recognize him at first. He was wearing jeans; a plaid shirt, sleeves cut off; and a green-and-yellow DeKalb cap with a flying-ear-of-corn logo. Why did an ear of corn have wings?

And he'd cut his hair.

She stared too long. She tried to hide a smile.

"You said to blend."

"I said *blend*. It looks like you're ready to make a mockumentary."

"A mockumentary *with love*."

"Ha!"

Dorothy sniffed his leg and wagged her tail.

So she didn't hate all men. Olivia told him what was going on.

"You gonna keep her?"

"She's not mine to keep."

"Yeah, but we can pretty much bet Bonnie Murphy is going to prison."

"We don't know that. I plan to see if I can find information on any local rescue groups. Maybe I can find someone to foster her. And I'm not a hundred percent sure she's the right Dorothy. Or even Dorothy at all. She responded to the name, wildly so, but maybe her name is really something that rhymes."

"Like Smoreothy."

"Bellamorothy," she said.

"I've heard Bella is the most popular dog name."

"I used to go to a dog park and if someone shouted Bella, half the dogs looked."

"I'll bet she's the right one. Maybe she just hates cops."

"Without knowing her history, I really can't say. She might have been abused before they got her. By a big guy. Next time I meet with Bonnie, I'll ask her."

"And put in a good word for me?"

"I'm honestly not sure, Will." She repeated what Murphy had said the night before. "She's fragile."

"Okay. I'll let it go for now. And I'll head to the Machine Shed first thing in the morning and see if I can get any local gossip on Conrad Murphy."

Once Will was gone, Olivia gave Dorothy a bath in the tub. She was a good sport about it. She'd been a good sport about everything so far.

Olivia dried her with a towel, then lifted her so they were face-to-face. "Fidorothy?"

12

The Machine Shed was near the motel, so Will decided to just walk there. He wasn't sure what a real machine shed was but figured it must have something to do with farming. He grew up in Bel Air, born with a silver spoon in his mouth, some would say. But that hadn't kept him from trying to be his own person and not spend his life living in his father's shadow. He had goals. He had ambition. And yeah, maybe early on it had been about being someone completely different than his dad. It was why he'd changed his name. But now he wanted to be him.

Yet he'd set a car on fire.

What the absolute hell? If that wasn't a sign of someone who was seriously messed up, he didn't know what was. He'd never done anything that stupid before. After he'd seen Olivia at the airport and recognized her, he'd spent his entire flight trying to figure out how to get her into his story. And he had to admit to having a bit of a crush on her after seeing her in *Private Dick Chick*. When he realized her rental car was the only one left other than the Cadillac, he figured he could get her to ride with him, and they would become pals, and she would be his Harper Lee and on and on, and what was wrong with him? As he'd driven from the airport in Garden City, he'd felt his story slipping away, panicked, and had done the dumbest thing he'd ever done in his life.

He was going to take full responsibility for it, but people went to jail for stuff like that. To prison maybe? So yeah, now that he thought about it, he could see he was trying too hard. The story was that important to him. Like something he felt was his final shot. He'd become the creep in his own piece. Certainly no sympathetic character. Nobody would be rooting for him. *He* wouldn't even be rooting for him. He was going to have to come clean to the rental company and the insurance company. But not now. Later. Once he got his story. Maybe he could spin it so people would still cheer him on, or at least not hate him. Somehow.

At the café, he took a seat near the sunny front window, where he could look out on the street. The interior of the place was like something you might see in a movie, with red-and-white ruffly curtains. There were yellow flowers on each table, and the napkin holder was one of those metal ones he hadn't seen since nursing a hangover at Denny's.

Most of the customers were guys, and they were ordering big meals, hearty meals. Will guessed the kind of meal a person might want if they were going to put in a full day of hard labor.

He slid the plastic-covered menu out from behind the napkin holder and opened it. The prices were shocking. They were practically giving away food. The offerings had names like Tornado and Double Twister. Cyclone. Aunt Em's Coffee Cake. Will wasn't sure if he should be charmed or embarrassed for them.

"Where you from?" somebody asked.

It took him a few seconds to realize the guy was talking to him. Was he still that obvious?

"I'm working at that spread down the road." *Spread*? Did anybody really say that?

"Carmichael's?"

Will nodded and slid the menu back between the metal napkin holder and the salt and pepper shakers. "Yeah."

It must not have been a trick question, because nobody argued or pointed out the fallacy of his reply.

While he waited for the waitress to take his order, he listened to nearby conversation. Pretty much everybody was talking about the murdered child and Bonnie Ray-Murphy. It would have been weird if they hadn't been talking about it.

The waitress showed up, pen and pad of paper in hand. She was small and thin, her dark straight hair tied up in a tight ponytail. Maybe in her early twenties, wearing a uniform that was also straight out of a movie, a red-checked dress with a white apron. Then he wondered if it was some sort of *Wizard of Oz* thing too. Had to be.

He decided to order a big meal like the guys had ordered.

The main focus of the conversation around him was where they'd found the boy's body. In a well, which Will already knew, but he didn't know the details. So while he waited for his food, he recorded the talk on his phone, hoping it just looked like he was reading and responding to messages. Public place. Not illegal.

The well is on the Ray farm. I saw it yesterday when the crime scene tape was still up. That place with all the trees, where the house burned down.

Why didn't they fill it in?

It was hand dug. I leave my hand-dug well for wildlife.

You shouldn't.

How could a kid walk that far?

Wasn't he at the grandma's house?

My kid walks that far all the time. And he was used to walking across the field to his grandmother's. Nothing too weird about that. I think it was an accident.

Kid number three?

I know it's weird, but that's why it's an accident. A tragedy.

Yep.

Yep.

Yep.

When Will's food arrived, he hid his phone under a napkin next to his plate of two eggs over easy, hash browns, pancakes with chunks of butter, served with coffee so black it was like looking into someone's dark soul.

He'd use that in his story.

The other customers wolfed down their food. Will tried to eat everything, but he ended up asking for something to put the leftovers in.

The waitress took his plate, returned with a carryout container she placed in front of him. Then she tore a piece of green paper from her pad, returned the pad to her apron pocket.

What he owed wasn't the only thing on the paper. At the bottom, near the total, was a little extra info, something she'd added.

You aren't fooling anybody. We all know who you are.

Did she mean the clothes? Had Olivia been right? Had he gone a little too far in his attempt to blend? His cap was backward. He shifted it around, looking up to see the waitress standing there watching him with a faint smile and a rise of her eyebrows.

She turned the paper over.

The other side contained a phone number, along with more writing.

Call me if you want to talk. I know a few things.

Maybe she'd be his best lead. Maybe she knew if Conrad Murphy was seeing anybody.

He paid and left.

Then, thirty minutes later, from his motel room, he called her.

She suggested meeting that night at a bar twenty miles away. He agreed, but he also started wondering if this was some kind of prank. Especially if everybody knew who he was. Why twenty miles away? Maybe so nobody in town saw them?

He thought about letting Olivia know where he was going in case he was kidnapped or killed or at the very least left naked in the middle of nowhere with no phone, but he decided to keep it to himself. She'd want to come. And even if he went alone, she'd want to know what he found out.

Nope.

He hoped to redeem himself in Olivia's eyes, but he wasn't sharing his story with anybody.

While he had his phone out, he went to his voicemail, scrolled down to one he listened to a lot. Too often, some would say.

Hey, Will! Just wanted to tell you happy birthday. Wish I could be there to help you celebrate. We'll do it up right next year. I'm heading to Manhattan for a book signing. Weather is bad, but the show must go on. Love you!

Will and his parents had been living in New York City at the time, trying it out for a few years since it was the center of the publishing world. Father and son hadn't been getting along that well. Will had lost his swimming scholarship due to an injury that shouldn't have happened. Diving while drunk was a bad idea. He'd decided to attend his dad's signing and surprise him.

His dad was late.

He and his mom had sat there in folding chairs, staring at the empty podium, waiting and waiting, their worry growing with each passing minute. They started by just explaining it as bad roads, couldn't get there. Then maybe he'd been in a wreck, and he couldn't call. But it was the worst of all possible news. He'd died in an accident on the way to the signing.

Will was putting his phone away when he got a text from Olivia asking if he could watch the dog. It was a welcome distraction from his sad memories.

No problem. I'll meet you at the motel.

13

The Ray place was located about four miles outside Finney and down a long dirt road with fields on both sides. No other homes or signs of life within sight. Nothing to break the horizon other than grain elevators and a cluster of trees where a house might have once stood. Kansas was so vast and flat that it made Olivia feel disoriented but at the same time hyperaware of the earth itself and how, without gravity, she'd just float away, untethered.

She stopped the car halfway down the lane and got out. Just stood there feeling the setting, breathing in the scent of earth and fields. She'd left Dorothy with Will. She'd planned to leave the dog in the crate she'd purchased at the farm store, but Will had agreed to watch her for a couple of hours while he did some online research in his room. It seemed the best solution even though Olivia had no idea if he knew anything about animals. But she didn't plan to be gone long. He could surely just pet the dog occasionally when she wanted a little attention.

The map app had given Olivia a choice of two directions to the Ray farm. One would have taken her over the tracks where the accident happened. *The* accident. She'd decided not to go that way even though it was the shorter route. She wasn't ready to visit the tracks yet. She didn't even know if she was ready to see the Ray farm.

Did any of it seem familiar? The way the air felt? The way it smelled? Those were the questions she asked herself. And the answer was still no.

Yet, it *was* oddly familiar.

The wind managed to lift her short hair. It created waves in the front of her black T-shirt. Did it ever stop blowing here? And if it did, would that itself feel ominous? Right now, the brisk breeze was tolerable, though warm. But it carried that signature dirt with it. She ran a tongue over her lips and could taste Kansas.

She'd heard about a woman on Etsy who sold jars of dirt from every state. And people who bought it to eat. Dirt connoisseurs, they called themselves. They rated the states. She'd heard Iowa had the best dirt, but that Kansas was near the top. She thought she'd tasted a little bit of salt in her lick.

Maybe she wouldn't go to the train tracks at all. Ever. The place of death and loss. Maybe it would be too much. Maybe not going was okay. Even with no memory of the event, it could be too much to bear, made all the stranger knowing that accident, that small fraction of time, that one mistake, was the moment her life had taken a new direction—into the only life she knew.

She stood in the middle of the road, hands on her hips, and stared at the house looming in the distance as if she and the building were having some kind of a showdown. A two-story white farmhouse, the starkness of it feeling like an Andrew Wyeth painting.

What was the name of the one with the woman in the field? *Christina's World*. Yes. His most famous work. It had the lonely beauty that could trigger a tightness in your chest and a sharpness in your throat. The house stood out there looking brave and strong and alive, surrounded by nothing but not caring about the vast barrenness, almost seeming to like it, embrace it. It was something she'd seen in photos hundreds of times.

Seeing the house now, for real, knowing that Ava Ray had dragged herself across fields for miles to get home, made it feel even more like the woman had lived the painting.

It was all so heartbreaking.

And the girls . . . those poor, poor girls.

Olivia had to remind herself that *she* was one of those poor girls and had been left behind in the car—Mazie, Ava's daughter, probably already dead. The other child, Bonnie, still alive. Bonnie had somehow had the resilience and foresight to leave the car. Some speculated that she'd seen her mother wander off and had gone after her, to collapse in the field where a search-and-rescue dog found her forty hours later.

Olivia got back in the car, closing the door. The tight seal created a pod of peace, an escape from the noise of the wind, plunging her into a muffled, surprising quiet. She sat there a moment, then put the car in gear and slowly approached, the tires crunching over gravel.

Once she reached the property, she realized the farmhouse wasn't just a single tall and solitary building. The road view had been deceiving. The home was actually perched on a rise. Behind it were several parked cars near a large metal building that looked like a warehouse. There were red double doors. Above them was a hand-painted sign that said: Pie Farm. Home of the Famous Blue Ribbon Pie.

Olivia had called before coming, not wanting to spring herself on a grieving grandmother who'd not only lost three grandchildren, but maybe lost those children at the hand of her own daughter. On the phone, Ava had told her to come to the house, so Olivia veered to the right, parked, and walked up the wide steps.

Despite the wind, it managed to feel beautiful and tranquil.

There was a wooden swing attached to the porch ceiling, and hanging plants—pink and purple petunias that smelled sweet, bravely and innocently living on while the world around them was bathed in darkness. Olivia allowed herself a moment to take in this setting too, see if anything about the house felt familiar now that she was here, on the porch. She and Mazie had been friends since they were two, and they'd spent a lot of time together.

Again, nothing.

Before Olivia could press the vintage brass bell, the door was opened by a tall woman who at first just stood there on the other side of the screen, seeming to be giving herself a moment of her own, either bracing for another human or trying to figure out how much Olivia had changed since she'd last seen her.

Seconds later, she swung the screen door wide, giving Olivia a better look. Mrs. Ray, if indeed it was her, had gray hair, long and straight and pulled back. A slightly chipped front tooth that was oddly charming. She was wearing a long yellow-and-pink apron over faded jeans and a white T-shirt that had the name of her company, *Pie Farm*, across the top. Flip-flops. Tan arms and face.

"Hi. I'm Ava."

This was the person who'd been driving the car. The story was that her husband had found her here, in the house, after the accident. She'd walked all the way home from the wreck, injured, bloody, and had started preparing breakfast the way she always did. In shock. Just shut down and on autopilot.

Strange that Ava hadn't moved away, at least out of the house, but maybe she found it comforting. And how could a person outrun such a tragedy other than by taking the path Olivia had taken, a brain injury that wiped it all away?

Beyond Ava, in the shadowy recesses, women bustling around in the kitchen. Olivia got the sense that it was a gathering of people there to support someone during loss.

Ava opened the door even wider and invited Olivia in.

She introduced her to the three women making sandwiches and pouring drinks and arranging plates of cookies. Now that she was inside, Olivia could see there were even more people in the space, visitors meant to comfort. A couple sitting off in the living room to the right of the kitchen, plates in hands, talking softly to a man who might have been a minister. He was dressed in black and just had that look about him.

The three women in the kitchen walked past Olivia, smiled, and joined the others in the living room, leaving Olivia and Ava alone in the kitchen.

"I didn't realize you were having an open house." Was that the name of it? Olivia had never dealt with that kind of thing, and it wasn't done much in California. But she'd seen movies. People just seemed to come and go. Was there a start and stop? How was it that the bereaved were expected to feed people? That seemed unfair, but everybody was eating.

"I think I should come back another day," Olivia said.

"This is a great time for you to be here," Ava said sweetly. "Perfect." She had a stoic presence about her. Maybe she was a descendant of one of those strong Dust Bowl women, the ones who hadn't killed their families.

"Are you hungry?" she asked. "There's plenty of food. Way too much."

Even her voice was comforting. Olivia felt like she was safe, that even if a tornado hit, they'd all be okay because Ava would figure out what to do.

You ever know a person who just copies you?

Ava couldn't have been reflecting her. People Olivia had met in her life often told her she was strong, but they usually meant because she just kept going. She just kept living. And if you thought about that very deeply, everybody was strong. It was hard to keep going when bad things piled up around you.

"The community has been bringing me food for days," Ava said with a tone of confidentiality. "There was also food at Bonnie's house that I brought here. It just keeps coming."

"Is your business open today?"

"Yes. But that's a blessing, really. We are only closed on holidays. And I have standing orders to keep filled. I supply stores all the way to Wichita."

The space was warm and inviting, like something out of a country farmhouse magazine, a place that spoke of the past despite the modern and expensive-looking appliances.

Ava poured coffee into a white mug and offered it to Olivia, who shook her head. Then Ava grabbed a pint of cream from the fridge, added a little to the cup, replaced the cream. All done in the space of a few seconds, all muscle memory and not much else. She leaned a hip against the counter and planted one foot on her knee in a flamingo pose as she drank the coffee.

Olivia was surprised by her casualness. But she liked it.

"When I first started, my pies were made right here, in this kitchen," Ava said. "You probably saw the building we use now. The actual pie factory."

Olivia nodded.

"It's weird how it happened. I never wanted a big business, but here I am. And it's a good thing."

Time was ticking. "I heard Bonnie might get out of prison at least for now, until the trial," Olivia said. "What do you think about that?"

"I think it's fine as long as they keep her away from the baby. I'm not saying she hurt her other children. I just think it's a good precaution."

"I agree."

Ava was staring, making Olivia feel uncomfortable. She finally spoke words that weren't a surprise: "They sure did a good job on you."

It was the same thing Bonnie had said.

"I saw you right after the accident. Your face looked like raw hamburger. I also heard you can't remember anything. Is that right?"

Olivia couldn't hide her surprise. Hardly anybody knew about the extent of her memory loss.

Ava must have noted her discomfort and bafflement. She said, "I stayed in touch with your father. He was a good man, and I'm sorry about your recent loss. He kept me up to date on everything."

That was news to Olivia.

"I kind of felt like you were my own daughter sometimes because you and Mazie were so close."

"I wonder if we'd still be friends," Olivia said. "If she'd lived." The weird what-ifs a person came up with.

"I've wondered that too. You were inseparable. I started babysitting for you when you were two. You were here all the time."

"I wish I could remember."

"They were good times. Wonderful times. But the accident was awfully hard on Bonnie. More than we knew. We thought she was doing okay. She didn't seem that affected by it. She grew up, had a normal childhood, got married, and then everything started. She was in the car, you know. I do think that had to impact her even though she didn't show it. We were coming back from the state fair. I'd entered two pies. And didn't get a ribbon for either one."

"Guess you showed them," Olivia said.

"Guess so." Ava laughed, then said, "Bonnie has a learning disability. If you visited her in jail, you might have noticed."

"I wasn't sure." There had been a discrepancy in grammar, and Bonnie's speaking patterns were certainly less fluid than her mother's.

"I took her to doctors, and they ran tests. Nobody could ever find anything physically wrong, but most tended to blame the train wreck and the trauma. Not physical trauma, but mental. There's also the speculation that her brain actually fried out there when she was lying in that field."

"Poor thing."

"Yes."

Before she forgot, she told her that Bonnie wanted a breast pump.

"I'll take one to her. It really wouldn't be a bad idea, whether we use the milk or not."

Then Olivia cautiously broached one of the main reasons she was really there. It was personal, and she felt uncomfortable about asking. "I wondered if I could see Mazie's room."

Ava put her cup aside. "Oh. Well, I should have thought of that, I guess." For the first time in their brief encounter, she seemed a little flustered, but quickly recovered. "I haven't changed anything," she said. "I do take comfort in the room. Maybe you will too. I like to sit in there and think about her, especially on the days when things are really tough. Like now. I don't know what she'd think about Bonnie. I think maybe she'd understand that trauma can cause a person to do unnatural things. And that maybe it wasn't Bonnie's fault."

It sounded as if Ava thought her daughter was guilty. "I'd like to see it." In truth, the thought of seeing the room, especially knowing nothing had been changed, made Olivia feel uneasy. It was too close to the location of the accident. Too real now, when Finney and all that had happened here had always just seemed a weird curiosity, like a book she'd read over and over and knew by heart but wasn't part of her life.

Olivia followed her up wooden steps to the second floor, spotting a door at the end of a hallway. "Does that go to the attic?"

"How did you know?"

How *did* she know? "Most of these houses have attics." But in her head, she could visualize a room with a dollhouse and board games.

"You two played up there sometimes. And you were here a lot. Maybe you remember."

Did she? Was she finally remembering something?

Ava opened another door. The sound of the metal knob and the way the door creaked open, the way the floor was uneven. *It seemed familiar.* Olivia knew if someone were to drop a ball, it would roll to the far corner of the room they were looking at.

"Go ahead." Ava turned on the overhead light and stepped to one side. "Go on in."

The floor was worn yellow vinyl. Maybe old enough to be asbestos. Floral wallpaper, pink and yellow, a bed with a pink bedspread and a throw pillow with a red octopus on it. Olivia stepped inside, turned to see Ava standing in the doorway, leaning against the jamb, watching with her arms crossed. She seemed to be waiting for something.

"She liked octopuses," Ava said, noting where Olivia was focused now. The pillow on the twin bed. "Octopi, I guess. I thought about naming my business some play on the word, but decided against it in the end. Couldn't come up with anything that really worked."

"I like Pie Farm."

"It's fine."

"It's simple." Olivia wanted to touch the pillow, but she also felt repulsed by it. "I like octopuses too," she said vaguely, trying to remember if she'd actually held that pillow, marveling at how much the octopus on the pillow looked like the one on her arm. She felt her mind slipping. "I think I might remember this room."

"You were here a lot. You always said you two were twins. You even looked alike. She sometimes spent the night at your house, but most of the time you came here. She didn't like the mortuary. It scared her, and here you both could just run wild and laugh and be kids."

On the surface, Ava appeared to be moving along, business as usual, probably compartmentalizing her sorrow to pull out later when she was alone. Olivia had employed that same method after Cecil Hotel had died. She was still employing it at times when the grief became too much.

There were shelves attached to the wall, lined with children's books. *The Baby-Sitters Club* and stuff like that. A ceramic unicorn lamp with a ruffly white lampshade. A Trapper Keeper. Olivia had forgotten about those. Did kids still use them to hold papers and pencils? Did they still make them?

"Those were the school supplies we bought," Ava said. "School was supposed to start in a week, and she was so excited."

A little desk. A lunch box with a unicorn on it. A purple hairbrush that still had hair in it.

"I don't know if you can see this." Ava flipped the switch on the wall and the room went darker.

There were glow-in-the-dark stars on the ceiling, made with stickers, the kind that absorbed the sunshine and continued to shine at night for a few hours.

Olivia liked stars too.

So did a lot of people.

"She wasn't old enough to know for sure what she wanted to be, but an astronaut was the last thing she was obsessed about. Who knows? Maybe she would've become a detective like you."

"Maybe." Olivia humored her musings. "We could have opened a business together."

There was a music box on the desk. Wooden, with a little figure holding balloons. Olivia wound it up and opened a tiny drawer as if she'd done it several times.

It felt familiar, but, as Ava had said, Olivia had stayed there a lot. And yet, even before the music began to play, she knew what she'd hear. A song by George Harrison.

She felt weak, like she wanted to drop to the floor. Something felt wrong, very wrong. Her head began to pound, and she visualized the metal plate shifting against her brain. Keeping her back to Ava, she closed her eyes a moment and waited for the pain to subside. The idea of remaining in the room any longer was another heap of unsettling.

She somehow managed to keep her voice steady. "Thank you. I think I've seen enough for now."

"Sure, honey."

They went back down the stairs and outside. She needed to see where the boy had been found. She'd heard the well was on Ava's property. Should she tell her she had Bonnie's dog? Or probably had Bonnie's dog?

Oh, the photo.

She pulled out her phone and showed Ava the picture she'd taken outside the shelter. "Is this Dorothy?"

"Yes!"

"I'm watching her, at least for a little while."

Ava took a step away so she could beam at Olivia. "You're a good person. I always felt sure about that. And it's just nice to be able to show you around. Not the best of circumstances, I know, but you make this whole nightmare feel not as awful. It's almost like having Mazie here."

"Happy to be a diversion." Olivia tucked her phone into her pocket. "I don't mind at all."

"You're more than just a diversion. You're practically family. And since you might never be back here again, I want you to take some good memories with you when you leave."

They walked down a sidewalk that led to the massive metal shed. Inside were workers in hairnets and white aprons involved in various tasks, from dumping flour into giant vats to placing small mounds of dough on a conveyor belt. Ava introduced Olivia to a few people who were within earshot. They smiled and waved.

One woman shouted, "I loved you in *Private Dick Chick!*"

Ava didn't ask, and Olivia wondered how many people had watched that show. Had Will seen it? She hoped not.

"I think the most rewarding thing for me has been employing local women who otherwise wouldn't have jobs. Some of them are single moms. Some are trying to save up for college."

"It's a very good thing. Do you just hire women?"

"I don't want men to feel I'm biased, but yes. I do. All women, even my drivers. Not that I flat out wouldn't hire men, but my plan has been women supporting women, and I feel good about that. And I pay above minimum wage. It's a business that is female owned in an area where it's hard for women to even find jobs."

The two of them walked to another section, where the dough was being pressed into pie tins, then another area, where apple filling was injected before the tins went into an open oven with shelves of pies moving in a slow circle.

"Remarkable."

"They'll bake for forty-five minutes," Ava said.

At the far end of the building, two women were sliding cooled pies into boxes with cellophane windows for viewing the product. Ava picked up a pie and carried it to a table, where she cut a slice, using a triangular spatula to slide it onto a paper plate. She tried to hand the plate and white plastic fork to Olivia.

"That's okay." Olivia put her hand up, palm out.

"Oh, you have to try it straight from the oven."

Olivia disliked pie of any kind, but she really had a thing about apples. She wasn't sure why, but she especially hated them.

"You really need to try the pie. Come on. I'll be offended."

Olivia took the plate. Balancing it on the palm of her hand, she jabbed the fork in the pointy end of the slice and lifted a hefty glob. Without giving herself time to shudder, she popped the sample into her mouth, chewed fast, smiled, swallowed. She tried not to gag. It was awful. "Do I taste nutmeg along with the cinnamon?"

"Yes, you do!" Ava looked happy and proud. "That always goes in my apple pies. So what do you think? I mean, we are mass-producing them, but I try to retain that homemade touch."

Olivia pretended to take another bite, then put the plate aside. "Delicious."

Ava took her arm, pulling her closer as if they were old pals. "Before you go, I want to show you the orchard. You're also kind of like having your mother back. She and I were good friends. The best of friends. And I'm so sorry for your loss."

"Thank you."

In the orchard, she explained, "We expanded the grove over ten years ago, and now I grow most of my own apples. I think when the trees are producing more, it will be all my own apples in a few more years. An acre of trees."

"Wow." Olivia had little concept of how big an acre was, but it looked like a lot. She checked her watch. She'd been gone longer than anticipated. She wondered how Will and Dorothy were doing.

"I'm going to need to go," Olivia said. "But before I do . . . Could you point me in the direction of the well where Henry's body was found?"

Unlike the request to see Mazie's room, this one didn't seem to surprise Ava. "You always were a morbid little thing."

Wow. And yet it wasn't as if she'd never been called morbid before. Anybody who worked a homicide case ran into that reaction eventually.

How can you stand seeing dead bodies? You must like it.

"Well, you and everybody else," Ava said, softening her comment. "And your dad *was* a coroner, so maybe it runs in the family. Or maybe death is commonplace for you."

"It's not." But Olivia could see how a person might draw that conclusion. And she had no doubt her past had something to do with her decision to go into detective work.

Ava gestured. "Come on. I'll take you."

"That's not necessary." She shouldn't have to revisit the spot where her grandchild died.

"I need to go back there," Ava said. "Just make myself do it. And I see it in my mind all the time anyway. I imagine myself just standing there, talking sweetly to him. I might make a place for me to sit. I know it seems weird, but I think it would make me feel closer to him, being in the spot where he took his last breath."

She led the way.

As they walked, Ava talked about Bonnie.

"Her firstborn died a few days after birth. Crib death, they called it. The second child died on Bonnie and Conrad's property," Ava said. "You probably read about that. She was two. Got up in the middle of the night. We were having a heat wave, and the power had gone out. They pulled their mattresses outside on the lawn to get some relief. Slept outside. Most we can figure, the girl wandered away. I don't know if you've ever gotten lost in a field of corn, but it's easier than you think. I've known people who've been lost for days. But by the time search-and-rescue dogs were brought in and the baby was found, it was too late. Poor little dear heart died of heat exhaustion. It was a hundred and fifteen for almost a week straight."

"Such a tragedy." Olivia paused and considered her next words. "Would you say the parents were in any way neglectful?"

"What?" Ava seemed taken aback by Olivia's question, and even a little angry. "Not ever. No. Poor Bonnie. Not her fault at all. And those kids were a handful. All of them."

"Sorry. I had to ask." A mother wouldn't want to think the worst of her own child, but at some point a person had to face reality.

Olivia realized they were heading for the stand of trees she'd noticed on the way in. After walking down the driveway, they ducked through barbed wire, Ava moving through the loose strands with practice and Olivia more awkwardly, requiring assistance in getting her shirt unsnagged.

They followed a beaten path through the grass, then into a thicket of deep, dark woods that was refreshing after being in the bright sunlight. In the far distance, between patches of light and shadow, Olivia saw yellow crime-scene tape.

Upon reaching the tape, Ava tore and pulled it from the tree trunks where it had been strung, finally appearing genuinely upset. "Why is this still here? They said they were going to remove it." She wadded it up and stuffed it in an apron pocket.

"That's a well?" Olivia wasn't sure what she'd expected, but a large hole in the ground surrounded by rocks wasn't it.

"Hand dug," Ava told her. "It's how they used to do it in the old days. This has probably been here since the Dust Bowl. I never had it filled in, because it's a haven for wild animals. They come here to drink and get out of the heat. But I'm having someone bring a load of dirt and will fill it in." She let out a sob. "Too late. Seems silly to do it now."

"There's one baby left."

"That's true." She nodded, swallowed, still looking upset. "It never seemed worse than having a pool or a lake out your back door. But a person had to keep an eye on those kids every second. That was impossible. Bonnie came over, and we were in the kitchen, canning jelly. We realized Henry was gone. And because of what had happened before, we went straight to the cornfield. Just figured the same thing again. We shouted and we ran. Couldn't find him. Somebody said they saw him walking down the road, heading home. If you knew that kid, you woulda believed it too."

It wasn't just a hole in the ground. As Olivia got closer and her eyes adjusted to the dark, she saw it had been fashioned by stacking large round stones about two feet high. She dropped to her knees and leaned over, pulled out her phone, and turned on the light. The sides of the well had been lined with the same round stones.

"Who found him?" Olivia asked.

"Conrad."

Olivia got to her feet. "I'm so sorry." She felt a little more sympathy for Conrad Murphy.

14

Whenever rude people asked about the night the train killed her daughter, Ava told them it was almost an out-of-body experience. Like she was watching a movie, or watching herself from a safe distance. She'd heard it was common for people experiencing something so traumatic. Like soldiers on a battlefield just started functioning on autopilot. It's how they got through killing another human being and saving themselves.

They were coming back from the state fair, where Ava hadn't won anything for her pies. Nothing!

She remembered driving up the incline to the railroad crossing. It was a spot she'd driven hundreds of times, no, thousands, she guessed. She wasn't from Finney County. In fact, she'd never really been accepted until the kids died and her pie business took off. But she'd been around forever, definitely long enough to know how that particular spot, located less than five miles from home, had a bad and sad history, and the mothers in town were always trying to get the county to put up lights and a crossing arm. Or why, once an arm was finally in place, the arm was always in the down position with no train in sight, forcing locals to drive around it, training them to ignore it.

That was what happened that night. The arm was down.

Ava stopped. Waited. No train in sight.

In Kansas, where a person might wonder if those people who believed the earth was flat could possibly be right, you could see for miles. But that night, that late in the growing season, the crops in the field near the tracks maybe hid the train. Ava was never sure. Or maybe her brain was exhausted. It was almost three a.m., and they'd spent the day in Kansas City, where both girls, now sleeping in the back seat, hadn't placed in their tap-dancing performances, but they'd at least enjoyed the trip. Bonnie was back there too, sandwiched between them. Florence Welles was asleep in the passenger seat beside Ava.

They said most car accidents happen within five miles of home. Maybe she was just anxious to get back to her own bed.

She inched the car forward. She drove around the arm.

It wasn't her car. It belonged to Florence and her husband. A manual transmission that Ava wasn't used to driving.

The engine died.

And there it was.

A train.

Flying across the open prairie, hurtling toward them.

Ava had been told they traveled at speeds up to one hundred miles an hour in this section.

Straight. Good visibility.

She stared in disbelief at that single giant headlight illuminating the twin metal tracks.

She turned the key in the ignition. In her panic, she forgot to put in the clutch. She did so now, turned the key again, didn't give it enough gas, and it died again.

That was about the time she went on autopilot. No thought, just doing. Just self-preservation.

She unhooked her seat belt.

Screamed at everybody to get out.

She did scream, right?

Opened her door. Stepped out onto the tracks.

This was probably where her foot caught, because one of her shoes was later found wedged between the metal track and a railroad tie. Her other shoe was never found.

She stumbled to the rear door. Opened it.

The train horn was one continuous blast now, with no break. Just that loud, brain-scrambling chaos.

She looked up and saw two men in the locomotive, their mouths open.

Then, the next thing she knew, she was gone. Out of there. Like she flew away.

But of course she didn't.

And she lost hours.

Later, when the sun was coming up, she found herself at home in the kitchen, making breakfast for her family, for her daughters who were back in the car on the tracks. Maybe her brain just couldn't accept what had happened. Like some homing pigeon that just knew where to go, she'd walked across wheat fields in the dark to her house.

Nobody was there.

She'd thought that was strange, and she felt lonely. Later she found out that her husband, Mack, had been at the crash scene. And there Ava was, one bare foot leaving bloody prints on the linoleum floor as she moved numbly between the stove and the kitchen table, sliding fried eggs onto the waiting plates.

The familiar exercise brought her comfort. The normalcy of it.

This is what I do. Cook and care for my sweet family. I live for them.

She was sitting at the table, hands in her lap, staring at her own plate of food when the kitchen door opened with such force it hit the wall. And her husband was suddenly in the room with her. He pulled her out of the chair, wrapped his arms around her, and held on, sobbing, petting her head, making strange and awful noises, talking, some of his words penetrating the protective fog around her.

"People are looking for you," he said. "I thought you were dead."

"I'm fine."

He held her away from him and seemed to really look at her. Something in his expression told her she wasn't fine.

Mack was a good man. Salt of the earth. Farmer. Hard worker. Not given to much emotion, but a solid guy. Didn't drink or even smoke. Went to church most Sundays. Believed a woman's place was in the home. Felt no responsibility for anything that went on in the house. That was Ava's job. But he *was* a good man. Good enough.

Ava had gone to a community college but had found math hard and dropped out.

She was a little intimidated by people with degrees. She didn't know why. Like a piece of paper made them smarter than her. She had skills. Like winning blue ribbons at the county fair for her jam and pies. And she was a good mom. A great mom. But she often felt resentful toward Mack because it seemed like he'd been a bait and switch. When they first met, he'd been so funny and full of life. Then, as soon as she got pregnant with their first, he quit drinking and found Jesus.

She didn't have a problem with Jesus, but the nondrinking Mack was so dull. Not the person he'd been when they married. And yet she knew he was what most women wanted. And even though he'd changed, it was weird to see him crying and upset. That hadn't been a part of either personality. It almost made her want to laugh, but she knew that wasn't the right response.

She asked him where the kids were, in particular their daughter Mazie.

He let out a choked sob. "Dead! Mazie is dead and Bonnie is missing!" He looked frantic. "Did you walk here from the crash?"

"I think I must have." She put a weak hand to her forehead. Pulled it away and saw a small piece of dark dried blood on her fingers. "I just wanted to come home."

Time seemed to jump forward again. Mack helped her take a shower. The next thing she was aware of was being in bed, the covers over her. And the handmade quilt his grandmother had given them as a wedding present. It was intertwining circles, representing wedding rings.

She looked up at Mack and said, "You're a good man."

He seemed confused. Maybe he thought she'd forgotten about the train wreck and how it was all her fault. She hadn't. She was coping as best she could.

15

Marveling at the level of relief she felt upon leaving the Ray farm, Olivia drove back to the motel to pick up Dorothy, taking corners with care, hoping the boxed pie on the dash that Ava had insisted she take didn't end up on the floor. But so what if it did?

She spotted a man with a familiar long, lanky stride strolling down the sidewalk. He had a dog on a leash. Olivia pulled up beside Will and Dorothy and lowered the passenger window. "What are you doing?" Since she wasn't sure how much he knew about animals, she hadn't imagined his dog sitting involving a walk. But she was later than she'd anticipated, so she was more surprised than annoyed.

He gestured toward the dog and shrugged as if to say what he was doing was obvious. And it was. "Taking Dorothy for a walk. And you know what? I think a dog might be a secret weapon. I took her to the park just around the corner."

Where they'd sat that first day with their shakes. It had two swings, a slide, and a little bit of grass.

"There were some moms there with their kids, and we started talking. The kids wanted to pet the dog. I asked some casual questions, and suddenly I had more information in five minutes than I've gotten the entire time I've been here."

She wasn't sure it was the dog. A decent-looking guy in a small town where there were very few men his age. Olivia noticed he'd toned down his clothes. He'd ditched the flannel with the sleeves removed and was sporting a T-shirt instead, along with jeans and nondescript running shoes. The DeKalb cap was still on his head.

"Get in," she said. "You can tell me all about it."

He put Dorothy in back, then settled into the seat beside Olivia.

"Is that pie?" he asked, spotting the box on the dash as he closed his door.

"Yeah."

"What kind?"

"Apple."

"I love apple pie."

"Then this is your lucky day." She handed him the box.

She wasn't expecting him to eat it right then and there, but he opened it, grabbed one of the forks Ava had thoughtfully supplied, and jabbed it through the top crust, pulling out an impressive load that went right into his mouth. He nodded as he chewed, swallowed, then said, "That's damn good pie."

"You can have it. I don't like pie."

"Not any kind of pie?"

"No."

"That's not right."

"So I've been told."

"I found out a bit about Conrad Murphy," Will said around a mouthful of food. "Maybe stuff you already know."

"Shoot."

Will continued to eat, balancing the open box on the palm of his hand.

She felt queasy just thinking of those slimy apple slices.

"Murphy actually grew up in town," he said. "Not a farmer."

"I did not know that."

"Well, good. I guess I'm not so worthless."

"You aren't worthless."

"He and Bonnie met in high school. She got pregnant. They got married when they were both seventeen. Her dad gave Bonnie and Conrad a hundred acres. Conrad quickly found out he didn't like farming. Got a job as town marshal. They cash rent the land. I have no idea what cash rent means, but that's what I heard."

"You got all that at the park?"

"A little at the gas station when I was shopping for ice cream. You might know that Bonnie's father died about ten years ago. Some freak accident."

"Corncrib." She'd read about it.

"I guess that's a thing. Death by corn. The silo is filled with picked corn. At first, I pictured cobs of corn. You know, like the kind people boil or grill. But it's just the kernels. Like they have a machine that picks and removes it from the cob all at the same time."

"A combine."

"There's all this other weird stuff. It's picked wet, but it's supposed to be a certain moisture content before it goes into a silo. If it's too wet, it can harden when it dries. The corn is removed from the bottom, leaving a top crust that looks solid and safe. But in Mr. Ray's case, the crust was about an inch thick. He walked on it and fell to his death. His wife found him."

No wonder Ava seemed numb to tragedy. At some point a person just had to stop feeling or the pain was too much to bear. *Did anybody have anything to gain from his death?* she wondered. "It's something that happens sometimes, along with people getting smothered by corn," she said.

"How did the first kid die?" Will asked. "I keep forgetting to look that up."

"Sudden infant death syndrome. Or what some people call crib death."

"Crib death. That's kind of weird, right? The grandfather dies in a corncrib. Another kid died in a cornfield. The mother, Bonnie, was found in a cornfield after the train wreck."

"Wheat field. I always heard it was wheat."

"Regardless, we've got a big corn theme going on. I mean, you might want to start looking at the corn. Maybe the corn needs to go to prison. Okay, bad joke, but it is odd."

"There is a lot of corn here."

He pulled off his cap and turned it around, pointing. "And the logo on this cap. I had to research it for my book. Designed in the thirties, but I still don't know why it has wings. I don't want to say it was a copy of another popular logo at the time, but it was." He shook his head. "Who knew there was a place where corn can kill you."

"And where you can get lost and die not far from your front door," she said.

"Or just be walking along and fall in an open well."

Or get hit by a train.

He tossed his fork in the box, closed the lid, and put the pie back on the dash. "You should try my pumpkin pie," he said.

"I don't think so."

"I make a pretty good one. It has cream cheese in it. I'll invite you over when we get back to civilization."

He probably wouldn't, but it was an interesting thought. Their . . . friendship continuing beyond this place. He had a certain charm, and she'd begun to notice things about him that weren't annoying, things she found almost attractive, like the dimple in one cheek and his slightly crooked smile when he was trying to be funny. The way his eyes looked blue sometimes, but green at others. Long, thin fingers. The way he tucked a pen behind his ear, with no thought, only habit, probably started years ago as affectation but turning into something more of a signature habit. The patting of a breast pocket, looking for his little gray reporter notebook.

She didn't think about relationships much. She had too much going on in her life between her job, her grief, and her health. A guy didn't fit into the picture, and she hadn't met anybody recently and not so recently. She was suspicious of anybody who was above average in the looks department. The top three things she went for were smart, kind, and funny. SKF.

Like the town and everything that had happened here, he was beginning to seem like a real person to her. So she was intrigued by the idea of maybe seeing him again in a different setting, back in her real life.

A woman with a baby stroller was heading for them on the sidewalk.

"Hi, Will," she said in a singsong voice as she passed.

"Hey, April."

She continued on her way.

Olivia put the car in gear and pulled away from the curb. "Kinda think it wasn't just the dog."

16

Will didn't immediately recognize the girl from the Machine Shed, because she was dressed in regular clothes. Jeans, sneakers, T-shirt, and her hair was down. But a few moments after he ducked into the dark bar, he spotted her in a booth in the back. He crossed the room and slid into the bench seat across from her.

"Maybe you don't drink," she said, "but I went ahead and ordered beer for both of us and onion rings to share so the server doesn't bug us."

There were two glasses of dark beer on the varnished wooden table. He imagined her opening some capsule to roofie his drink. She had long, fancy fingernails, always suspicious.

"Thanks." He picked up the glass and took a swallow to show her he trusted her even though he 100 percent didn't. He started to wish he'd let Olivia know where he'd gone.

The onion rings arrived in a red plastic basket with a greasy paper liner. The server pulled a bottle of ketchup from his black apron and asked if they needed anything else. Two head shakes and he was gone.

The girl put some ketchup on one corner of the paper.

He chose an onion ring, held it close, examined it. Dark and crispy on the outside. Smelled . . . not so great, but he was trying to act like a local. He dabbed the onion ring in ketchup. Took a bite. It was nasty, and the onion was slimy and hot. Probably something he'd regret eating in about thirty minutes.

The girl started talking.

"I graduated from high school two years ago," she told Will right out of the gate. Maybe to set boundaries and let him know this was in no way a date. Her name was Imogene, and she probably would have been one of the popular girls in high school. Maybe a cheerleader, not in art club. He imagined her senior photo, and even though big hair wouldn't have been in style, that's what he saw in his head.

"Are you old enough to drink?" he asked.

"Close." She shrugged and glanced across the room. "They never card me here. Don't worry."

"I will, but okay." Anything for a story. *Almost* anything.

"I used to babysit for the Murphys," she told him. "My classmates were jealous because everybody called the dad Murphy Hot Cop."

"As one does."

"I didn't babysit much, because the parents hardly went anywhere and she was a stay-at-home mom."

He pulled out his phone and placed it on the table between them. "Do you mind if I record this?"

She suddenly looked tense and uneasy. "No, please don't."

"No problem." He put the phone away and patted the breast pocket of his shirt. "What if I take notes?"

"I guess that's okay. But don't use my name."

"I won't."

He dug out his reporter's notebook. He liked to use it because it was narrow enough to fit into any pocket. He flipped it open, clicked his pen.

"When I started babysitting for them," she said, "the first kid was dead already."

"Crib death."

"Yeah. So it was just the girl. Henry and Calliope weren't born yet. But there were weird things that always bugged me."

"Like what?"

"Like there were no rules. No instructions for me. Nothing about when to eat or what to eat. She could take a bath or not take a bath. Go to bed or not go to bed. Sometimes I even wondered why I was there at all."

"Do you think the parents didn't care?"

"I don't think Hot Cop had much to do with anything that went on in the house. That was Bonnie's territory. And it wasn't like she didn't *care*. It was more like it was maybe too hard for her."

"Overwhelmed, possibly?"

"Maybe. I don't know. I was a kid myself. I'm still kind of a kid, but you know what I mean. I knew it was weird, and I tried to figure it out, but I might have been way off. I got the idea she didn't want to be a mom. That he was the one who wanted a family. Well, that's what I heard too. It wasn't just my impression. I don't know if it's true, but it kind of seemed that way."

"What was the girl like?"

"I hate to say this because she's dead, but she was a huge brat. She had to get her way or she'd have a wild tantrum. I don't think she was used to being told no. I can see how both those kids wandered off. Probably never told they shouldn't do that. I don't think Bonnie knew how to handle them, so she let them do whatever they wanted." She sighed. "But I sure wish none of them had died."

"It sounds like one of those situations where Child Protective Services should have been called. Do you know if they ever were?"

"I'm not sure we have anything like that around here. Seems like something cities have, but yeah."

He didn't want her to feel worse than she obviously did. People, neighbors, friends on the periphery of tragedies often felt guilty. "We've all heard of situations where they are contacted, and the kids are left in the home and end up dead, so I'm not saying you or anybody else should have stepped in. I just wondered if they were ever involved."

"I ask myself all the time if I should have said more. And who do you report it to? The father is a cop. I told my mom, but she blew it off. And everybody felt sorry for the family too, because of all the bad things they'd gone through, so I think people let it slide."

"I get it."

"And then there's all that other weird stuff." She pulled out an onion ring, and he watched her eat it, trying not to shudder. As she munched, she seemed to be weighing her words, not giving much thought to eating the greasy food. Although she did pull a couple of napkins from the metal holder, fold them, and wipe at her chin just below her mouth. "The sacrifice stuff," she finally said. "That's what I really wanted to tell you about."

"Sacrifice?" This had taken a weird turn. He looked over his shoulder to see if he was being pranked. There were other people in the room. Some eating at tables, a few at the bar. Nobody paying any attention to the reporter and waitress in the booth.

He'd written a few Halloween pieces on haunted places. One of the most popular had been a road where cars supposedly rolled uphill. They didn't. It was an optical illusion, and all it would have taken was a level for anybody to determine that. Cars did roll, but they rolled *down*hill. And yet the town loved it, especially people in that teen-to-early-twenties age group. The story put the place on the map and drew tourists.

"People are afraid to talk because they really think there's some kind of . . ." She looked at the onion rings. Three left. They were big, and there was no way he was going to eat another one.

She picked one up, dropped it back in the basket. "Evil," she said as if deciding to just say it.

He leaned forward and really wished he'd been able to record this. Maybe he was going to finally have that breaking story. Of course there was evil here. Three kids were dead. He didn't believe the accident theory. And for the sake of a good story, he couldn't believe it. But then he wondered if she was talking about the onion ring.

"Evil exists," he said, nodding, looking at her, hoping she didn't get scared and stop.

"I'm not talking about an evil *person*," she said. "I mean an evil *entity*."

"Entity?" His enthusiasm dropped like a rock. She might as well have tossed a bucket of water in his face. He'd been a reporter long enough to know there were many people, too many people, who just wanted attention, and they were a waste of time. He wasn't big on ghosts or spirits or tarot cards or astrology. He was all about facts. Data. Proof. Had to be. Otherwise he could pretty much say anything and call it truth. "Care to explain that?"

"It all lines up once you think about it. Every time a kid has died, we've been experiencing a severe drought. Like all the fields that don't have irrigation are dying. And irrigation is expensive for the smaller farmers. Most of them can't afford it, and they depend on rain to survive." She leaned closer. "So get this. Every time a kid dies, it rains. A lot. Like a crop-saving lot." She dropped back against the booth, arms crossed, and waited for his reaction.

He didn't even try to hide his disappointment. "That's ridiculous." What a waste of time. It made everything else she'd said completely invalid and nothing he could use. Def not a reliable source.

"Look it up. The weather stuff and the deaths."

"I don't care. That's called a coincidence. It's a thing."

"Okay, I'll go with that. Let's say there's no evil entity. Maybe someone noticed that a kid died and it rained. They *thought* there was a connection. What about that?" Her face said there should be no dispute. "So there's no evil. Some people noticed the connection and thought the death of kid number one made it rain. And so somebody, some desperate farmer, decided to keep the sacrifices going. And then there was another coincidence." She put air quotes around *coincidence*. "It rained. Third time, rained again. That's all fact. Kid died and it rained. Three times. So who knows, maybe someone . . . I don't know. I don't know." She waved her hands, suddenly appearing embarrassed. "Oh God. I feel so stupid now saying it out loud. It seemed like I'd really solved it when it was in my head. It's stupid. I can tell you think I'm an idiot. I was hoping I could share it with somebody who isn't from here, because I sure as hell won't say anything to anybody who lives in town."

"No, no, no," he said. "It's not stupid." Once she removed the entity, it made a little more sense. "Someone could be superstitious. Superstition is real. Look at all the sports players who do weird things like don't change their socks for a whole season. What you're saying *is* weird. It's out there, but all theories are worth sharing and considering. That's how we get to the truth. Those theories are then proven or dismissed."

That seemed to make her feel better, and he kind of regretted it because she revved back up.

"There's other stuff too," she said. "More. I don't want to talk about it right now, because I haven't decided about sharing it. These people around here watch out for one another. I've lived in the area all my life, and loyalty is important. They keep their mouths shut. They lie to protect the community. Or they look the other way."

This was feeling promising again, but he didn't want to seem too interested or get his hopes up.

She checked her watch. "I gotta go. Maybe we can meet again sometime. Maybe not. I have to think about it. I saved your number."

"Okay. Thanks." Once again he got the feeling she was just playing him. "Call me anytime."

She left. He paid, left a nice tip.

She was still in the parking lot when he stepped outside. It had cooled off, but the air felt thick and damp. It looked like Imogene had stopped to talk on her phone. He was just about ready to make himself known when she put her phone away and got into a little white car. Without noticing him, she drove away.

On the drive back to Finney, the moon was half full and he could see a lot of stars, maybe the Big Dipper. Most of the ride, he felt like he was the only person on the two-lane road. He didn't get the chance to see much sky in LA.

After returning to his room, he thought about telling Olivia what had happened, but again decided to keep it close for now. He sent a few text messages to people back home, the neighbor who was keeping an eye on his apartment, feeding his cat, and getting his mail. His mother, who was off on a photography adventure in Canada. She'd probably forgotten he wasn't in LA. She replied with some nature photos he thought were very nice. She might or might not include them in an upcoming photography showing she was having in Beverly Hills.

A wave of loneliness washed over him, and for a moment he thought about seeing what Olivia was up to and if she'd learned anything today. But then he decided he'd been bugging her enough. Let her initiate the next thing, if there was a next thing.

He'd thought having someone like her in his story would help to round it out and give it more authenticity and interest, but he also didn't want to make a pest of himself. Or a bigger fool of himself than he had already. The stunt with the car might go down as the dumbest thing he'd ever done. He hoped it was anyway, because he couldn't imagine what any dumber thing might be.

Since he hadn't recorded the conversation with Imogene, he pulled out his laptop. Before he forgot the details, he went through his written notes, transcribing everything to a Word file, adding stuff he hadn't taken the time to write down, careful to be as exact as he could. How far it was to the bar from his motel room, what the sky looked like on the way there (orange and pink, with a few clouds, those deep-black silhouettes again), time he arrived, approximate temperature. Anything that would help the reader visualize the event. The way a letter on the bar sign was out so it said **OPE**, no *N* for *open* illuminated, and how few cars there were in the parking lot, but it had been early and a weeknight. All those details were important when writing nonfiction.

As he was working, he heard a vehicle outside, saw headlights through the curtain, heard doors open and close. Probably people checking in for the upcoming Mazie Ray Days, which might make a nice background for his story.

Once he'd finished writing up his notes, he got off the bed and pulled the curtain aside. His room was on the back side of the motel, where there wasn't much action or traffic. He spotted a few cars, signs of increased room occupation, but no people. Beyond the parking area was a field that seemed abandoned.

He was only just now realizing he'd romanticized this whole trip, and he honestly didn't know how much longer he could stand to be here. If it wasn't for Olivia, he'd be tempted to head back to LA tomorrow, but he didn't want to leave her alone, with no one watching her back. Not that she needed anyone. She could take care of herself. And not that he was any kind of a back-watcher, but he felt it was the two of them against the town. That thought reminded him of the nonsense Imogene had been spouting about babies being sacrificed to bring rain. Such a waste of time. Or was it? Was there anything to the superstition?

He took a shower, brushed his teeth, got into bed, and decided he'd try to get the rest of the story from Imogene tomorrow, regardless of how ridiculous it might be. Then he'd think about returning to LA, give up his dream of winning a Pulitzer.

He was almost asleep when he got a text from Imogene.

Let's meet again and I'll tell you everything. It has to be told.

17

Late the next morning, Will headed to the café. He was wearing the yellow-and-green cap with the flying corn, but he'd left the plaid shirt with the missing sleeves back in his room. Glancing around, he could see that his local attire had been a stretch. People didn't really look a whole lot different than what he was used to, except for the Instagram influencer crowd.

At the café, he sat at the table he'd used the day before. Someone other than Imogene put a glass of water and silverware in front of him.

"No Imogene?" he asked.

"Didn't show up."

The waitress was maybe in her fifties and had clearly been doing this a long time. He felt her pain while also feeling intimidated by her.

"She didn't even call," the woman said. "So I'm doing the job of two people."

"Is that unusual behavior for her?"

"I don't know. I just started working the morning shift, but I'd say it's typical for people her age."

He fiddled with the menu, pretending to read it. "I'm not sure that's fair." Imogene hadn't struck him as someone who'd flake like that, but then he recalled what she'd said about human sacrifices, and he decided flaking might be exactly what she'd do. Seemed like he might have lost his only lead, and it was a weak one.

The café door burst open and a woman practically fell inside. Her face was red, her eyes large. She seemed like someone lacking total awareness of her surroundings. "Where's Imogene?" she screamed to anybody who would listen, turning herself around, swaying. "Has anybody here seen my daughter?"

The people sitting at tables appeared stunned.

"She always comes home when she says she's coming home," the mother said. "Always. Has anybody seen her?" She looked around, from person to person.

Customers shook their heads.

"She was meeting someone last night," she said. "She just said she had to go out. It was late. She left, and I haven't heard a word since. I know something's happened to her!"

The waitress's demeanor softened. She put an arm around the upset mother, hugged her, gave her shoulder a pat. "Girls are like that. She probably overslept. Just give it a little time."

"Not my girl. She's very responsible." Imogene's mother moved toward the door. "I gotta go. Gotta talk to the marshal." She lunged for the door, paused in the opening, turned back. "If you hear anything, any of you, let me know." She burst into tears and left.

Will sat there as stunned as anybody else. More than anybody else.

It took some time for him to realize the world was turning again and the waitress was looking at him, pencil in hand, waiting for his order.

He slid the menu back behind the napkin holder. "I just remembered something I have to do." His mouth was almost too dry to talk. Feeling robotic and jerky, he left the café. Outside, he pulled out his phone and searched social media, looking for any recent information on Imogene, but found nothing.

He walked aimlessly.

He lost track of time and began to feel weak. His watch said it was early afternoon. How long ago had he been at the café?

He spotted a photo taped to a light pole and approached it for a closer look.

Imogene.

Under the photo were those familiar all-cap letters that spelled **MISSING**.

His phone rang. It was Olivia. He didn't answer. She'd never called him before, only texted. Had she heard about Imogene? Did she know he'd met with her? No, she couldn't know that. Could she? She was a detective though. Maybe she'd followed him.

This looked bad.

He had to get out of town. That's what he needed to do.

He walked very quickly back to the motel. In his room, he pulled out his leather suitcase that had belonged to his father, put it on the bed, and started tossing in clothes. Could he just drive to the airport and get a flight once he got there? He'd need to call and switch his ticket, a return flight for a date he'd just randomly chosen. And that airport was small. It might not even have flights out every day. He could drive. Just get in his car and drive all the way back to LA.

He felt queasy, yet he knew he should eat. His brain wasn't working right. He'd go to the gas station. Get something. Maybe a slice of pizza from that little heated thing that turned. Instead of walking, he drove. Might need to get away fast. As he was heading into the station, he had to navigate around a group of people clustered on the sidewalk near the ice machine and the bundled wood.

"Her car's been found," one of the guys in the group said. "Out in the middle of a field." He caught other snatches of conversation that might or might not have been true.

There was blood on the front seat.

They need all the help they can get for a search party.

Instead of going inside for food, he returned to his car and followed the crowd out of town.

He knew he was in the right spot long before he got there. Traffic slowed, and there was a police car with silent lights going. Someone directing traffic.

He pulled to the side of the road, half in a ditch, got out, and walked toward a group of people and officers gathered near the edge of a field. He and other volunteers were given orange vests and long poles and directed to walk side by side in a straight line so they could be sure every inch was covered.

They took breaks. Shade tents had been set up with food and water. There were even two portable toilets.

He started feeling queasy again. His hands shook. She was dead. Of course she was dead, but who and why, and did his meeting with her have anything to do with it? And what about the stuff she'd said she wanted to tell him? Something that needed to be told?

He couldn't continue searching. He was getting too light headed.

He left his vest and stick with a woman in one of the tents. There were plenty of people to take his place. *Oh great.* Olivia was there too, her face swimming in and out of the crowd. She must have heard about the search party and had come to help. Maybe that was why she'd called. He should have answered. Not answering looked suspicious.

It took him forever to find his rental. The sun was beating down, and his face felt hot and sunburned. He'd forgotten he wasn't driving his own car, his real car, the one he drove in LA. When he finally found the rental vehicle, he noticed flies crawling along the seam of the trunk, where the lid met the body of the car.

That's strange.

He dug the fob from his pocket and pressed the trunk-release button. It popped open a few inches. He raised it the rest of the way and staggered back, almost falling down, holding his hand to his mouth and nose.

His mind refused to process what he'd seen. He was distantly aware of other people nearby. Someone let out a gasp.

"What's that smell?"

Someone else said, "Oh my God!" Another person screamed.

He couldn't look, but in his mind, he could still see what was in the trunk, just flashes, as if one still image would be too much for his brain to process. Long, shiny brown hair, a tan arm, folded legs—a girl, curled up in his trunk almost like she was sleeping.

Had this all been some trick to get him out here? Had someone put her in there while they were walking the fields? Was she actually dead? Was she in on it too? Like some sort of freaky sick game to get back at him for the backward cap and the shirt with the sleeves cut off? Was there really a group of people who thought dead bodies could make it rain?

No. Stupid. Too stupid.

But how was that harder to believe than this? A dead girl in his trunk?

Maybe not dead. He needed to check. Make sure.

He was vaguely aware of a lot of activity. People running, screaming, yelling for help, saying they'd found her.

Will forced himself to step closer to the trunk. Flies hit him in the face, and with a frantic motion he tried to shoo them away. *They'd been on her.* He leaned in. He reached down and touched her arm. Cold, but not that cold.

He'd seen two dead bodies in his life, and those had both been from a distance, both gunshot victims. This was something else, something personal, something that hurt his heart and scared the hell out of him. Somebody put her there. Somebody wanted to make him look guilty.

He moved his hand from her arm to her wrist. Felt for a pulse. Maybe this was an actress with really good makeup. But he could feel the absence of Imogene. She'd been fire and sass. There was nothing here. No presence.

He felt hands on him, pulling him away from her, forcing his arms behind his back. The metal of handcuffs went around his wrists and clicked into place. He was shoved to the side, pushed in the direction of a nearby police car. He glanced to see who was leading him off.

Marshal Murphy, a grim expression on his face, his jaw muscle rigid. Will recognized him from the press coverage, especially the heartbreaking picture of him outside the farmhouse cradling his one remaining child.

"Will!"

He looked up and saw Olivia standing near the edge of the mob. Her expression was the only one that was more concern than hatred.

"I'll meet you at the jail!" she shouted.

People scowled at her.

If he made it to the jail.

Right now it looked like pretty much everybody in the county wanted to kill him. Then he had the dumbest thought. This was his fault. He'd wanted to inject himself into this story. *Good freaking job, Will.* He thought about his neighbor, and he thought about his cat, and he thought about his mother and how her photography trip was going to be ruined. And then he started crying because Imogene was dead. He might or might not have killed her, but he was pretty sure it was his fault.

18

Once Will was hauled off in the police car, Olivia planned to follow. That was until she spotted Marshal Murphy sauntering around, shouting orders. No yellow tape, people too near Will's rental car. An ambulance eased close and parked; the back doors opened. Two people pulled out a gurney.

She looked at the body in the trunk, making some visual assessments without touching anything. Not her place to step in, but back when she worked Homicide, she was a firm believer in observing the scene for a good length of time before anyone made a move to touch or gather evidence.

"You can't take the body away," she told the people with the gurney. "Someone needs to cordon off the car, a crime-scene team needs to be brought in. I'm sure the county has one, and this needs to be properly processed."

Murphy overheard the conversation and approached. This was the first she'd seen him since the night at the morgue. He seemed more intimidating in the daylight, with his bulging arms and severe-looking mouth.

"We do our own evidence collection," he said. "You don't have any authority here. Or anywhere, for that matter."

She pulled her phone from her back pocket and began scrolling through her contact list. "I'm going to call a crime-scene specialist from

Wichita, and she'll have people here very quickly. Until then, I'll stay where I am to make sure nobody touches the body." There was no way in hell she was going to allow the scene to be sloppily processed. One of the easiest ways to get Will out of jail would be determining how long the girl had been dead.

"I can arrest you for obstruction," he said.

"Can you? Do you really want to cuff me in front of this crowd of people?" She looked around. She was keeping her voice low, and nobody was near enough to hear, but she'd talk louder if she needed to. "I'm simply demanding you do the right thing. I think you've got enough attention on you right now, what with Bonnie and all. Do you really want more? Because I can also make sure you get national press coverage. I know a lot of people, and this story can be everywhere very soon. About how you tampered with a crime scene."

He scowled.

In her previous job as a homicide detective, she'd met a lot of people in the field. Those acquaintances were almost a community, where everyone was connected in some way or another, no matter where they lived in the country. Her old friend Coco Sandoval, for one. She'd not so recently transferred from LA to the Kansas Bureau of Investigation, located in Wichita.

She called Coco, letting her know there was also a vehicle that would require transport. "We're going to need a tow truck to haul this in for a thorough processing," Olivia told her. Will certainly didn't have a good record when it came to rental cars.

"Is this connected to the possible filicide case there?" Coco asked.

"Maybe. I don't know. The mother is currently in jail, so that rules her out. The victim is Imogene Griffin, a twenty-year-old woman who went missing. Body was found in the trunk of a car. Fully dressed, no outward sign of sexual violence. Bruises on the neck that look like finger impressions. Body is in advanced or complete rigor."

"A hot car will skew those findings."

"Yep."

Had Imogene known something? Maybe about the recent murder? Olivia didn't like to jump to conclusions, but that was all she had right now. "Might be no connection at all between the two cases," she said, "and yet here are two deaths in a town that had zero until the children began dropping. I'd really like to get an official window for time of death because right now I have a friend sitting in jail."

"A close friend?"

Was she surprised? If so, maybe because Olivia kept people at a distance, even people she worked with like Coco. "I said *friend*, but really just a recent acquaintance. We took the same flight here from LA to investigate the case."

"FBI?"

"No, reporter for *Hard Times*."

"You have my sympathy."

"He's okay. A little flaky. It's kind of us against the town. They aren't wild about our being here. And they are not going to be happy to have you processing the scene."

"Tough. I'll make sure we do it right. I have to say that a body in the trunk is highly suspicious. He's going to have to have a damn good alibi. Can't blame them for tossing him in jail."

True. Had he charmed her with a fake persona? After all, he had most likely set fire to his car.

"We're stretched thin right now," Coco said, "but I can have boots on the ground in four or five hours."

"Sooner would be better, if possible. The marshal wants to process the scene himself, and I think the whole town is probably going to support that decision. I'm not sure I can hold them back that long."

"I'll see if I can get a chopper. This sounds intriguing. Wish I could come myself."

"How do you like it in Kansas?"

"It was tough the first year. Real culture shock, but I've settled in. Still not crazy about those wide-open plains. I don't know why. But it's beautiful too."

"I understand. Feeling that way myself right now."

"I'll get in touch with the right people and have a team there as quickly as possible," Coco said. "I'll keep you in the loop. And in the meantime, try to keep everybody away from the scene."

"I'll do my best—and, Coco? I'd like to talk to you about something related." Seeing what she'd witnessed today when it came to processing crime scenes, she could pretty much bet not nearly enough evidence had been collected when all three children's bodies were found. Zero would be her guess. "Give me a call when you get a chance so we can talk about it. Maybe tonight?"

"Sounds good."

"I'm dropping a location pin," Olivia said. "Should be plenty of room for a helicopter."

After disconnecting, she walked over to Murphy. "Someone from the KBI will be here, soon I hope. In the meantime, what about a perimeter? I'll bet you have some of that bright yellow tape we could put up?"

He did.

She was surprised he actually had any, but she could see he wasn't very familiar with using it.

Olivia stuck around until the helicopter showed up. By that time, townspeople were shouting at her and shaking their fists. She was expecting fire and pitchforks at any moment. One big guy said he wanted to kill her.

Murphy, bless his heart, walked over and hushed him up. "I don't want to hear any of that kind of talk," he told the guy.

It was too late to visit Will at the jail. After a brief conversation with the crime-scene team, she headed back to the motel, worried about Dorothy because she'd left her alone for several hours. The dog was agitated but didn't seem too upset. Some snacks, a walk, and cuddles, and Olivia felt forgiven. Once evening rolled around, her phone rang. A call from Coco.

They talked a bit about their lives, and then Olivia brought up the real reason for the conversation. "As you've no doubt heard, this is the third child to die in the Murphy family, and there is one more at home. Bonnie Murphy is still a suspect, but with little or no evidence, she's going to be released soon."

"Oh wow."

"Yeah. So anyway, you know how small towns often combine the job of coroner and medical examiner. There was not much evidence collected. I'd at the very least like to have a tox report."

"Me too."

"Maybe some touch DNA from the clothing or skin, but that can be difficult due to a water death. I'm way overstepping here. I'm a private citizen, but they are burying the latest child soon. I think it's too late to stop it, but I'm wondering about your department possibly getting a court order to exhume the body."

"We're on the same page there. I'll see what I can do. Good talking to you. Is that Cecil Hotel I hear whimpering in the background?"

"No, Cecil died a few months ago."

"Oh, I'm so sorry. He was a great dog, but I'm glad you have a new pup in your life."

Olivia glanced over. The dog was staring at her, looking way too sweet. She told Coco goodbye and ended the call. Then she gave Dorothy a good petting, cradling her face, saying, "So what did you see, when did you see it, and do you need to go into witness protection?"

It was a joke, but why had Murphy tried to get rid of Dorothy? She still might have some nasty tricks up her paws, but so far Dorothy seemed like the perfect dog. And if he wanted to dispose of her because she might be connected to a crime, why didn't he just shoot her and dig a hole?

"I'm sorry for even thinking that, Dorothy," Olivia told her.

But it didn't make sense. Maybe he just couldn't bring himself to do it. Although he seemed like someone who might relish something that awful. She had to remind herself not to allow her personal reaction to him color her perspective. It could really skew a case.

And then there was Will. Had he killed Imogene Griffin? That's what she needed to find out.

19

Who would have thought she'd be back in the same jail, sitting on the same stool, holding the same phone just days after meeting with Bonnie? The big difference? This time Olivia was talking to Will.

"I didn't kill Imogene," he said.

He looked bad. Wrinkled clothes, he needed to shave, his hair was a mess, and his eyes were bloodshot.

"Why didn't you tell me you were meeting with her?" Olivia asked. "That alone looks suspicious."

"I wanted an exclusive! A scoop! And I also knew you might want to come along. And she might not talk if you were there."

"Bloody hell."

"I didn't do anything wrong. You believe me, right?"

"I don't know. I'm not sure if I can believe anything you say."

"I get it. I wouldn't trust me either." He let out a groan and buried his face in his hands. He mumbled something about just wanting to be the next Truman Capote. Then he looked up at her. "He didn't win a Pulitzer. You know that, right? I was gonna win one for him."

"Oh, come on."

"No, really. And for my dad. I guess I was really doing it to prove myself to him. Too late to make him proud of me, but that's where my head has been."

"Let's forget about that for now. They can't hold you any longer than seventy-two hours without an official charge."

"I had a body in my trunk. I think they can pretty much do anything they want. But here's the thing. She knew something, and she was afraid to tell me."

"You think someone might have killed her to keep her quiet?"

"Maybe." He seemed reluctant to continue, but he finally shared some of what Imogene had told him when they met at the bar. "The Murphys. Dysfunction on every level it sounded like," he said. "The mother. The kids. The hot cop."

"I've called some people. A coroner will be involved, someone from the outside. We'll establish time of death and prove you were elsewhere. You were elsewhere, right?"

"Yes!" His reply was a scream of anguish.

Overacting?

20

An officer unlocked Will's cell. "Come on out," he said with annoyance as he swung the door wide and stood to the side. "You're free to go."

"Is this a joke?" Will asked.

"I wish."

"All righty then." Will followed the officer down the row of empty cells. He'd had the area to himself all three days, but he'd heard Bonnie was in a section by herself. "What happened?" he asked.

The officer ignored him.

Olivia was waiting for him in the lobby, and when he saw her, he let out a sob. It just shot out of him. She looked like an angel, otherworldly, with an errant shaft of sunlight finding its way inside the building, specifically destined to fall on her short red hair. Kind of Joan of Arc, now that he thought about it. Why, she was beautiful. Powerful, in control, someone who got things done in a calm manner. Maybe it was just dust in the air, but it seemed like she shimmered. He made a mental note to write that down.

He should have known she'd get him out.

In his relief to find himself a free man who was not heading to his own hanging in the town square, he dashed for her and embraced her with both arms. It took a little bit for him to realize she wasn't as excited about the reunion as he was. He didn't want to stop hugging her, but he let go and stepped back. Was he free for good, or just out for now?

He also realized he had tears in his eyes, but he suddenly didn't care. He was free. He wasn't dead.

"Here are your things." The officer who'd led him from the cell handed him a Ziploc bag with his phone and keys and his flip notebook and pen. And his sunglasses, which he slipped on before he and Olivia stepped outside.

He stood there in the great outdoors, took a deep breath. Even nasty Kansas seemed like the most beautiful place on earth. Maybe he should think of moving here. He suddenly wondered if the jail had made a mistake in releasing him and would soon realize it. "We should run. Before they change their minds."

She gave him an awkward pat, kind of a *buck up, kid* thing. "Everything is fine. You're being a little dramatic, but I guess I understand."

"I was there forever."

"Three days."

"It seemed like three months. It was awful."

She frowned and looked at him more closely. Now that she was no longer in that shaft of light, she wasn't glowing. But man, her eyes were a deep brown, and such an interesting complement to her hair.

"Did anyone harm you when you were in there?"

"Yes!"

"What? Tell me!"

"If by *harm* you mean serving me really bad coffee."

She laughed.

She had a great laugh too, something deep that burst from her. Was he falling in love? He had no memory of what that felt like. This was more like the kind of thing he remembered from high school, and he was too damn old for crushes. He shouldn't have watched *Private Dick Chick* so many times.

"I don't understand how I'm standing here, a free man," he said.

"They had video footage of you at the gas station buying ice cream approximately the same time Imogene died. Time of death got you off."

"Good thing I like ice cream."

"That by itself might not have been enough, but it looks like your car was tampered with. The door and trunk have scratch marks on them that appear to have been done by a crowbar or something similar. So the theory is that somebody popped the trunk and disposed of the body. Unfortunately, there's no footage of that. The motel has outdoor cameras, but the lenses had been spray-painted black. But that also helped your case. Somebody didn't want to be seen breaking into your car."

"That's a lot of detective work."

"It's what I do. Oh, one more thing. Imogene had an ex-boyfriend who used to beat her and is now a prime suspect. He was texting with her the night of her death."

"Might have seen us together. Got mad."

"Yep. Poor girl."

"You're good."

"Anyway, all of that combined made it so they simply couldn't hold you any longer. And believe me, they wanted to."

Her car was parked in the small lot next to the jail. He was tempted to ask if they could put the top down, but he didn't want to be an even bigger pain in the ass than he already was. But once in the passenger seat, once they hit the road, he lowered his window and leaned out. Now he understood why dogs loved to grab some air. Freedom, man.

"I'll bet you're hungry," she said. "You want to get something to eat?"

"Not at the café."

"No, not the café."

"What about one of those pizza slices from that weird and hypnotic slow-spinning oven at the gas station?"

"I was thinking you might prefer to go to a nearby town for something more substantial. And maybe a place where nobody knows you."

"Like the opposite of *Cheers*."

"I guess."

"The jail food wasn't bad." Home-cooked stuff he'd imagined being prepared by some woman wearing a cheerful apron, smiling sweetly as she pulled the fixins out of her oven. Weird Midwest food, like meatloaf and mashed potatoes and gravy. Green beans with a slab of butter. Coffee that was thick and bitter, like something reheated after sitting out overnight. His stomach heaved a little just recalling it.

He realized it could have been worse, and he appreciated that unknown person going to the trouble to actually cook meals for him. Although the first night after eating, he'd felt sick to his stomach and had moaned and told the guard he'd been poisoned.

"I'd really like a slice of that pizza," he said. "I'll wait outside though. Pretty sure everybody in there will recognize me."

"Pretty sure you're right. Okay. It's your day."

"Get Out of Jail Free Day." He tried to laugh but couldn't.

"Too soon?"

"Think so."

She parked and went into the gas station with its attached convenience store.

As Will waited in the car, he kept thinking of things to add to their dinner. He sent her several texts, and by the time she stepped out the door, she was carrying two white plastic bags and a six-pack of beer, the bags stretched and weighed down with, hopefully, the snacks and ice cream he'd requested. He didn't drink beer that much, but today seemed to call for it.

At her motel room, they dumped the goods on the long dresser. Will put the ice cream in the freezer compartment of the tiny fridge while Olivia fed Dorothy. Then they took her for a quick walk around the motel.

"After you were arrested, I went to the office and asked to see the footage," Olivia told him. "The desk clerk tried to pull it up. Everything was black. We went outside and found the cameras like that." She pointed. "I don't think Murphy was even going to ask. So that led to a closer examination of your vehicle."

He wondered what would have happened to him if she hadn't been around. He might have gone to prison. He might have died mysteriously in jail.

Back inside, they ate the pizza slices and both of them drank two bottles of beer. Something made in a little nearby town. It was actually very good.

"What are you going to do now?" she asked, leaning back against the headboard of the bed, her feet crossed at the ankles, Dorothy beside her.

"I don't know." He got up from the only chair in the room and began picking up trash. "Maybe go home. I mean, *home* home. California home." He didn't mention that he'd been thinking about it even before the arrest. "But I wonder if I need to stick around."

"Might be good to get out of here." She didn't look fully convinced though, but then she was hard to read.

He thought about the book he'd planned to write. And he thought about leaving her here, to the wolves. He didn't like that. "You think I should pack it in and leave?"

"Totally up to you." Then she added, "Just an FYI. The Murphy child's funeral is tomorrow." Kinda sounded like a challenge to him. Or a dare.

21

"It's a wild day for a funeral," Olivia told Dorothy as she latched the door to the dog crate. And by *wild day*, she meant the wind was getting more intense by the minute. It was amazing the roof didn't fly off the motel.

"Be glad you're safe in here, and not out there. Although with a name like Dorothy, the weather might be perfect for you."

The dog whimpered and began digging at the blanket, making a nest. She was a good girl. She barked occasionally, but she didn't seem to do so when left alone, not that Olivia had heard or heard about, anyway. It was a relief to find she could endure a crate and almost seemed to like it at times. No need to feel too guilty.

Olivia's phone alerted her to a message.

Figuring it was Will, she checked the screen. It was from her doctor's office. Her surgery had been rescheduled for a week from today. That was alarmingly soon. She'd hoped to put it off for a long time. Maybe forever. The message added that a surgical slot had opened up, otherwise the wait would have been months.

We tried to call you, but nobody picked up. Doc says we need to move on this. Please confirm the date with yes or no.

She hesitated before confirming with a yes. Then she tucked her phone away and grabbed her bag containing her camera and telephoto lens.

She was wearing a black dress along with black sandals, both items she'd picked up at the antique shop she'd spotted her first night in town, the vintage garment the very one she'd noticed in the window.

When she stepped outside, the door was practically ripped from her hand. She grabbed it and struggled to pull it closed, finally accomplishing the task while the wind sucked air from her lungs. The daytime sky was so dark that streetlights were on. Even the birds weren't singing from nearby trees—asleep, thinking it was night.

She'd thought the event might be postponed due to the weather, at least the burial, but a check of social media had shown no mention of cancellation. Although she wasn't feeling very guilty about the crate, she was worried about leaving Dorothy alone with a possible storm coming.

She locked the motel door, ducked her head, and ran for her car, not at all enjoying the feel of such a flimsy frock and unsubstantial shoes. She was used to dressing for battle. Yet, while the wind was unsettling, she also found something oddly invigorating about it. She rarely experienced extreme weather. The storm made her aware of nature and the environment in a way the streets of LA never could.

Still, other than that brief moment in Mazie's bedroom, nothing felt familiar. It seemed that part of her memory was really and truly gone. And she could admit that it wasn't just the risk of dying that made her reluctant to have the surgery. It was the fear of forgetting. Forgetting everything that was left. Herself. This person in this body. Maybe she'd wake up, if she woke up, to be not even a version of herself but somebody completely different.

Maybe she'd wake up an asshole.

Will was waiting next to her car. He was dressed in black slacks, a white long-sleeved dress shirt, and a black tie that was whipping in the wind. The rental company had refused to rent another vehicle to him this time. Understandable. One burned up, and another had a dead body in the trunk. She'd told him he could ride to the funeral with her.

She slid behind the wheel, and he got in the passenger seat.

"I have to hope we're dressed appropriately. I, at least, want to go to the cemetery." Burials could sometimes flush out the suspicious or elicit odd reactions from attendees. She planned to find a good spot to do some serious people watching.

"You look nice," Will said. "And I'm pretty sure black is always appropriate for a funeral."

"I hate to dress up. It feels like I'm wearing a costume."

"I like to. I don't even mind suits. I would have worn one, but this was all I brought."

The typically empty streets were packed with cars. She caught sight of three vans with satellite dishes and network logos, prepping for live broadcasts.

She parked a block from the church, wedging her car into a spot that provided a full-windshield view of the building, a stone structure with a massive single spire with outdoor speakers that must have been connected to the organ, because she could hear that distinctive dirge despite the howl of the wind. It was always a curiosity to see impoverished small towns with such impressive churches, many of them now abandoned or turned into condos.

"There's a hydrant right here." Will pointed out the side passenger window.

"I'll leave if anybody confronts me about it. But I think those people are all at the funeral."

"It's a stereotype, but are you getting the feeling that people can get away with more in small towns?" Will asked.

"And not just murder," Olivia said. "There can be a lot of corruption in small towns. I don't want to malign them all, because that's unfair, but in my experience, I've found a surprising amount of all types of crime because nobody is overseeing it."

Will nodded, then said, "I've never been on a stakeout."

"This isn't really a stakeout. And I'd have guessed you had been in similar situations, waiting for some celebrity to appear."

"I'm not paparazzi." He sounded a little miffed. "I've never done that kind of work." His voice took on a thoughtful tone. "Not that I wouldn't for the right story . . ."

"Didn't I read a piece you wrote about the actors on *Gilmore Girls*? A where-are-they-now story?"

"It was *assigned* to me."

"I have nothing against that kind of writing. I found it informative."

"That was before I started writing for *Hard Times*. Gotta do what you gotta do."

"I learned that Amy Sherman-Palladino didn't write season seven. That was informative."

"It went to hell, right?"

"Kind of flatlined. But I don't think it was horrible."

"My article was written before *The Handmaid's Tale*."

"Oh my God. I screamed when I saw Rory in that."

"Me too."

More talk. Some munching of snacks. Then the giant wooden doors to the church opened. Two people stepped to the side while maintaining a hold on the doors to keep them from slamming shut on the exiting attendees.

"Looks like they're coming out." Olivia grabbed her camera with the telephoto lens and aimed it at the front of the church. As people appeared, she pressed the shutter release.

"Oh my God," she said.

"What?"

"There's Bonnie!"

"Bonnie Murphy?" Spoken as if Will thought that couldn't be possible.

Olivia was having the same reaction. "Yep." She handed the camera to him.

"I wonder if they got special permission for her to attend the funeral," he said as he looked through the camera lens. He pressed the shutter a couple of times. Passed the camera back.

"All of this has been way too fast," Olivia said. "The funeral, the lack of complete autopsy. Why the hurry unless there's something to hide? I'm gonna say Bonnie's out for good. I don't even see the ankle monitor she's supposed to be wearing. The death will be officially ruled an accident, and the world will continue to spin. With one more baby left to die, either by neglect or murder."

Bonnie; her husband, Conrad; and Ava all ducked into a black limo, the kind supplied by funeral homes.

"I'd like to be a fly on the ceiling of that vehicle," Will said. "What do you think they're talking about? Are they all in it together? At least the cover-up?"

Were Ava and Conrad protecting Bonnie? And then where did Imogene fit? Did she fit? Was she simply or unsimply killed by a jealous ex-boyfriend who found out she'd met with Will? "I can imagine Ava rambling about pie. Apple pie, rhubarb pie, peach pie."

"Don't forget pumpkin."

Once most of the attendees were in cars, but before the procession left, Olivia put her camera in the bag, started her engine, and headed for the cemetery, hoping to beat them there.

"There's no way to be inconspicuous when driving a red vintage Cadillac," she said.

"Sorry about the rental car. Are you ever going to forgive me?"

Maybe—if her surgery went wrong and she forgot about the rental fiasco. She chuckled to herself, and he shot her a puzzled sideways glance.

She was able to park in an area far from the burial plot and behind a clump of trees that she hoped would at least partially hide the car.

They got out and practically crept forward, Olivia with her camera bag slung over one shoulder. They found a spot under a tree, in the shade, not too close, but close enough to see that the grave had already been dug, a crew loitering nearby, not being as inconspicuous as they should have been as they waited for the service to be over so they could fill in the hole and go home to gossip about it.

There was a tent and a large rug and folding chairs for the family. The black hearse arrived first. It was unloaded by several men with shiny white foreheads that were usually covered by caps. The casket was positioned above the grave, where it would be lowered once the service was done.

Cars parked in a random mess, in no particular order. People emerged from vehicles, all moving toward a central location like metal being attracted to a magnet. Walking across graves and through dead grass burned by hot sun and lack of rain. A flock of crows passed overhead, and the wind blew skirts and jackets in a way that made the clothing look like wings. The sky was getting even darker, and funeral-goers cast nervous glances overhead.

Olivia pulled her camera from her bag and squinted through the viewfinder again, quickly noting Bonnie standing between her husband and mother.

She silently passed the camera to Will.

"That's some weird shit," he said under his breath as he looked through the lens. After a minute, he passed the camera back.

"I don't like this," Olivia whispered. "At the very least, she should be somewhere under suicide watch."

"Is there anything about this town that makes sense?"

"I thought maybe it just seemed that way to me because of my history."

"No, it *is* weird. Somebody put a body in my trunk."

She thought about how Will had ingratiated himself into her Kansas existence, and she felt both annoyed and grateful to have someone outside the town circle as an acquaintance. He was probably the only other person to get just *how* weird this was.

Everyone in Finney and beyond seemed to be there. The crowd was that big. If people had been talking, there would have been a roar. The wind had quieted, but the sky was threatening, and Olivia thought she heard rumblings of thunder from the far distance. She hoped Dorothy wasn't afraid of storms. Her old dog had been terrified of storms and fireworks. If Dorothy had that phobia, she shouldn't be alone.

Dogs could break and fix your heart.

"And I think it's going to get weirder," Olivia said as she watched a new parade of vehicles enter the cemetery and head toward the burial plot, this after attendees were already in place, the minister in position next to the grave site, holding a Bible, the graveside service ready to commence.

The black sedan was moving a little too fast, seemingly on a mission. Bringing up the tail was a white emergency-type van. When it was close enough, Olivia read the lettering: *Kansas Bureau of Investigation.*

They were here to stop the burial and get the body. Much better than an exhumation. A thrilled *zing* shot through her. She stuck her camera away and adjusted the bag on her shoulder. "I've got to get a closer look."

"Right with you." Will was already moving.

They stopped near one of the few mausoleums on the grounds. Using it for cover, peeking around the corner, they were close enough to hear but hopefully far enough away to go unnoticed.

A woman with black hair exited the sedan and strode forward, stopping near the minister. Olivia heard something about a court order to confiscate the body for a thorough autopsy.

"We'll be respectfully taking it to Wichita and will release it for burial as soon as we're done. We'll try to do everything in a timely manner," she added.

The crowd roared now. Mouths dropped open and people turned to one another as if to pantomime *Well I never!* And yet, even from a distance, Olivia could pick up a certain salacious satisfaction in the group. How many were there for the spectacle, nothing more?

Conrad Murphy began waving his arms and shouting. Others joined in, yelling at the woman too. The agent's team gathered behind her, as if they might need to defend themselves and her.

Then the marshal, whom Olivia realized was wearing his whole marshal outfit, including the hat, caught sight of her standing near the mausoleum and redirected his anger, marching across the grass, pointing at her, shouting, "This is your doing, isn't it?"

Will looked at her and mouthed, *Is it?*

She blinked in admission.

His eyebrows lifted. "Good one."

At least somebody was happy.

She put her camera and case aside, and she and Will moved closer. Olivia wondered if Coco was in the group, but she didn't see her. Most were wearing blue polo shirts with the Kansas Bureau of Investigation logo across the back that matched the logos on the cars and the white van.

As the crowd watched in shocked disbelief, the casket was affixed with a chain of custody seal that was signed by one of the agents. It wouldn't be broken until the body arrived at the coroner's office for the autopsy. Much would have already been lost through the embalming procedure, but she hoped they'd be able to find evidence to support that the death was either accidental or murder. And if it was murder, the killer needed to be held accountable.

The casket was full size rather than a child's, white with gold trim, which seemed an odd choice, but maybe it was all they had on hand— yet another detail that made the burial feel rushed. Once the casket was inside the van, the double doors were slammed closed.

And then, almost as if it had never happened, the convoy of vehicles circled the perimeter of the cemetery and continued their slow procession out the gate, leaving the mourners standing there with no body to bury.

Moments later, barely leaving people time to process one oddity, another replaced it. A rusty pickup truck came flying through the gate and down one of the dirt lanes, the wheels kicking up a cloud of dust. The vehicle veered off the path and cut straight across the grass, bouncing, sometimes airborne, finally coming to a sharp stop not far from the mausoleum.

The truck door creaked open and a woman jumped out.

Dark hair disheveled, barefoot, wearing a stained nightgown. She had a rifle tucked under her arm, cradling the weapon as if she was used to holding and shooting one, drunk or sober. Her gaze moved around the crowd. She finally locked hard on Olivia and Will.

And lifted the rifle.

Looking down the barrel, she began to walk straight for Will. "This is called taking the law into my own hands." She tripped, caught herself, and stood, swaying a little. "There you were, sitting in the café, acting like you didn't know where she was or what had happened to her. And she was in your trunk all the time."

Imogene's mother? Must have been.

A few drops of rain fell, but the woman didn't seem to notice. Her eyes never wavered, like someone in combat who knew one blink could result in a lost kill.

Nobody tried to stop her. Everybody seemed transfixed. But then a man shouted, "Come on, Irene! Do it. Pull the trigger. Kill that son of a bitch!"

Will made a strangled sound, but Olivia didn't chance a look in his direction. Like Irene, she kept her eyes on the target, *her* target, the woman with the gun, never wavering, watching for any chance to disarm her.

Other people joined in the chant against Will. And many, instead of running from possible gunfire, began moving closer. An angry mob.

A woman said, "We'll back you up, Irene! Say he had a gun and threatened you with it. It takes a village!"

Several began to chant the phrase "It takes a village."

"Village of the damned," Will whispered.

Conrad Murphy materialized from the cluster of people. He surprised Olivia by trying to calm Irene. "Put the gun down. Let's talk about this."

"Shut up, Murphy," Irene said. "If you won't do your job, I'll have to do it for you. You let this murderer free. You even let your wife kill your own kids. You are pathetic."

People gasped. Olivia gasped too. At her audacity. But grief made a person not care what anybody thought. She felt sorry for Irene.

"This is not helping anybody. Will did not kill your daughter," Olivia said, inching closer. She realized she felt invincible at the moment, and she understood why. This place, being here, didn't seem real. There was a good chance she'd die soon anyway. A week from now. Might as well go out with purpose.

If Irene shot her first, maybe Will could get away. He wasn't exactly worthy of her bloodshed. She'd rather die for somebody else, somebody she loved, like her father, if he were still alive. Or—*sorry, Will*—even her dog, Cecil, if he were still alive. Her mother, if she were still alive. Even Mazie Ray, someone she couldn't even remember. But here she was, risking her life for some Truman Capote wannabe. Guess it made as much sense as anything.

"Oh really?" Irene said. "I don't believe you. I think you're both a couple of carpetbagging liars. Outsiders who think they know what's best for us. Well, you don't."

"We want to find out who the killer is as much as you do," Olivia said. "Almost as much, anyway. Don't divert the focus away from finding your daughter's murderer. And that person is still out there, running around loose. He might be right here, at this funeral. But we need to find and follow evidence. That takes time."

"This has nothing to do with you," Irene shouted, tears streaming down her face. "What are you even doing here?"

The raindrops got larger. They were so cold they stung. Irene glanced up, appearing surprised, as if trying to figure out what had hit her.

The rain increased, then diminished, and then a few small hailstones began to fall with such randomness that they seemed a joke. People ducked and ran for their cars and pickups. Irene glanced nervously at the churning cloud above her head and muttered something about how the town was cursed.

Conrad Murphy and Irene had made a good point when they asked what Olivia was doing there. She'd done what she'd come to do. The boy's body would get a thorough autopsy, and Will was out of jail. Even Bonnie was out, although Olivia didn't know how she felt about that. Why *was* she here? She and Will should get the hell out while they still could, before their heads were stuck on pikes at the edge of town.

Olivia hadn't kept up on her hand-to-hand combat, but she recalled the basic moves, all muscle memory now. She could still kick or dive. In a fraction of a second, she mentally measured the distance and knew she had to choose the least pleasant maneuver, launching herself into a move that, over water, might be slightly unpleasant. This would be more like diving to catch a ground ball.

She dove. She grabbed Irene's leg and pulled.

The woman fell hard, gun flying.

She surprised Olivia by fighting back. She rolled, straddled Olivia, grabbed her by the front of her antique dress, ripping the fabric but still retaining enough of a hold to lift her head and slam it hard against the ground.

Will shouted and ran for them.

Someone yelled, "Girl fight!"

Someone else grabbed the rifle. Maybe Murphy. Seemed like Murphy because Olivia thought she spotted his cop hat. Hard to know anything much beyond the pain, which was a red-hot poker of agony flashing behind her eyes.

She screamed in front of everybody, curled into a ball, and cradled her head. The screaming eventually faded to a keening wail, then shifted to shallow panting as she tried not to move.

Then, thankfully, she blacked out.

22

When Olivia busted him out of jail, Will had thought about how she seemed so strong and capable of anything. To see her curled on the ground shook him to a degree he never would have expected. But she was a force, and she was rare. A person just knew when they were in the presence of somebody special, and she was all that and more.

Backup arrived in the form of another police car. Irene Griffin was cuffed. Murphy and two other townspeople were bent over Olivia. Farther away, the locals who hadn't left stood and watched like a bunch of drenched crows. The hail was over, and the rain had almost stopped. A few drops pattered against leaves, the wind was gone, vanished, and the sun was trying to shine, everything shimmering.

Will was used to standing back, not getting involved, not because he was a coward, but because he typically didn't care enough to bother. Right now, seeing them, people who had been chanting for his death moments ago, a cop who'd just stood there while Olivia had basically saved Will's life, he felt a rage building inside him.

He strode forward, pushed the two people nearest her away. "Don't touch her. I'm calling 911."

She must've heard him, because she moved a little and said, eyes closed, "No." Her voice was a wispy thread. "Don't. Just help me up and get me out of here. Back to the motel."

"You need to go to the hospital." He leaned closer, looking for damage. Her face was wet from the rain, but he didn't see any blood.

"Keys . . . in my pocket."

He didn't approve, but he was on board with getting her out of there. Once she was in the car, he could drive her to a hospital.

He straightened, pointed at the people nearby. "Stay away from her. I'm coming right back."

He marched away, picking up her camera bag as he passed the mausoleum where they'd been earlier. He stepped over and around and on some graves, then hopped in the car and drove across the grass, much like Irene had done, coming to stop a few yards from Olivia.

Shut off the engine, opened the passenger door wide.

Everybody but one person had done what he'd said and had kept their distance.

Bonnie Murphy was sitting beside Olivia, holding her hand and stroking her arm, crooning softly to her.

Seeing that, he had to wonder if maybe she hadn't killed those kids. Even though her child's body had just been swept away from her, she was thinking of Olivia.

With Bonnie's help, he got Olivia to her feet. Looping one of Olivia's arms behind his neck, grasping her wrist, another arm around her waist, he and Bonnie slowly escorted Olivia to the car.

"She needs a doctor," Bonnie said. To Olivia: "You need to go to the hospital." Bonnie looked at Will and mouthed, *Just take her.*

He nodded.

But of course Olivia was on to that plan.

Once they had her reclined in the passenger seat and he was driving away from the grave site, slowly even though he wanted to blast out of there like a bunch of demons were after them, he took each bump as carefully as possible, easing the car through the gate, turning down the highway that led back to the heart of Finney but also Dodge City, a much larger town that most likely had a hospital.

He stopped at the crossroad where he'd need to turn right to medical care or left to Finney.

"Motel," she said softly. Then louder, "Take me to the motel."

He put the car in park and shifted in his seat. "Let's look at you. Open your eyes."

She did.

Both pupils were the same size. That was good, right? He felt for her pulse in her wrist. Seemed a little rapid.

She closed her eyes.

"Okay, but my backup plan is to take you to the hospital if you aren't looking better in an hour."

A few minutes later, he pulled to a stop with the bumper just inches from the sidewalk that ran the length of the motel. Tidy windows, six orange doors.

He helped her into the room, where she carefully lowered herself onto the bed, easing down on her back, head on a pillow, arm across her eyes. Dorothy was in a crate, and she began barking. The sound bounced off the walls and practically shook Will's metal fillings.

"Dorothy," Olivia whispered weakly. "Shush."

"Should I let her out?"

"Yeah."

He unlatched the door, and she shot past him, jumping onto the bed. Olivia slipped off her sandals using her bare toes, her arm wrapped around the dog. "Look in that bag under the TV," she told Will. "There's some medication."

He opened the wrong one first and found two guns. He quickly closed that, found the bag she was talking about, and unzipped it. She wasn't kidding about medication. *What the?* He'd heard she'd had a lot of surgeries, but the amount of pain medication made him wonder just how successful they'd been.

Not very, he'd say.

She told him what she needed. "Two of them," she said.

From the refrigerator, he pulled out a bottle of water, opened it.

She propped herself up on one elbow, took the pills from his palm, and swallowed them, then lay back down with a sigh. She seemed all angles now and bones that didn't want to move. He touched her arm, near the octopus tattoo. Her skin was cold even though the room was warm. He pulled a blanket from a high rack in the corner and covered her with it.

"Thanks," she mumbled. "I'll be fine. Just need a few minutes."

He sat down in the chair. "I'm not leaving."

Her phone rang. She struggled to pull it from her dress pocket. He helped her, looked at the screen. "It's somebody named Ezra."

"My assistant. I should answer that."

"I'll get it." Will answered instead. He introduced himself and told Ezra that Olivia wasn't feeling well.

"How do I know you haven't abducted her?" Ezra asked.

"I guess you don't." He put the phone on speaker and pointed it at Olivia. "Tell him you're okay."

"I'm okay," Olivia said. "I have a headache."

Will heard Ezra's sharp inhale. "I knew this would happen. You need to get home. Now."

She didn't move.

"She's falling asleep." Will stepped out of the room and closed the door so they could continue their conversation without disturbing her. "She got in a fight saving my life from a rifle-wielding funeral-goer, and she was hit in the head."

Ezra muttered something about white people.

Will walked over to Olivia's car and leaned a hip against it, feet crossed at the ankles.

"She's supposed to be taking extra care of that head," Ezra said. He seemed to hesitate before adding, "She's scheduled for surgery in a week, and she already cancelled it once. It's something she needs to have done. And instead of resting, taking it easy, walking on the beach or whatever she wants to do to relax, she's flying to Hellhole Hillbilly Redneck, Kansas, risking her life for some woman who probably murdered her own kids. And now you, some guy who stole her car, killed a waitress, and thinks he's Truman Capote, whoever the hell that is, is taking care of her. Very reassuring."

Will winced. "So you've heard about me. And Capote wrote *In Cold Blood*. I highly recommend it."

"She needs to get home. That's what needs to happen. I don't want to come to Kansas, I don't even know where Kansas is and I don't want to know, but I will come if I have to."

"This has all been very enlightening."

"Well, damn. I suppose that means you're going to write about it."

"And what if I do?"

Everything had happened so fast that Will really hadn't had any time to process it. Now he thought about how the body had been whisked away and how Imogene's mother had arrived in the rusty truck, how she'd been wearing a dirty nightgown and carrying a rifle like it was part of her. All of that was pure gold, just dropped in his lap. How could he *not* write about it? He felt a small thrill just imagining nailing that scene. "How do I know if she needs to go to the hospital?" he asked.

"How much has she told you about her health issue?"

"Nothing. I didn't even know she had one. Well, other than old injuries. I knew about that."

"She doesn't like to talk about it, but since she might need emergency care, I think you should know at least a little. The deal is, she could die at any moment. Like have a massive brain hemorrhage, and that would be it. Or she could have a stroke, a big one.

"I didn't want her going someplace without good medical facilities, where she doesn't know anybody. The surgery will correct the problem and essentially save her life, but she cancelled to go there and do . . . I don't know what, because that woman with the three dead kids, it's sad and all, but she seems guilty. I mean, she is guilty. It's just *how* guilty is the question. Like is it second-degree? Is it some situation where she has unaddressed and untreated mental health issues and doesn't deserve to get a first-degree manslaughter charge? Whatever it is, I don't approve of Olivia risking her life to be there for someone who could be straight-up evil. But anyway, she's got a metal plate in her head that needs to be removed and replaced with something else. It's putting pressure on her brain and causing bad headaches. She shouldn't be exerting herself, and she shouldn't be getting into physical fights with anybody."

Will thought about how Irene had slammed Olivia's head against the ground. He felt dizzy and his vision started to blur. He stepped blindly into the shade of the motel, felt for the brick of the wall with one hand, and lowered himself to the sidewalk. He really wanted to lie down on it, but he pulled up his knees and leaned forward, waiting for the spell of dizziness to pass.

"I guess I'm glad you're there," Ezra said grudgingly. "You aren't friends, and she hasn't known you long, but it sounds like you are kind of looking out for her."

Will thought about how he'd rented the compact car out from under her and how he'd set it on fire so she'd give him a ride. "I haven't been the best of friends," he said, "but I'm going to try harder. The big question is, should she go to the hospital right now?"

"Give her a stroke test and keep an eye on her. You can Google it. I've had to do that a few times, and she's always come out of these episodes on her own. But she's never taken a blow to the head. Give me your cell number, and I'll text you her doctor's info. That'll be your best bet if she isn't recovering like she should. I'll check back in a few hours."

"Okay."

Back inside, Will woke Olivia and made her go through a series of tests he'd found online. First, he turned out the lights, plunging the room into semidarkness. When he turned the lights back on, he checked her pupils. They reacted properly.

He handed her a coffee cup. "Take this." With very little movement of her body other than lifting her arm, she grabbed the cup with no problem.

"I haven't had a stroke."

Her face was symmetrical, no drooping of one side.

"Other hand," he said.

That was fine.

"Show me your teeth."

Her smile was even.

"Keep your eyes closed and raise both arms."

That was fine.

Holding his phone up to his face, he read more instructions. "Repeat this sentence. *Don't cry over spilled milk.* I have no idea why they want you to repeat that one, but there you go."

"Don't cry over spilled milk."

"I think you're good. Can I get you anything? Food? Something else to drink?"

"No. Just let me sleep. Take Dorothy for a walk and feed her. She gets a half cup of dry food and a couple of treats."

"Done."

"Thanks."

"No problem."

If not for what was going on with her, the past few days had been some of the most exciting in Will's life. He couldn't wait to get back to his room and write down the day. Of course if he was still sitting in jail for an alleged murder, he would not be feeling the same way.

He took Dorothy for a walk, then fed her.

As soon as she'd eaten, she jumped onto the bed and curled up next to Olivia. He checked to make sure she was asleep and not dead. She was breathing evenly, and her color looked better. Her face was very pale, but her lips were no longer tinged blue. And now that her face *was* so pale, he could see indented red lines down one side, across her chin and forehead.

Scars.

She looked fragile right now. So strange that just yesterday he'd marveled at how she seemed so strong, like a superhero. But even superheroes needed help from time to time. And even superheroes had sidekicks.

He smiled at that thought, sat down in the chair, and pulled out his phone. Normally he would dictate into the Notes app, but he didn't want his voice to disturb her, so he typed his narrative of the day, his fingers moving quickly and silently.

As had often been the case since his dad died, Will had a strong and bittersweet urge to call and talk to him about the story he was working on. Could a child make his dead father proud?

23

Olivia's medication knocked her out, which was the idea. She got up once to use the bathroom, but she mostly had little or no idea of time passing. She was aware of Dorothy sleeping next to her, her presence comforting, but that was about it. At one point, she thought Will had left, but when she stirred in the morning, cracking her eyes, she saw him slouched in the chair, arms crossed at his waist, head forward, asleep.

She must have made a sound.

He came awake with a start and looked at her, a visual check to see if she was okay.

He was a hard person to get a handle on. That guy from the airport, the guy who took her rental car out from under her, seemed like someone else. Who was the real Will LaFever?

"Thanks for looking out for me," she said.

"You saved my life yesterday."

She pulled the covers up higher, over her shoulder, rolled away from him, moving carefully, testing for pain. It seemed to be gone, but the medication had left her feeling heavy and groggy and stupid. Without opening her eyes again, she said, "I don't know about that. Irene might never have pulled the trigger."

"I think she would have. Intentionally or not. She was out of her mind. I'm going to go get some coffee. Do you think you could eat anything?"

"Not yet. Coffee. Maybe juice."

He left. While he was gone, she shuffled to the bathroom and washed her face and brushed her teeth. Changed out of the black funeral dress that was torn and stained from the fight. Put on a T-shirt and gray yoga pants. Looking in the mirror above the sink, it was no surprise to see she was pale and that her scars stood out deep and red. She opened a container of special foundation and applied some to her face. It did a pretty good job hiding the red lines.

She touched the back of her head and felt a lump where her skull had been slammed against the ground. Irene's strength had taken her by surprise. She'd thought once she disarmed her that would be it.

She was back in bed when Will returned with coffee and juice. He placed them on the end table. "Gas station fare again. Sorry. Best I could do." Then he fed Dorothy and took her outside. By the time he got back, Olivia was feeling slightly more human, although her brain was sluggish.

"I had weird dreams," he said. "I was supposed to decide on a day I'd like to relive, and I actually couldn't think of anything." He seemed disturbed by that. To have never had a day he wanted to relive. She wondered what her choice would be. Certainly a day before her father and Cecil Hotel had died. What about way back, when her mother was still alive?

"I've only had one dream in my life," she said, her blunt confession surprising her. "And I don't dream that one very often."

"Everybody dreams," he said. "Every night. Some people just don't remember them. Next time when you wake up, try to remember."

"I've tried. There's nothing there." It seemed to be tied to her lost memories. "But sometimes, a lot of times, I wonder if *everything* is a dream. This is a dream. This motel room. This town. You."

If she thought about it too hard, she experienced a falling sensation, and sometimes she would even find herself crying for seemingly no reason, only to realize she was crying because she didn't know if she was alive or dead or in a coma. And did it matter if this was the world she existed in, whether just in her own brain or in a real space?

It mattered to her.

If she had the kind of memories most people had, something to anchor her, keep her feet on the ground, keep her body from feeling like it was floating away, then maybe the unknown of surgery wouldn't be so bad.

"I have some bad news." He grimaced. "Your tires have been slashed, and somebody spray-painted a message on your car."

He might as well have said the sky was cloudy. Yes, her brain was sluggish. She took a sip of coffee, then asked, "What's the message?"

"*Go home.* No profanity. No drawings. Just, *go home.*"

"It seems kind of counterproductive to slash the tires."

"My thought exactly."

Ezra sent her a message congratulating her on stopping a shooting. He included a video of her in the cemetery, diving through the air to take down Irene.

Really, it was amazing she didn't have a broken arm or worse.

"You're a meme," Will said, scrolling through his own phone, then turning it to show her. "This is my favorite so far." Someone had cut up footage, mixing it with video from *The Matrix*, along with music and special effects. Even she was impressed.

"And to think I came here hoping to keep a low profile," she said.

They both laughed, and Dorothy wagged her tail.

She called the rental company and broke the news to them about the vandalized vehicle.

"Ah, man," the guy said. "Poor Caddy! What's the deal with that town? Is it cursed or something? Also, we don't have any more cars."

"Let's just get the tires repaired and I'll continue to drive it."

"Can do."

She ended the call. "Looks like I'm going to have to drive around with the words *go home* painted on the side," she told Will.

"Could be worse," he said.

"How?"

"Could be a penis. Kids love drawing those."

"I have the feeling the vandals were adults." Although she couldn't dispute the practical nature of the message. *Go home.* Not bad advice.

24

Do all the houses look alike here? Olivia wondered as she pulled onto Bonnie's property, hoping to find her there. White, two stories, big front porch, a baby swing attached to a tree limb. It was a surprise visit, and she'd brought the dog. After spending most of the day in bed, she was finally feeling close to normal, and she had a few things to do before leaving town.

Bonnie was home. Barefoot, dressed in a yellow cotton skirt and a white top, her hair in frizzy braids that looked as if they hadn't been rebraided in a while. A lot of loose strands that somehow worked for her. She stared at Olivia for a long moment, then smiled a little and asked her to come inside. She seemed floaty, disconnected, sedated. And she probably *was* on medication to help her cope with everything. Olivia felt slightly guilty visiting her at all, but she'd asked her to come to Kansas, and Olivia still had her dog.

Bonnie gave Dorothy a little pet, almost an absent-minded one. "We don't let dogs in the house."

Olivia was already inside, the dog on a leash beside her.

"Oh, never mind." Bonnie waved a hand. "Conrad isn't here."

She wandered around, pulled out a couple of glasses, got a pitcher of ice water from the refrigerator, filled the glasses, and handed one to Olivia. Everything was robotic, as if she was trying to figure out what she was supposed to do, then relieved when she decided. "I'm so glad you weren't hurt at the funeral yesterday. I was worried. What do you think about Will LaFever? Do you like him? He's cute."

"Oh, I don't know. I don't really even know him. We aren't anything alike."

"That doesn't always matter."

Olivia took a drink of water. It was almost too cold for her teeth. "How do you feel about being released?" she asked.

"I'm not sure. I was ready for a death sentence. I am guilty, you know."

Olivia couldn't even muster up any surprise. Guess they were both numb.

But then Bonnie elaborated, explaining the guilt any parent would feel. "Of not watching my children as closely as I should. My mind wanders sometimes, and kids are so hard to take care of. They're always moving. They never stop unless they're asleep." She paced. She walked to the screen door and looked out, as if expecting someone. Or afraid someone might show up.

Olivia put her glass aside. "I understand Imogene used to babysit for you."

"That's right. So awful what happened to her."

"Do you have any idea who could have done it?"

"Well, we know it wasn't me." She laughed.

It all felt very inappropriate, but she seemed to move to a different drummer.

Olivia looked down at the table. "I see you've been reunited with the breast pump."

"Yes! My mom brought it to the jail shortly after you stopped to see her. Thank you."

That would be pretty amazing if that was all her trip accomplished. A breast pump brought to jail.

"I was afraid I'd dry up, but you can increase your milk if you still have some. So I've been pumping away. I mean, I want to do as much as I can for my kids." Her voice trailed off.

The whole thing was so sad.

"My mother is going to keep my baby, and I can only have supervised visits, where I'll nurse her."

"That seems wise."

"You have an octopus tattoo. Mazie loved octopuses. She used to have a stuffed pink one that she'd sing to." She started drifting around the kitchen, holding her skirt, singing the song "You Are My Sunshine."

Olivia just wanted her to stop.

When she finally did, she said, "I looked for that stuffed octopus but could never find it."

Olivia had a flash, a real memory from the real time with her father. They were at a café, and a woman met them there. The woman sat down, and she and Olivia's father talked. And wasn't it part of a long drive? A trip, maybe the only trip they'd ever taken? Yes. As the woman got up to leave, she reached into her bag, pulled out a pink octopus, and handed it to Olivia, saying, "I thought you might want this." Or something like that.

"Look, we're twins." Bonnie was holding her necklace so Olivia could see it. She laughed. "That's what Mazie used to always say."

"Your mother said I was the one who always said that." Who was the woman in her memory? Why had the meeting seemed so clandestine? And what about the stuffed animal? Had it been *the* octopus? The one Bonnie couldn't find?

She tried to remember the woman's face, but it had been so long ago. She seemed to recall dark, shiny hair, kind of like Bonnie's. Kind of like her own real color.

"No, it was Mazie," Bonnie said.

"Oh." Olivia's reply was vague.

When the woman left the café, Olivia had been excited about the stuffed animal. She'd hugged it to her chest, trying to keep her father from taking it away. But he'd pulled it from her grasp, and, as they left, he'd shoved it in a trash container. She might have cried. He might have told her to be quiet, that they'd get a different stuffed animal.

Her thoughts tumbled in confusion. The whole thing was so preposterous, so B movie. But she'd been in the business long enough to know that humans did horrible and peculiar things. What if she hadn't really died that night? Or rather, what if Olivia Welles had died that night? And Mazie, the person who loved octopuses and said things like "We're twins," had lived? That would mean the person standing in the kitchen beside her would be her sister.

No.

So stupid.

Just no.

She and Mazie had been best friends. They said the same things and liked the same things. The room at Ava's had been so familiar because some part of her damaged brain had fired and recalled it. Yet the sights, smells, textures, had seemed more real than real life. Was that memory? Real memory? That acute sharpness, shine, and sparkle?

"Oh no." Bonnie looked out the window. "Oh no no no. You can't be here. He said you can't be here."

With her mind still struggling with this newest possible revelation, Olivia joined Bonnie at the window and saw Murphy getting out of the police car.

"You need to hide." She started shoving Olivia.

"He's already seen my rental," Olivia said. "Can't miss that."

"Tell him you had to bring something here. Tell him you've only been here a few minutes."

Olivia pulled herself together and sprang into action. She grabbed Dorothy's leash while Bonnie literally pushed her out the door and onto the porch. They both watched Murphy stride across the yard. Dorothy lunged, taking Olivia by surprise, the leash flying from her hand as Dorothy ran fast for Murphy, barking and circling him.

He kicked. The dog dodged. "Get that mutt away from me."

Bonnie crouched and called the dog. Dorothy ran to her, and she picked it up, shooting Olivia a warning look.

"Olivia just got here and is just leaving," she shouted to Murphy. She handed the dog to Olivia. "And she's taking Dorothy with her. She came by to see if I wanted her, but I told her she could keep her. That's good, right?"

It would be easy to read into Dorothy's dislike of the man, but some dogs just disliked certain people. Cecil had hated large men and large dogs.

"Don't ever let me see you here again," he said. "If I do, I'll arrest you for trespassing and harassment. And I'll make sure I have enough evidence to hold you longer than your murdering friend. He might be out of jail, but that's not going to last. He *will* be convicted."

Olivia didn't like leaving Bonnie with Murphy, but she also didn't want to do or say anything to make the situation worse. She looked at Bonnie. "Would you like to come with me?" Olivia asked.

Bonnie's eyes got big. She shook her head and took a step back, toward the kitchen door.

"We could just go get some ice cream." Olivia shrugged and tried to make it seem like a casual invitation. "Put the top down on my car. It could be fun."

"Our kid just died," Murphy said. "We don't need to have fun."

"Okay. I just thought a change of scenery might be nice."

"Get out of here. Now."

She looked at Bonnie. Bonnie nodded and mouthed, *Leave.*

There was nothing more Olivia could do. She got in the car, Dorothy in the passenger seat, and left. After putting some distance between herself and the Murphy farm, she headed straight to Ava Ray's house. She wanted to see that bedroom again. And she also wanted to ask Ava a few things. About the time she met with her father in a café. And maybe she'd even ask her about the night she died.

25

As Olivia drove to Ava's farm, the grain elevators were black silhouettes against a blue, blue sky, looking like some midwestern velvet painting. She hoped Will could do the area justice, maybe not spend too much time dwelling on the sense of despair and loneliness, but get down the magic of it, the nuanced beauty that was big and powerful as well as quiet and subtle. A place where the light fell in a sad way.

She didn't call Ava to let her know she was coming. She wanted to deploy the element of surprise so the woman would have no chance to tidy the house or coach anybody or prepare herself.

There were several cars in the driveway near the factory, and Olivia could smell the baking pies. She controlled the urge to gag. The day was unusually chilly; the storm seemed to have cooled things down. She parked in the shade, lowered all the windows several inches, and left Dorothy inside the car. She'd be fine. Olivia went to the farmhouse, hoping she'd find Ava alone.

Ava answered the door and seemed glad to see Olivia. "I was just feeding the baby. Come on in."

Olivia followed her into the kitchen.

A pan of water sat on the mint-colored vintage-look stove, no flame under it. Ava plucked a baby bottle from the pan, dried it with a dish towel, shook the contents, and tested it on her inner wrist. "Luckily,

Bonnie's milk didn't dry up when she was in jail, so she's been pumping like crazy. My freezer is full of breast milk."

"That's great." Olivia's response was robotic, her thoughts on other things. And what else could a person say about a freezer full of breast milk?

"I told her she might want to start selling some of it."

Olivia couldn't imagine anyone wanting to purchase breast milk from a mother who was a suspect in the deaths of her children. Or maybe it would be just the opposite. Maybe people would pay top dollar for a potential murderer's milk.

Ava lifted the infant from a nearby bassinet.

This was Olivia's first in-person look at the child. Maybe six months old, a girl with wispy white hair. She was one of those kids who might eventually turn into something. Sometimes pretty babies got ugly and ugly babies got pretty.

She watched Ava feed the child.

She was old enough to sit up, but Ava cuddled her in the crook of her arm and crooned to her. While she fed her, the baby patted the bottle and made cooing noises as she drank, staring with unblinking eyes at her grandmother.

Ava smiled at Olivia. "I know this is a horrible situation, but I love being able to bond with her this way. I never bottle-fed the other children." A cloud passed over her face. Most likely as she thought about their deaths and how they were no longer part of her life. And yet she managed to create a quiet scene of motherhood, of grandmotherhood.

The child fell asleep before finishing the bottle. Ava wiped her mouth with a soft-looking white cloth and put the baby back in the bassinet. It felt like the perfect life even though it wasn't.

"I was wondering if I could see Mazie's room again," Olivia said.

Ava appeared surprised, then said, "Okay. Of course."

They went upstairs.

Olivia wandered around the room. In her mind, she imagined two girls laughing, playing with marbles on the floor, and watching them roll.

She tossed her purse on the bed, then picked up the octopus pillow and hugged it to her chest. Put it down, looked at the books again. Took one from the shelf. Recalled the scent of paper and ink. Put the book back, then paused in front of the vanity dresser with the large mirror. She touched the purple brush she'd seen there before. Young girls all seemed to like purple. Most of them, anyway.

The room was stuffy, with a rectangle of light falling across the pink bedspread. She could smell Ava behind her. Fabric softener, ginger or cloves, and coffee.

Olivia picked up the brush, stroking a thumb over the black bristles. She thought about running it through her own hair, but then had another idea, a better idea.

"Sit down."

"What?"

"Sit." Olivia smiled. "I'll brush your hair."

"Well, that's silly."

"Oh, come on. It's soothing to have someone else brush your hair. How long has it been since anybody did that?"

"I don't even remember. Probably not since I was a kid. And I'll bet I didn't like it."

Olivia laughed. "Let's see." She pulled out the small wooden chair, white to match the vanity. "Come on," she coaxed. "Sit down."

Ava sat down. "I can't stay long."

"Just a little bit."

Now they were both facing the large mirror. Ava removed the stretch tie from her hair, and Olivia began to slowly brush the woman's hair. It was straight and shiny, gray, that pretty kind of gray that some people actually used dye to achieve. Several strands collected in the bristles.

"How's that feel?" Olivia asked, brushing with one hand and smoothing with the other.

Ava let out a sigh and smiled. "I have to admit, it *is* nice. So strange that it feels better when someone else does it."

"Weird, right?"

"It's very relaxing." She closed her eyes. "And makes me kind of sleepy."

"I keep trying to remember the old days," Olivia said. "And there's nothing there." She leaned forward, putting her face right next to Ava's and looking at their reflection. Ava's eyes opened with a start. She watched Olivia in the mirror.

"But I did remember something that didn't happen here. Something that happened years after the accident," Olivia said.

"Oh. What?"

Olivia kept her face next to Ava's. "Did you notice that our eyebrows are kind of the same?"

"No."

There were those things a person knew in the deep-down heart of themselves. Things you never fully reveal to yourself, or things you know are true but simply can't face. They're always there, running in the background, creating the parts of you that hurt in a way that hurts forever. Olivia might have always known. Because she'd always felt the push/pull of Kansas. Ever since she could remember, she'd felt the fear, along with the revulsion. And also the curiosity. But the mind protected itself just like the metal plate in her head had protected her. And people believed the lies their loved ones told because those things made them feel better when they believed.

"And our lips," Olivia said. "We both have full bottom lips and a smaller upper lip. But the upper lip has that same pronounced dip in the center."

"That's what lips look like."

"And the jawline." She touched her own jawbone.

"You've had a lot of surgeries." Ava let out a nervous laugh. "I'm guessing they used a classic face as a template. I must have a classic, boring face."

"Yeah. That's probably it. Or—" Olivia pressed her face close again. "We might be related."

Ava stared back at Olivia in the mirror, her eyes large. Was that fear in there? Yes, Olivia was pretty sure it was.

Olivia straightened and walked across the room to the bed, where she'd tossed her purse. She opened it and stuck the brush inside. "I'm going to take the brush with me. I don't often deal with DNA, but I have a friend at a lab who will turn samples around pretty quickly."

Behind her, Ava let out a gasping sob. She jumped to her feet, her hair, hair that had looked so pretty, now wild, framing wild eyes and a turned-down mouth. "No, don't. Please."

"There's only one reason I can think of for you to be against that idea." Even though Ava was right in front of her, Olivia felt herself mentally pulling away, trying to shield herself from further emotional trauma.

She turned her thoughts back to happier times, to the past and her father. Memories, warm and wonderful, rushed at her, one after the other. Some came like snapshots; others practically put her right there, in the scene, the images so vivid and clear. Her dad walking with her on the beach, his hand big over hers. That glimpse was immediately replaced by her first day of school, then all the doctor appointments he'd taken her to. All the times he'd been there when she awoke from every surgery, even the ones that had briefly killed her.

Then there were all the times he'd read to her. She'd loved the Berenstain Bears. The silly and corny jokes they'd shared. His were the corniest. Teaching her to ride a bike even though he was scared she'd fall. Running beside her, not wanting to let go. But she'd pedaled faster, and he'd had no choice. She broke free and rolled on without him, leaving him by himself in the middle of the street. Maybe the truth was he hadn't deserted her. Maybe she'd left him.

And then there were the moths.

She'd been terrified of their unpredictable flight. Then one day she'd found a dying moth on the windowsill and had felt bad for it. The tiny creature was so beautiful and fragile, the body soft.

"You're nothing to be afraid of," she'd whispered.

Her father had come into her room, put his arm around her, and told her the most amazing story . . .

With a start, Olivia realized Ava must have said something. She was looking right at her with glistening eyes. Olivia was still caught up in the memory, thinking about what her father had shared that day. To Ava, she said in an almost dreamlike voice, "Do you know there's a moth in the Amazon that drinks the tears of sleeping birds?"

"What?"

"It's true."

"That's horrible."

"I think it's lovely."

Ava reached for her.

Olivia flinched and took a step away.

"It wasn't my idea!" Ava said, pleading in her voice. "It was all your father. He pushed me into it. You know how he was. So forceful. He could convince a person black was white if he wanted to. And he had a savior complex."

Olivia kind of understood why her father had done it. Switched the girls and lied about it. Her mother—well, his wife, not really her mother—had been the love of his life, the kind songs were written about. And yes, that might have changed if she'd lived, but both his child and wife had died. And maybe he'd planned to tell Olivia at some point, but after so much time had passed, and so many lies told, he just couldn't do it. And then he met someone else, got married, had two children. A do-over that had ended up working out well for him.

And it explained why he'd gone from being a doting father to someone who didn't seem to want anything to do with Olivia. Two reasons, really. One, he had a new family and didn't need her anymore. Two, she was a constant reminder of what had happened and of his own deceit he could no longer face. So he'd moved on and pretended it never happened.

He sometimes called her on her birthday and Christmas, but those dwindled over time until a few occasional awkward attempts at contact from his wife, then finally nothing until the call that told Olivia he'd died.

And still no confession. He'd gone to his grave with the secret.

She should have hated him for that, but she couldn't. He'd been out of his mind with grief, and he'd carried on as best he could. He'd gotten her all the surgeries she needed, with the best doctors. Or maybe it was a way to redirect his grief and give himself a sense of purpose. And once she was well, and once he'd moved on, he accomplished what he'd meant to accomplish.

What she couldn't forgive him for was how, for so many years, she'd wondered what she'd done to alienate him. She'd go through conversations in her mind, looking for some big or small thing. A stupid argument about politics or art. She knew he'd been disappointed when she became a detective. At the time she'd thought it was because he'd wanted her to go into another field. But now, almost laughably, she realized he'd probably thought she might be more in the mindset to discover the truth about herself. So his letting her think it was something she'd done . . . that might be impossible to forgive.

"Can I hug you?"

Maybe that's what Ava had said before—words that hadn't penetrated Olivia's memories.

"You look like you could use a hug," Ava said. "I could too."

What a routine reaction to a tragic event that was almost Shakespearean in scope. "Absolutely not."

Ava recoiled at the rejection, then looked down and back up, a stricken expression on her face. "I did what I thought was right for you," she said. "And I still think it was right. Not a hundred percent right, but the best. Was it a lie? It was. But I'd do it again. For you."

"I deserved to know the truth."

"It was fraud! You father could have gone to prison."

That was a possibility.

"Your father knew you would need so much surgery, maybe for the rest of your life. He had insurance. We didn't. Your mother was dying. Well, Florence was dying, and he hoped knowing you would live would keep her alive. And it did. For a while. Then she got that infection, and her body couldn't fight it. But she was able to go to her next life knowing her daughter would live."

"But that's not true."

"I know, but wasn't it a good lie?"

"No. It wasn't."

"Please, don't say anything to anybody. You know the truth, that's all that matters. My family is going through enough. Bonnie is going through enough. Please, please, please, don't tell her." Tears started falling from her eyes. "I don't think she'd ever be able to forgive me."

Olivia wondered if Bonnie actually knew. Or suspected. Is that why she'd called her?

"Please, don't tell anyone," Ava begged. "You can't tell anyone. No one can ever know. It has to be our secret. My reputation will be ruined in this town. Nobody will ever talk to me again or trust me. My business will fold, and all the workers will no longer have jobs."

"I won't say anything yet," Olivia said. "But you should tell Bonnie soon."

"You don't know her. You don't know how this will upset her."

"What about me? I'm pretty damn upset right now."

"You've had a wonderful life! You got out of Finney! You went to college. You didn't get married at seventeen and start having babies like both Bonnie and I did. You got out! And I'm glad you got out of here. And without this place, the history, the memories to drag you down, you were able to succeed in life. I'm proud of you! I'm proud of myself for having the guts to do it. To give you a better life. You should really be thanking me!"

Wow. She was really spinning this. "I know you met with my father once, but did you really keep in touch?"

"For many years, yes. It was more often me reaching out to him to find out how you were doing. I'd beg for pictures, and he'd sometimes send them. Oh wait. I have some." She turned and rushed from the room. Olivia heard a drawer open and close, and then Ava was back with a little wooden box.

It contained several photos, all of Olivia, mostly from various schools, but there were a few others. One taken at Disneyland in front of Sleeping Beauty Castle. Another at a beach that might have actually been Venice Beach. Ava pulled them out one at a time and shook them in front of Olivia's face. "See? See? I didn't forget you! I never forgot you!"

"Did he send you money?"

"What?"

"Money."

"Why would he do that?"

"To keep you quiet."

"Oh, that's horrible." She snapped the box closed and glared. "That's a horrible thing to say."

"I can probably find out."

"Go ahead. You'll find nothing."

She hated to end it like this, but things were devolving quickly, and Olivia really needed to get away from Ava and think, process. She also felt a weird and overwhelming sense of relief, because her life had always felt like a big question mark. So many things had been answered here today in the space of a few minutes.

"I have to go."

"You aren't leaving town, are you?" Ava asked. "I want you to come to the parade! You could drive your car. Oh, that would be perfect. I'll ride with you."

What the . . . ? Olivia couldn't possibly think about anything as mundane as a parade, and she knew it would take time to fully grasp all she'd learned in the past hour. Right now she didn't know if she hated Ava or felt sorry for her. Or loved her a little, even if it was with that misguided love a child might feel for a parent who deserved no love.

"I'll get back to you on that." Or not.

She left the room, but she could feel Ava's presence moving behind her. Halfway down the stairs, Olivia felt a vibration in her pocket. She paused on the landing, pulled out her phone, and read the text. It was from Coco Sandoval. Most of it was regarding the autopsy of the body they'd grabbed from the funeral.

I have some preliminary autopsy findings on the Ray boy. You were instrumental in this, so I wanted you to be the first to know the results. Keeping this information close for right now though. Still waiting on some labs, but ethylene glycol was found in the tissue. Even after embalming.

Ethylene glycol. Antifreeze.

Olivia replied, letting Coco know she'd call her later. Then she smiled grimly, tucked the phone away, and looked back up at Ava, who was still at the top of the stairs, her hair loose and wild around her face. She looked better, younger, with her hair swept back. There was something crone-like about her now.

"Bad news?" Ava asked.

"I guess you could say that."

Ava was waiting, hand on the banister. It was hard to read her expression. The stairwell was dark, and her face was in shadow. But

Olivia could feel how distraught she was. And even though she'd never been a cruel person or someone who took satisfaction in revenge, she couldn't help but feel a bit of satisfaction. A satisfaction that led her to push further. She didn't want to mention the antifreeze, told in confidence, but she could share one other bit of news that Coco had included.

"That was my friend from the Kansas Bureau of Investigation. The bodies of the other two children are going to be exhumed."

Ava just kind of melted. With one hand gripping the railing, she sat down hard on the stairs, mouth open, eyes large.

Without saying anything else—because where did a person take the conversation from here?—Olivia went down the stairs. She reached the kitchen just in time to hear a door slam. She looked at the bassinet.

It was empty.

26

Olivia ran out of the house and down the porch steps.

Bonnie, yes, it was Bonnie, racing for a truck, clutching the baby in her arms.

Olivia shouted after her, and Bonnie stopped and turned.

"Stay away! Stay back!" she screamed. "This is my baby! Nobody can have my baby!"

"We just want to make sure she's okay," Olivia said.

"She's fine! She's with me!" Bonnie lifted her high. The baby was crying and wriggling, terrified. "I'll throw her."

Olivia froze, both feet planted firmly on the ground. "I'm not coming any closer." She didn't want to drive her to harm the child.

People in the pie shop had heard the commotion. A few were walking toward Bonnie, behind her, unseen, the bakers moving forward in their white aprons and hairnets. Oh, the gossip was going to fly tonight. Maybe not even tonight. A couple of people seemed to be recording the drama. Someone else, a young girl, was madly talking into her phone. The family's story had been the center of their lives for so long, overshadowing everything else. Did anybody ever resent that? Or did it make their own stories feel bigger?

"I want what's best for the baby," Olivia calmly told Bonnie. "And I'm sure you do too."

"I do. I do." She shifted the child, cradling her against her belly now. "Remember when you took down Irene at the cemetery? That was so good."

"We have to protect the people we care about. I want to protect you." Olivia tilted her head in what she hoped was a friendly, sweet, unthreatening way. She smiled and looked at the baby. "She's so beautiful. I'd love to hold her. Would you let me hold her? Just for a minute?" Olivia stepped closer, extending her arms, continuing to smile.

Bonnie, surprisingly, gave her the child. Just passed her over, then waited for the cooing and admiration to ensue.

Instead, Olivia stepped away quickly. Two of the bakers came forward and grabbed Bonnie. Not roughly, but by both arms in case she decided to lunge. Ava was there now too. After looking down at the baby in her arms, Olivia passed the child to the grandmother, who made a sobbing sound of relief and hurried her toward the house.

Safe.

The women released Bonnie, and she ran to her truck, got in, slammed the door, and drove away in a cloud of dust. It happened so fast, and saving the baby had been the main focus. Nobody thought to stop her.

Shortly after Bonnie took off, Olivia got in the Cadillac and headed in the direction of Finney. She wondered if she was possibly in shock, because she felt nothing, numb, now knowing what she knew about her father's lies. But before going back to town, she had one more thing to do, one more place to see. She hadn't wanted to go there, but now she felt like it would pale in comparison to everything else.

The train tracks where she died.

27

Sometimes the buildup created unrealistic expectations.

Olivia had seen the place so many times in her mind and in photos that the reality was a letdown, and she was thankful for that.

Tracks. They were just tracks.

The sky was just sky.

The fields, just fields.

She tried to spot the Ray house in the distance but could only see the peaks of the grain elevators that reminded her of the Tin Man's hat.

The road had a wide gravel shoulder where she was able to park and get out, snapping Dorothy's leash to her collar, allowing the dog to come with her.

It was, as always, windy, the gusts especially strong today, traveling over humid acres of corn. In the far distance, an irrigation system was making a slow path around the field, the *click, click, click* of the water the only sound other than the wind.

The town had raised money to erect a little park, just a corner carved out of the nearby field, but it had a shade tree and two benches. There was a monument that stood eight feet tall with the date of the crash and the names and ages of the two victims.

She ran her fingers across the carved letters that spelled Mazie Ray. But *she* was Mazie, standing here alive and not so well. Once the news hit every corner of the community, would they cross that out and add Olivia? Who would really care? She liked the idea of an error on the granite, making it a kind of monument to the deceit and the lies. A false life.

Would she change her name? She didn't think so, because her business was tied to Olivia Welles, yet the idea of coming up with someone completely new was intriguing, as always.

She turned away from the little park to view the vastness again, breathe it in, feel it all the way to her bones. After taking in the landscape, she walked the tracks, sometimes balancing on the metal rail, sometimes stepping on the wooden ties, Dorothy at the end of the leash. In her mind, Olivia imagined the train whistle howling from a distance, getting louder and louder, the car not moving.

She finally left the tracks and made her way down the embankment. This was the direction Ava must have taken. And Bonnie had spotted her and tried to catch up, only to pass out in the yet-to-be harvested wheat.

Bonnie had been sun blind for days.

Olivia heard a horn for real. The signal began to chime and flash, the arm dropped to keep vehicles from crossing. She saw a few hands lifted to windows of the passenger cars. Then the train was gone.

Back in the Cadillac, before leaving the monument, she called her father's wife.

"Oh, hey, Olivia," Maureen said, sounding surprised but genuinely glad. "Good to hear from you!"

Olivia felt a surprising rush of affection. She'd never really given Maureen a chance. But she wasn't calling to chat. "Did you know?" she asked bluntly.

"Know what?"

"That I'm not my father's biological daughter."

Maureen let out a choking gasp.

"Not only that," Olivia said, her voice and body shaking, "I'm pretty sure I'm actually Mazie Ray, and that Olivia Welles died the night of the train wreck."

"What on earth are you talking about?"

"He didn't have any message for me? A letter? Anything? Or maybe a deathbed confession? He just left this for me to find out for myself? Or worse, never find out?"

"I'm so sorry. This is all news to me. I have to sit down."

There was a very long pause.

Maureen had always come across as unflappable, but Olivia imagined her reaching blindly for a chair. How old was she now? She was picturing a woman in her fifties, but she was much older than that.

"There was never any hint that you were other than who he said you were," Maureen finally said, her voice strained. "Oh, Olivia. I feel so bad. Are you sure about this?"

"Yes." There was still the DNA to process, but at this point that seemed more of a formality.

"I didn't know. I promise. You should come up for a visit. We can talk. I wish we'd stayed in touch over the years. I wish I could give you a hug."

That might be nice. Olivia's phone alerted her to another call. She ignored it.

"Come visit. I'd love to see you." Maureen's voice brightened. "The girls would love to see you."

"I can't right now, but maybe I'll drive up to your place someday. I'll explain it all then." Maureen might even see something about it on the news, some side piece connected to the Finney deaths. She thought about Will, wondered if he'd break the story.

She didn't mention her surgery to Maureen. Olivia had a will, but her dad had been the beneficiary. She'd need to update that. And leave her measly bank account to who? The Venice dog-rescue group? With no updated will, it would probably go to Ava. *Egad.*

"Take care of yourself," she said. "And tell the kids hi for me." Kids. They were adults now, but still Maureen's kids.

She ended the conversation, drove back to Finney, where she fed Dorothy, then put her in the crate. She checked her phone. She had missed calls from both Coco and Ezra, but she didn't feel like talking to anybody. Not even them.

She stepped out of the motel, locked up, got in her car, and drove to the morgue.

There was no place like home.

28

At the morgue, Olivia pulled up to the back door where she and Will had slipped inside the other night. Ezra called again. This time she answered.

"Sorry. I can't talk now," she told him.

"This will only take a minute. It's about the autopsy."

"I already got it from Coco. Antifreeze."

"No, not that one. Imogene Griffin. Got some DNA from her that matches the cop."

"Murphy?" Wow.

"Yep."

She got out of the car and walked toward the morgue door. Someone had put a padlock on it since she and Will had visited. Remaining on the phone with Ezra, talking and listening, she scoped out the area, looking for another way in the building.

"Honestly, that's not a surprise," she said. "Now that I think about it. Murphy didn't secure the crime scene, and he was all over it. I mean, he practically set up a picnic in there."

"Well, did he have a picnic in her vagina?"

She stopped in her tracks. "Oh." She wasn't that surprised to hear his DNA was on file, most likely with CODIS. It was standard proce-dure to collect parents' DNA when dealing with the death of a child, and it would have looked odd if he hadn't supplied a sample. It might have been uploaded so long ago that he'd forgotten about it.

"Yeah."

Her mind pieced together the details. A young babysitter. An abusive boyfriend. An unsecured crime scene. None of this meant he killed her, but he was definitely number one on her suspect list now.

She spotted a first-floor broken window. "I've got to go."

"I'm gonna keep tabs on you. Still watching you with the Find My app."

Intrusive, but also a little comforting to know he was tracking her. He started to say something else when she hung up.

She walked around the building, dead grass crunching under her feet. She sidestepped piles of debris, some that had been pilfered from inside, some that looked like various stages of attempted and failed construction or repairs. She found and dragged concrete blocks and boards close to the broken window, stacked them, climbed.

The panes had been shattered, but some shards remained. She knocked out the remaining glass, and it fell with a crash. She reached inside, felt for the sash latch, unlocked it, and was able to raise the windowless frame up and out of the way enough for her to duck inside, at first straddling the windowsill, then sitting on it, both feet inside, to drop to the floor.

She was making no attempt at stealth. Screw that. She was beyond caring, at least not now. She was mad, getting madder by the minute. Mad at her father, Ava, and anybody else who might have suspected the switch.

Also mad at herself.

Yeah. Maybe that was really it. Because she had to look inward and question whether she'd always known. In the world of crime and denial, she'd learned many people subconsciously chose to ignore what was right in front of them. Immediate family of people who killed. That creepy uncle who raped his niece. Everybody pretended it hadn't happened, even the niece. That weird case of an adult who claimed to be a family's missing kid when even his eye color was different from the lost child. Excuses could always be found. They'd *needed* him to be their child. Maybe she'd needed to be Olivia. Because if she had questioned it, what would that have meant for her? That she'd no longer have had a father, and she might have been sent to Kansas to live with complete strangers. Harold Welles *was* her family, the only family she'd known. So maybe she'd really done what had, subconsciously, seemed best for her.

She took the stairs to the morgue area, stepping over the pile of bricks in order to access the secret room. Now that it wasn't the dead of night, she saw rows of glass-block windows that supplied murky light. She picked up the child's clothing from the metal gurney and pressed it to her face and inhaled deeply. She rubbed the rough, frilly fabric between her fingers, trying to trigger even a faint memory.

Nothing.

She levered herself onto the gurney, feet dangling, then spun around to lie down, hands still clutching the dress to her chest.

She closed her eyes.

29

This was where Olivia was born.

She tried to imagine how it happened. The two girls had been pronounced dead at the scene by her father and brought to the morgue. How long had she been here before it was discovered she was alive?

Sometime later her father had arrived, grief-stricken, his wife in intensive care. He'd come to tend to the girls, maybe put them in a cooler at the very least. And he'd discovered one of them alive. And maybe at first, due to the severity of their injuries, he'd truly gotten them mixed up.

It might have been fanciful of her, but she imagined her father leaning over, maybe holding her hand, speaking the name Olivia. She'd opened her eyes and saw the joy and surprise leap into his. And then began the long journey to rebuild her face and body.

"I knew you'd come back in here."

She actually did open her eyes.

Marshal Murphy was standing in the crumbling entry. A shaft of sunshine fell from somewhere, and she could see the slightest of movements had stirred up dust that was floating and visible. If not for the light, they would have no idea they were breathing in ghosts.

She didn't get up. She put the blue dress aside and repositioned herself to get a better look at him, lying on her side, one elbow on the gurney, head propped by her hand.

"I found out something surprising today," she said. "I'm not really Olivia Welles."

He took a few steps closer, hands on his belt, like maybe he was thinking he might need to pull his weapon, which was holstered on his hip, snap open.

"That's kind of old news," he said.

"You knew?"

"Ava told me. I wasn't supposed to tell Bonnie, but I think she always suspected. I never said anything though. I don't even know why Ava told me. Kinda wish she hadn't. Maybe she thought I'd figure it out."

"I want to talk a little about Imogene."

She sat up in one smooth movement, speaking conversationally, her feet unable to touch the floor. "All this human stuff is so predictable. Here's what I think happened, and feel free to correct me if I'm wrong." She braced her hands between her knees and casually swung her feet, trying to keep an easy tone. "Imogene was babysitting for you and Bonnie. One night you gave her a ride home, but you didn't take her straight home. Instead, you pulled off on a cozy side road and you two had sex. Now it might have been fully consensual, but she would have been a minor at the time. What was she? Fourteen? Even younger? Sex with a minor is a felony, you know. And my guess is she wasn't the only one. Then you found out she was talking to Will LaFever, and you started worrying that she might say something. Maybe you confronted her, or maybe you just had sex with her again, then killed her. Or you killed her and had sex with her. Seems like killing just comes easy in this town. What's one more? I'm not sure how you framed Will, but I know cops have all the magic tools it takes to open cars with ease.

"Am I at least a little right? I like to think my skills have gotten sharper over the years, but truth is, when you've been in the business as long as I have, you keep seeing people doing the same stupid stuff."

"You're talking nonsense."

He must not have known about the antifreeze. And he definitely didn't know about Imogene's autopsy.

He pulled out a set of handcuffs. "I gave you plenty of chances," he said. "More than anybody else would have. Stand up, turn around, and put your hands behind your back."

She got to her feet, stared at him, and smiled, realizing he was actually her brother-in-law. Then she started laughing at the Jerry Springer stupidity of it all.

"Crazy bitch," he muttered. "Turn around."

She did.

She put her hands behind her back.

She felt the cold metal of one shackle on her wrist. Before it latched, she slipped a leg behind one of his, caught his foot, kicked it out, pulled his weapon from his holster, and jumped away, all in a fraction of a second, cuffs clattering to the floor.

He flailed, hands and arms churning until he finally caught his balance.

She kept the gun trained on him. "Pick them up."

"You're going to go to prison for this."

"I doubt it. But, if so, we can go together." She pointed the gun at the floor, then back at him. "Cuffs."

He picked them up.

"You know what to do. Attach one to you and one to that railing over there."

"No."

"I don't really care. I can call for backup right now, or you can restrain yourself and have some time to think of a way out of this."

He complied and locked himself to the railing.

"Key."

He scowled and tossed her the key.

She caught it. "When I leave here, I might or might not call somebody to come and get you."

She sat back down on the gurney and put the gun beside her, pulling up one leg, hugging a knee to her chin as she regarded him.

"I'm guessing you don't know about your son's autopsy."

"Don't talk about him."

"I feel bad about this because you might not have had anything to do with it, but they found antifreeze in his organs. And finding it in the organs and tissue means the poisoning has been going on for a while. Poor kid. So that means the other children are going to be exhumed. Sorry. Not a great day for you. Also, why does Dorothy hate you? Is it just one of those things, like she just hates men in uniform?"

"Shut up."

"I think she hates you because she saw you hurting someone she cared about. That's what I think. I have a lot of theories. Do you want to hear more?"

"Not really."

With his free hand, he reached into his pocket.

She picked up the gun.

He pulled out his phone and lifted it in the air.

"Do you want to call 911?" she asked. "Oh wait. I hear sirens." Her phone pinged. She glanced at it.

A text from Ezra: Police are on the way. They are looking for Murphy.

She replied with talk-to-text. "Just follow my phone location. Party at the morgue."

30

Will stepped out of his motel room to see vehicles flying past, red lights flashing, sirens screaming. He heard them stop not far away, maybe near the morgue. Poor Dorothy howled a few times from Olivia's room.

He didn't have a car, so he ran on foot, sprinting across yards, then across the park where he and Olivia had drunk the Tornado shakes. Those were good.

Yeah, it was the morgue.

And Olivia's car was there.

He dropped from a jog to a brisk walk, trying to figure out what was going on as he drew closer. Three official sedans. State patrol, not county. Sirens silent now, but red lights flashing weakly.

The sun had gone down, but it wasn't completely dark yet. He almost gasped when he recognized Murphy standing with his hands behind his back. They'd cuffed him and were now sticking him in the back seat of a caged squad car. One officer was talking to someone in shadow. Will moved closer, close enough to spot Olivia's short red hair. She was conversing with a female state cop who was nodding and taking notes. Then the cop said something to Olivia, got back in her car, and drove off.

Will walked across the parking lot, hands in the front pockets of his jeans. "So, Murphy, huh?"

"Yeah."

"The kids?"

"No. I'm not supposed to tell you this . . ." She stepped closer, looked around, looked back at him, and whispered, "His DNA was found on—well, in—Imogene."

Will let out a deep breath. "Wow. That's not proof though."

"You're right. I wasn't privy to all the details, but I think Coco will find what she needs to make the charge stick."

His legs felt wobbly. Was he going to pass out? "I could use a drink. Something stronger than beer."

"I counted, and this town of less than three thousand people has five churches and four liquor stores, two of them with drive-thru windows. So we should be able to take care of that."

"I want to go in," he said. "Seems fun."

They drove to the nearest store and parked in the parking lot and went inside together. They were the only customers. Olivia picked up a fifth of bourbon. Decent color, in a square bottle. Nothing fancy, but it would do the trick.

"Hell yeah," Will said.

At the counter, he pulled out his wallet. "My treat. I'm the one who really needs it."

The cashier let out a little chuckle.

"No bag," Olivia said, grabbing the bottle. Will returned his wallet to his back pocket.

"Look at those stars," he said as they stepped out the door. "You don't see stars like that in LA."

Instead of getting in the car, he chose to sit on the hood, feet on the bumper. She sat on the other side and leaned her back against the windshield. She pointed up. "There's the Big Dipper."

"And Jupiter." He pointed too.

She unscrewed the cap, took a long drink, and passed the bottle to him.

The street in front of them seemed surprisingly busy for evening. "What are those cars doing?" He passed the fifth back to her. "I've seen the same ones go by three times."

"I think it's called dragging the strip. It's mostly kids behind the wheels."

"Oh, like *American Graffiti*. Wow. That's awesome."

His phone rang. He was just going to ignore it, but with a glance he saw the lock screen displayed his mother's face. "Gotta get this." He slipped off the hood and stepped a short distance away before answering.

"You need to come home right now," she said. "Get out of that strange little town before something else happens to you." She was back from her photography trip. He'd talked to her once since he'd gotten out of jail.

"I plan to."

"I have an art opening in two days here in Beverly Hills, if you need an excuse."

"I don't need one. I'll be there."

"Oh."

"You sound surprised."

She laughed, relaxed now that she knew he was coming home. "I was prepared for an argument."

He spun around on one heel and headed back for the Cadillac. Olivia was still on the hood, head tipped, bottle high, taking an impressive swig of booze.

"I'll see you day after tomorrow," he said.

She told him she loved him. He told her the same, and disconnected.

He clambered back on the hood of the car and took the bottle from Olivia. "That was my mom. She's worried about me, with the whole arrested-for-murder thing."

"Understandable. So you're going home?"

"Yeah. I couldn't sleep last night and kept thinking about it. Like it's time for me to go, and my mother is worried. I need to check in so she can see me in person, see that I'm okay."

A car honked. The occupants seemed to approve of their hood-drinking. Will and Olivia both waved.

"I don't know," he said. "I just don't feel like this is the right thing for me to be doing. I had an epiphany last night."

"Sometimes those middle-of-the-night epiphanies suck."

"Oh, I know. But this one hung in there and still makes sense." He held out the bottle.

She shook her head. "I think I've reached my limit."

He capped the container and braced it between his knees. "You've been a good influence on me. I need to set things right with the rent-al-car company. And I don't even know if I'm gonna write the story. It just seems so exploitative, especially now that I know you. That makes it more personal. More real."

"I think you could do it in a way that's not exploitative. Maybe you should think about it anyway."

"I will."

"I have something else I'll tell you," she said. "An exclusive, I guess. It's something I think I've always suspected deep down. But Mazie and I . . . we were . . . I'm just gonna say it even though it seems so corny. *Switched at death.*" She let out a snort.

"What? *You?*"

"Yeah. There's a story title right there." She explained what had happened, at least as much of it as she could. "I don't know it all yet, and I certainly don't know my father's side, and I never will. I think that's what bothers me the most."

"How are you doing?" he asked. She seemed so calm.

"Actually, not that bad. The bourbon is helping. And just sitting outside under the stars. That's helping. Hanging out. Helping."

"Yeah, but man. That's got to be tough."

He guessed she'd dealt with so much in her life, what was one more thing? He was going to miss her, and he was glad she lived in California. "I was talking to Ezra, and he told me what you've done for him."

"It wasn't really anything."

"I think it was. And you've helped me. You didn't save me from some heroin den, but you helped me see things a little differently, and see myself a little differently." Why was he talking so much? And about personal stuff he usually kept close. He lifted the bottle and saw how much they'd drunk between the two of them. And he understood. He wasn't slurring his words, but he was definitely buzzing. More than buzzing.

And he just kept going. "My goals weren't noble goals. I always knew that, but I'd like to make them noble, and I'm trying to figure out how I can do that."

"I kind of wish you'd stay," she said. "We arrived together. Seems like we should fly back together."

"I need to leave, and there are people who still believe I'm guilty. Honestly, I'm afraid of the people here. You should come with me tomorrow." Although he didn't think they'd harm her the way they might harm him. *He* might end up in somebody's trunk.

"Where is home? I'm having a hard time picturing you in your nest."

"Guess."

"When I first met you, I would have said sterile apartment, mostly because you seemed the type who wouldn't want to bother with things like a house or yard. But now I could imagine you living in some bunga-low near the beach somewhere with a few roommates. That's the house I want for you, the life I want for you."

"I live near Sunset Boulevard, above a café. Just me and my cat."

"That works too. You're not that far from me. Weird to think we've been living near each other. Less than an hour even if traffic is bad."

"I know. I checked out your address," he confessed.

"Have you ever done yoga on the beach?" she asked.

He must have looked horrified.

"Have you ever thought about it?"

"No. But if you're gonna do it, I'll meet you on the beach and we can do yoga together. Sunrise, sunset, I don't care. I'll give it a try."

They both settled back against the windshield. He pulled out his phone and held it high, taking a picture of them side by side. He didn't know if it was the booze that made the moment feel so special and made him feel like sobbing, or if this was really deserving of his emotions.

"You don't have a way to the airport," she suddenly said.

"I'm catching a bus." He told her the time. "It'll pick me up in some spot on the highway at the edge of town. Very old-world."

"You'll have luggage. I can at least drop you off there. And that will give you time to ride in the Mazie Ray Days parade."

"*Ride* in it?"

"Ava asked me to drive my car. Put the top down, I guess. I didn't know if I even wanted to see her again, but I think I'll do it. Kind of a nice wrap-up before I blast out of here."

"So let me get this straight. You're going to drive your car in a parade meant to commemorate a dead girl who isn't actually dead but is in fact driving a shiny red Cadillac in that very parade?"

"It does seem pretty strange when you say it out loud." She sounded even more into the idea.

"I have to be a part of this."

31

An hour earlier

Conrad Murphy sat in the back of the police car parked near the morgue and watched Olivia and Will LaFever walk away. Stupid outsiders. Really, you couldn't let anybody in. He'd known she was going to be trouble as soon as he heard she was in town. He'd had the feeling she'd be his downfall. Why in the hell had Bonnie called her? Curiosity, maybe. Her sister, after all. Or maybe she was trying to be a good mom for once and protect her remaining kid.

He'd never been sure if she'd had anything to do with any of it. Didn't want to know. Dealing with dead children was about all he could handle. The how and why were more than he could bear. To think his wife might have had anything to do with the death of his own kids was too much. Way too much. So he worked long hours. When he wasn't working and even when he was, he drank to kill the pain. Maybe to hide from himself. Because he was bad too.

When he'd seen Imogene talking to Will LaFever, he knew his life was about to change. She'd promised to never tell. She'd said she loved him, but he knew if it came out that they'd started having sex when she was fourteen . . . well, even the people of Finney might not look the other way. Especially if they found out Imogene wasn't the only minor he'd had a relationship with.

He hadn't meant to kill her. The idea had been to scare her. But then she'd started that stuff about how he'd promised to get a divorce and marry her, and how she'd had two abortions and still no divorce, and how she knew he was doing the same thing to other girls in town.

Even though she promised not to tell, he'd felt the change in her, the resolve. She'd seemed brave. And then she'd started screaming at him. Even though they were in the middle of nowhere, he had to stop the screaming.

The strangers, the outsiders, were to blame. Not him. Outsiders gave people ideas. Made them do things they wouldn't normally do, things that went against their nature. And so, even though it had broken his heart, he'd killed her. Fast and humanely. She'd only been scared for a minute and then it was over. Shortly after the deed was done, he got the idea to frame LaFever. Get the townspeople to hate him, make himself look like the hero. Olivia Welles would leave and that would be that. Everything would return to normal. It had been a good plan. Just not good enough.

32

Driving a red convertible in a parade wasn't something Olivia had expected to be doing when she'd flown to Kansas, but here she was. In a giant red Cadillac, moving slowly down the center of Main Street, the *In Cold Blood* guy from the airport beside her in the passenger seat, tossing candy to the kids lining the route. She never would have guessed this scene when she'd spotted him at the ticket counter that day.

Right now he was dressed in the same clothes he'd been wearing then. He was no longer attempting to blend in. No flannel shirt or cap with a yellow ear of corn on it. Today it was cargo pants, island shirt with straight tail and embroidery, the shirt she'd called his Hemingway. Sandals were back, all because he was going home. She'd been a little sad when he'd told her he was leaving, although not too sad because she'd be returning to LA soon herself. But it seemed like it should have been full circle, like they should have taken the same flight home.

Olivia was wearing a pair of denim cutoffs and a yellow T-shirt that said *Pie Farm* across the front. Behind her, sitting on the trunk area of the car, her feet on the seat, was Ava. She was smiling and doing that palm-out pageant wave, wearing a blue dress and white gloves. The side of the car where the graffiti spelled out *Go home* was covered with a banner that said *Grand Master.* Olivia wasn't sure what a parade grand master was, but it seemed the highest honor.

Bonnie was home. A woman who worked for Ava was staying with her, and there would be some mental health evaluations. It seemed unlikely that she would ever have custody of her remaining child, but time would tell. Olivia had made her own reluctant peace with Ava, at least for the time being since she had no idea what her own future held. She didn't want to leave Finney having any regrets. And there was something perversely satisfying about driving in a parade meant for her. Call it one final salute to the lie before the story went public.

If someone were to design the set of a small town, this would be it. Today especially, the weather was perfect. Blue sky, not too much wind for a change. People were everywhere, the sidewalks alive with smiles; adults and kids eating fair food, walking, chatting; babies in strollers; dogs on leashes; children laughing.

Olivia felt both connected and alienated. Weird to think this was her birthplace and she would never really, truly be a part of it. She wasn't sure if she wanted to be, yet she felt a pang and realized she wished she could stay a little longer. She didn't know where that feeling was coming from. Maybe a desire to learn more about her past or the yearning for something she could never re-create. Or just the charm of small-town life that would undoubtedly get boring after a couple of weeks. She tried to imagine herself living in such a place so far from the ocean and mountains and desert. The very idea made her uneasy.

In front of them were several girls in short white skirts. High school cheerleaders. Sometimes the parade would come to a halt so the girls could perform a cheer, most of their chants drowned out by the marching band directly behind the Cadillac.

But then the happy tone took a turn, and Olivia spotted a cluster of people holding signs and shouting.

Will shrank down in his seat, bracing his knees against the dashboard. "I knew I shouldn't have come."

"I don't think the signs are for you." One said MAZIE RAY DAYS and had a big dripping-red *X* over the writing. She didn't fully understand the gist of the protest until she read more of the signs.

STOP THE MADNESS. STOP GLORIFYING DEATH. STOP GLORIFYING DEAD CHILDREN. YOU ARE NOT OUR TOWN. THIS IS NOT WHO WE ARE.

"I think this might get hostile," Olivia said.

The words were no sooner out of her mouth than she saw a raised arm. "Duck!"

She expected a gun or an explosive device.

But no. It was a handful of excrement.

And it hit Ava square in the face.

That plop was followed by an immediate odor. Was it bad that Olivia's first thought was for the rental car? They were not going to be happy about this new damage.

From her limited experience, Olivia thought the odor smelled very much like the pig farm she'd driven past the other day. She spotted an opening in the crowd and decided to exit the parade down a side street.

"Don't," Ava said. "Rays don't run. That's not who we are."

A woman dashed up to the car. At first the occupants flinched. Until she handed a roll of paper towels to Ava. "Here you go, sweetie. I'm so sorry about that! Horrible people!"

Ava cleaned off her face.

"Go ahead and litter," Will said, seeing that she was looking around for a way to dispose of the towels. "I spotted some horses earlier, and I'm going to bet they have people who clean the streets."

"You're absolutely right," Ava said. "I made sure of that."

She threw out the white gloves that were no longer white, along with the towels. Then she continued to smile and wave to the crowd. And Will resumed tossing candy.

When they reached the end of the parade route, Ava asked Olivia to take her home. "I've got pies to pack up for the ice cream social this afternoon."

"You're coming back?" Olivia was surprised. Why would anybody do that to themselves? But then, she was an introvert and didn't understand a lot of what drove most people.

"Like I said, we don't run. And you should come too." She glanced at Will. "Both of you. There will be pie with homemade ice cream. And tonight, fireworks."

Will's eyes lit up when he heard the words *ice cream.*

"It's tradition," Ava said, "and I'm not going to let a few people ruin it for everybody else."

Olivia dropped her off at the farm, and then she and Will drove back to town, where he gathered his things and put them in the trunk of the car. They brought Dorothy along. The top was still down on the convertible, and the dog seemed to really enjoy the wind in her face as she sat on Will's lap, looking forward.

Olivia eventually pulled to a stop, puzzled. "Is this the place?" It was just the intersection of two highways, surrounded by cornfields.

"A fitting location," Will said.

They got out, Dorothy too. "This certainly wasn't the story I thought I'd be writing." He passed the leash to Olivia and unloaded his leather cases and backpack, putting them down near the highway. "And I certainly didn't think the day would end in pig shit."

"You know what they say. Shit happens."

"Always. It's been fun. A weird kind of fun, but fun. I'm going to stay in touch, and be sure to let me know when you're back in LA."

"I will. Maybe we can grab lunch somewhere." She spotted movement on the far horizon. "There's the bus."

"Okay, well." He held out his arms. She hesitated a moment before giving him a hug. She still wasn't sure she completely trusted him. But then again, she didn't really trust anyone.

She didn't leave until the bus had pulled away and she could no longer see him waving from the window. Then she headed back to town. It would feel lonely with him gone. And she wondered if they'd really ever see each other again.

33

The ice cream social was in a building on Main Street, where the sidewalks were wide and there was plenty of parking, across from the café where Imogene had worked. Half the street was blocked off with barricades. Past the barricades, a traveling carnival had set up. The Ferris wheel could be spotted beyond the trees. There was a Tilt-A-Whirl and a variety of the usual games. Most were things Olivia had only seen on TV. Never in real life. California had Disneyland and Knott's Berry Farm. The Midwest had traveling carnivals.

"You know the secret to really good apple pie?" Ava asked

She and Olivia were standing in the VFW hall. It seemed most small towns had such places for veterans to eat and drink. As Olivia understood it, the spaces could also be used for weddings and any kind of event that needed a kitchen, long and narrow lunch tables, and harsh overhead lighting. Ava had explained it all as they'd unloaded the pies that were now on tables that looked like they'd been around since World War II. And they probably had.

The walls were wood paneling, the floor, those suspicious squares that would most likely require abatement if ever removed. There were gold flag stands, one with the American flag, another with a Veterans of Foreign Wars, and one of Kansas. The Kansas flag was pretty, with a sunflower and a horse pulling a plow. The building had no interior rooms. Hence the word *hall*. Just one big space, the kitchen separated by a counter. This was where they ripped open bags of paper plates and dealt them like cards for quick serving.

Ava produced two knives and handed one to Olivia.

"I don't know," Olivia said. "Apples?"

Over the past several hours, Ava hadn't mentioned any of what had transpired yesterday at the house. And that was okay with Olivia. She'd decided to allow her this final bit of theater. Ava even seemed to have recovered from the public insult of the parade incident. In fact, she was almost buoyant.

"You're kidding, but it's actually true. Most people bake an apple pie with only one kind of apple." As Ava spoke, she cut a pie into six wedges. She was a pro, and Olivia marveled at the speed and neatness of the performance. Also the size of the slices. They seemed too big, but Olivia did the same, slicing and sliding triangles onto plates. A group of women appeared at the door, washed their hands at the sink, and joined them, grabbing knives and swirling and slicing pies as they chatted. Nobody mentioned the pig shit incident.

"I thought apples were just apples," Olivia said.

"Oh no, dear. And, horrors, sometimes some people don't even use baking apples."

Not a problem for Olivia, since she'd never baked an apple pie and never would.

"I mix varieties," Ava said. "I like to use the traditional Jonathan for the tart base, but I use something else like a Golden Delicious to add juice and sweetness. You don't need as much sugar that way, and it adds a better flavor. Kind of a surprising flavor."

More women arrived, these to make the ice cream.

It was a hive of activity, and everybody seemed to know their job. The machines, six in all, were plugged in and began churning away. Coffee was percolating in giant stainless-steel coffee makers that also looked ancient but impressive.

Ava had given her a crash course, so Olivia kind of knew the plan. People would file in the front door and out the back with their free dessert. Olivia wasn't much more a fan of vanilla ice cream than she was of pie, so she especially wished Will had been able to stay one more day to enjoy the homemade treat.

Once the pie slices were on plates, Ava removed her apron. Under it, like the first day Olivia had met her, she wore faded jeans. Today's T-shirt was pink, with the name of the town across the front.

She looked at her phone. "Oh no. I'm going to have to run home and check on Bonnie. Clara, the woman staying with her, says she's getting agitated. We have her locked in a bedroom. I know it seems terrible, but it was just for this event. To keep everybody safe."

"I'd better come too."

"No, stay here please. I'm used to dealing with Bonnie, and it will be easier if I go alone. If I'm not back when the ice cream is done, serve it without me. I'll get here as soon as I can."

"No problem."

She left.

Work continued.

Ava wasn't back when the ice cream was ready.

"We can't wait too much longer," one of the women fretted. "People are lined up down the block."

Olivia sent Ava a text to see if everything was okay.

No response, but if she was dealing with Bonnie, she might not have been able to reply.

She and several women scooped ice cream onto the prepped slices of pie.

Front and back doors were opened, and people began filing in one door and leaving through the other. It was obvious they'd done this before, knew the drill, and Olivia thought it was a nice gesture on Ava's part, especially after what had happened earlier in the day. She was definitely exhibiting grace under fire. Yet so many people were there, most likely due to all the recent events, that they ran out of pie.

"This has never happened before!" one of the women said.

People left in a huff. Others complained about how the recent publicity had brought too many outsiders to town, and now there wasn't enough dessert for everybody.

Olivia was fine doing without, but a few women came from the kitchen area, giggling, all holding white paper plates with a slice of pie and dollop of ice cream. They'd been smart, and when it became clear there would not be enough to go around, they'd grabbed and hidden theirs.

"This is my second piece," a woman said with a laugh. "I ate one before the ice cream was done. I think I deserve it."

Olivia sent Ava another text.

Pie is all gone!

Ava answered this time.

Fantastic! I hope you were able to get a piece!

Olivia just sent a smiling face in return. Let her draw her own conclusions.

"I don't feel very good," the woman who'd eaten two pieces of pie said. "I think I'm going to have to go home."

She'd hardly spoken the words when she reached for the counter like someone grasping at a ship mast during a storm. Then she staggered and ran out the back door.

"I'll go check on Brenda," a woman named Cindy said.

Minutes later, Cindy was back. "You guys, come and see this." She sounded scared.

Olivia and some of the other women stepped outside, shielding their eyes against the bright sun. Brenda was lying on the ground, under the shade of a nearby tree. Her face was ashen, her chest rising and falling rapidly.

"She said she wanted to go home, but I called 911," Cindy said. "They told me they'd get here as soon as possible, that they're getting a lot of calls." She pointed down the alleyway.

In the far distance, Olivia could see the top of a Ferris wheel turning, and she heard the music coming from the traveling carnival set up in the park where she and Will had perched on the picnic table. The calliope tune blasting from invisible speakers no longer seemed silly but had instead taken on the tone and soundtrack of sinister madness.

Brenda wasn't the only person on the ground.

There was a trail of bodies stretching from the VFW hall to the park. People lying on their sides, knees up, clutching their stomachs and moaning. Some were still upright, walking in small circles, looking at the sky, and talking to themselves as if hallucinating.

Olivia thought about how ethylene glycol was found in the tissue of the Murphy child. And she knew the early symptoms of the poisoning could come on fast, the main symptom being cramps and vomiting, but they could also include hallucinations.

The pie.

She ran past the people on the ground. Many were already connected to 911. She grabbed a phone from a woman and began talking to the dispatch operator.

"This is a mass poisoning," she said. "Probably antifreeze. We're going to need as many emergency vehicles as you can get from all the nearby towns."

She passed the phone back and heard more people, some on their knees, lying down, many calling in the emergency. She hurried through the crowd. Near the gazebo, she spotted a thicker throng of people still cradling plates in one hand and forks in the other.

"Stop eating!" she shouted.

A man looked at her with blank eyes, dug into his pie, lifted a forkload to his mouth.

With one hand, she smacked it away from his face. The pie and fork and ice cream went flying. "It's poison!"

"You crazy b—" He stopped cold and seemed to zoom in on something going on in his belly. The color drained from his face. He pressed a palm to his stomach and turned away.

To a man and a woman who weren't eating pie but looked as if they wanted to help, Olivia said, "Get garbage bags and start collecting this food!"

They nodded, glad to have direction, ran to the café, and returned with black garbage bags and more help.

Freakin' apple pie.

34

Even after spending most of the day wandering around town, Will still had two hours to kill until the airport shuttle picked him up to take him from Dodge City to Garden City. He found a bar that served food, sat down in a booth, and ordered fries and a milkshake while thinking longingly about the ice cream he was missing in Finney. He kind of wished he'd hung around. And yeah, he was worried about Olivia, leaving her in that godforsaken wasteland, but she could take care of herself and everybody else, including him.

As he dipped his fries in his chocolate shake, one of his favorite indulgences, he overheard a conversation from the next booth.

"You hear what happened in Finney?"

Will fully expected the person to launch into a story about the parade poop incident.

"They had an ice cream social, and people just started dropping like flies."

"Dead?" the guy across from the first speaker asked.

"Don't know. Just heard they collapsed, sicker than dogs."

"I'm never going to that town again. All those kids dying, now this. People say it's cursed, you know."

"I believe it."

"I take the long way around if I have to go to Wichita. Never drive through that evil place."

Nods of agreement before beer glasses were lifted to mouths.

Will pulled out his phone and checked social media. The first thing he saw was a video of the parade and Ava getting hit in the face. The second was a video of a person lurching, then dropping to the ground. People in the background were screaming and collapsing. It was pandemonium.

He tried to call Olivia. No answer.

He jumped to his feet. "I need a ride to Finney! Can anybody give me a ride?"

Several faces in the dark bar just stared at him. He opened his billfold and dug out some bills. Held them high in the air. "Two hundred dollars for a ride to Finney."

"Didn't you hear the news?" a woman said. "Something there is killing people. Nobody wants to drive to Finney."

"I'll go."

It took Will a little bit to find the person who'd spoken. A small, frail man in the far corner. The gentleman got to his feet and gripped the table. It looked like he might fall down otherwise.

"I ain't afraid of dying. I'll sure as hell drive to Finney for two hundred bucks."

Will put enough cash on the table to cover the cost of his food, then grabbed his belongings. "Lead the way."

The car was old. Like really old. Like something somebody had found in a barn excavation. Covered in dirt, mud dauber nests, bird droppings. The doors creaked when they opened them, and the interior smelled like mice and mothballs. But it actually ran, and old cars had big engines that could haul ass. The driver put the manual transmission through the gears, but after a few minutes on the highway, Will came to realize there would be no hauling ass.

"Can we go a little faster?" he asked.

"I said I'd take you to Finney, but I'm not gonna break the law. If you want me to do that, then I'll just pull over and you can get out."

"Okay. No, that's fine." Will leaned closer and looked at the speed-ometer. "I think you can go a little faster though. You're doing fifty."

The man scowled and pressed his foot down on the accelerator.

35

Bonnie hadn't meant to hurt anybody. Ever. It had just happened. The lady watching her, what was her name? Clara? Something like that. She'd been surprisingly fragile and easy to push down. Bonnie had expected more of a fight.

Right now, Clara was on the bedroom floor, screaming, one arm raised to shield herself from another blow. Her face was bleeding, and Bonnie thought her nose looked crooked.

"I'm sorry," Bonnie told her. "But I had to do it."

"Don't hurt me more!" the woman screamed. "Don't kill me!"

Now that was an idea Bonnie hadn't had. "Should I?" she asked. "I don't want you to call anybody."

"I won't, I won't!" Clara reached into her shirt, fumbled around in her bra, and pulled out a cell phone. She threw it across the room at Bonnie. It hit the wall and fell to the floor.

They were in the bedroom where Bonnie had been locked while her mother was at Mazie Ray Days. Clara had come in to bring her something to eat, and that's when the attack happened.

This was her mother's house, a home of great pain, great comfort, great confusion. Ava had been there recently, right?

Bonnie glanced at the ticking clock on the wall and the flowers in a vase. Some of the petals had fallen from the yellow blooms. Hadn't they been fresh last time she'd looked?

Wow. There were flowers everywhere.

As she cast her gaze around the room, at the flowers in the wallpaper, she saw where someone had peeled some of it off. On the wooden floor was a pile of curled paper scraps.

Interesting.

She stepped closer. Behind the paper, in an area of no paper, was some writing.

It said,

Don't forget about the baby.

Oh yes. The baby. *Her* baby. Just thinking about the baby caused her breast milk to release and drench the front of her shirt.

Bonnie had always been a problem. That's what her mother had told her ever since she could remember.

She tried to be good. She really did.

There was more peeled paper, and more messages.

Get out.

Run.

It looked like her handwriting, and yet she didn't remember doing it. But there was a pen on the desk nearby. And her nails were broken and the tips of her fingers bloody, maybe from digging at the wall.

Who did a person trust?

A message from herself to herself? When she'd always been a bad girl? When she couldn't manage to take care of her own children? When she was such a terrible wife that her husband had sex with their teenage babysitter?

He'd blamed that on Bonnie because she hadn't much cared for sex once the kids started coming. Just something to endure and get through. Like a chore as bad as cleaning the toilet. She shuddered.

A lot of things were her fault. The car-train wreck had been her fault too. She'd been jumping around on the back seat, and her mother had tried to reach her as she drove. Distracted long enough to drive over the tracks when a train was coming. Bonnie didn't remember it, but her mother had told her so and told her she'd keep their secret so Bonnie wouldn't be taken away. And after her father died, Bonnie was all Ava had left.

But Bonnie made more family for her.

Babies Ava could love.

Her prison bedroom was nice, with a TV and a really cozy bed. A padlock on the outside, not there now since the meal had been delivered.

She thought about lying down on the cozy bed. It would be so sweet to curl up there even though Clara was sobbing on the floor.

So much blood.

But then she heard a baby crying from somewhere far away.

Oh yes.

The baby.

She couldn't forget about the baby.

She bent down and picked up the phone Clara had tossed, and she stuck it in the pocket of her housecoat. It had big pockets. Under it, she was wearing loose pajama pants and a ratty old T-shirt. The T-shirt was purple, with a unicorn on it. Her other daughter had loved unicorns.

But she was dead now.

Henry was dead now.

Imogene was dead now.

But the baby, little Calliope, she was still alive.

The padlock was lying on top of a small table near the bedroom door. She slipped the curved shank in the hole. And locked the room up, turning the numbered dials to make sure it was secure.

But she had the feeling Clara wasn't planning on going anywhere. And where was Ava? Had she seen her earlier, loading the business van with pies? Had Bonnie helped her?

Yes.

"It will give you something to occupy your mind," Ava had said. Clara had been there too, helping. That was back in the old days of a few hours ago when Clara was well, without a broken face.

The baby cried again, and Bonnie jumped, remembering what she had to do.

She walked down the hall and found the room with the crib.

There was the infant, little Calliope, kicking her legs, crying, her face red and ugly.

Most babies were ugly. Just the truth. And the noise they made was enough to drive someone to drink.

Or worse.

She picked her up and bounced her in her arms, making a shushing noise. Surprisingly, the cries began to subside, then stopped altogether. Bonnie took the child downstairs, placed her in her padded travel seat, grabbed the handle, and went out the front door into the vastness of the world.

A white van was coming. Fast. It looked like a cartoon, flying up the gravel road, a long cloud of dirt behind it almost clinging to the ground to eventually disperse. Bonnie giggled, thinking about the van, as she carried the baby across the yard and into the cornfield.

She kept walking, and the child still wasn't crying. Odd about that.

She walked for a long time. So long and far that she might have reached the spot where she'd collapsed as a kid, when she'd left the wreck behind and had tried to follow her mother home. At one point, she couldn't go any farther. It was so hot, and the corn was putting off so much humidity. She did love that smell though.

And then she did what she had to do.

When she was done, she kissed the little girl goodbye, stood up, looked at the blood on her hands, then left the infant there, hidden by the corn.

36

Olivia drove eighty miles an hour.

The Cadillac's engine roared, and the steering wheel vibrated. She didn't slow down until she reached the turnoff for the Ray place. Quick right, and then the boat of a car fishtailed on the gravel. She regained control, let out a breath, leveled out at a steady forty, dust from the road billowing behind her in the rearview mirror, rocks hitting the undercarriage.

She made another right turn onto the dirt lane that led to the farmhouse. She hit a bump and was pretty sure all four wheels left the ground for a second. The car made contact again and kept going. She was beginning to love the Cadillac.

At the house, the white van with the logo on the side was parked askew in the grass, as if the driver had stopped as close to the front porch as possible. There was another car there too, a gray sedan of undetermined brand. The trunk and back doors were open, and she could see the front door to the house was open wide too.

Ava came barreling out, carrying two suitcases and various things tucked under her arm—clothing, a laptop—dropping some of her belongings on her way to the car. She hardly reacted to seeing Olivia. Tossed things in the trunk and passenger seat. Picked up what had fallen, one item being a can of spray paint.

"People in town are sick," Olivia told her. "Maybe dying."

"I heard about that." Ava slammed the trunk lid. "I had pig poop thrown at me, and I saw the signs people were holding. I'm not a popular person right now, so you know who they're going to blame. The pie maker. But you know who probably did it? Bonnie."

Olivia glanced around. "Where is she?"

"I don't know."

"I thought she was in a secured location."

"Me too. Clara, the woman I hired to watch her, was stupid. She opened the door."

"Where's the baby?"

"I don't know that either. I got here and found Clara locked in the bedroom. No Bonnie. No baby. My guess would be the baby is in the well."

Just casual, like it happened every day. And it was starting to seem that way.

Frantic, Olivia looked across the field to the grove of trees she'd visited previously. Why wasn't Ava doing anything to try to save the child? "What are we standing here for, then?" She raced toward the trees, ignoring the pain in her bum knee.

"If she's in the well, she's already dead, honey!" Ava shouted after her. "I don't even want to see it. Seen enough dead babies!"

Olivia ran across the driveway and through a field. She squeezed under and over rusty strands of barbed wire, plunged into the darkness of dense overgrowth, branches scratching her arms and bare legs. She spotted the old cement foundation of the house that had burned down years ago.

And there it was. The well. It seemed the vines, Virginia creeper, had grown just in the few days since she'd been there. She spotted broken branches and bruised leaves. Signs of passage.

Last time there had been no barrier other than the crime-scene tape, but someone had recently run strands of barbed wire around the area. Nothing that would stop a child.

Or a killer.

She slipped through the metal strands, snagging the back of her shirt, ripping herself free. She dropped to her knees beside the well, pulled out her phone, and turned on the flashlight. It was enough illumination to see the mossy stone walls of the hand-dug well. And, much lower, the reflection of water.

There was no body floating there, no arms or legs or clothing. She leaned forward, reaching her arm down deeper, shining the light.

Nothing.

She felt relief. But the child would most likely sink first and float later.

She heard twigs snapping behind her, then Ava's worried voice.

"Is she dead? I had to come."

"I don't see anything." Could she be there? Sunken in the water?

"Bonnie weighted the boy down with rocks," Ava said.

Nobody had ever mentioned that.

"You might not be able to see her." She let out a muffled sob.

They would have to call for help, but all emergency personnel were trying to save the lives of the people in Finney.

Olivia felt hands on her shoulders. She thought Ava was trying to coax her back from the edge. Motherly concern. That was until she shoved her with more strength than Olivia would have guessed she had. The women were strong around here.

Olivia tumbled forward.

Ava even helped with that, grabbing her legs so there was no chance of Olivia catching herself.

She tumbled down, arms outstretched, her phone cracking and flying from her hand to splash into the water. She grabbed protruding rocks, slowing her fall, until she hit water and plunged deep, headfirst, fully submerged.

Maybe *this* would be the sixth and final time she died.

37

Olivia played dead, holding her breath, clinging to stones so she wouldn't float and become visible. She looked up through the water and saw a beam of light.

Ava, checking to see if she was dead.

And then the light was gone.

Olivia surfaced, taking a deep breath but not a gasp, holding a cough, swallowing water, waiting. Once she hadn't heard anything for several minutes, she began the work of trying to get out.

The stones were wet and slick and covered with moss. She'd make it partway up, her foot would slip, and she'd crash down into the water again, waiting, listening, hoping Ava hadn't heard her. But Ava had her own agenda, which was to get away as quickly as she could.

Was she the murderer? Of all the children? Were they a team? Sometimes mothers and daughters killed together. And what about the train wreck? Had it really been an accident? And what about Conrad Murphy? Had he really killed Imogene? Or was he framed? Was this why she hated apple pie? Had Ava served her own children antifreeze pie? All this was tumbling around in Olivia's head as she tried to save herself.

Ava had walked all the way home that morning of the train wreck. She'd walked home and left two girls and her good friend in the car. Now, in light of this new revelation, Olivia could wonder if that had been intentional. Had she really been in shock? Or had she devised the whole thing, planned the whole thing? Or had it been a whim?

She'd approached the tracks, seen the train coming, decided to end all their lives except her own. Or maybe she'd planned to die too but had chickened out at the last moment.

There were long moments when Olivia felt like she couldn't do it, that she wasn't strong enough to get out of the well. But then, instead of trying to climb one side, she straddled her legs across the span of the wall, her feet on jutting round rocks. She reached above her, dug her fingers into crevices, and pulled herself up, inch after inch, carefully replacing one foothold with another and another.

Once she hit drier rocks, it went faster until she reached the well's lip. Careful, but in a hurry, she lurched forward until her stomach was pressed against the top, her hands reaching over the edge, touching grass, her feet pedaling like someone trying to get on a horse.

And then, a few more heaves and she was out, rolling to the ground, lying on her back, sky and trees above her. Her lungs burned, and her arms and legs shook uncontrollably, both from exertion and fear.

Olivia had died many times in her life, but apparently this wasn't going to be one of them.

38

Will gave his new buddy—his name was Charlie Morris—directions to the motel. They arrived to find the parking lot empty.

"Wait here." Will got out and ran to Olivia's room. He knocked. Dorothy barked from inside, but nobody opened the door. When he tried to peer through the crack in the curtains, he couldn't see anything.

He went to the office. "I need a key to room three."

"I can't just give you a key." Same young person who'd checked them in. But Will appreciated that she was doing her job.

"I came with her. You saw me."

"I can't give you a key."

"Have you heard about what's going on in town? Okay, how 'bout this? Come with me. Unlock the door. I just want to make sure she's not inside needing help."

The girl shrugged, grabbed a key off the wall, and together they walked to the room. She unlocked the door.

Olivia wasn't there.

Will hadn't really expected to find her, but Dorothy had knocked over her water and she was whimpering. He let her out, gave her a drink, snapped on her leash, and stepped back outside, closing the door behind him.

"You can't take the dog!" the desk clerk said. "Are you stealing that dog?"

"No, but thanks for your concern."

Once Dorothy was done peeing on a tuft of grass in a sidewalk crack, Will led her to the old man's car. She balked, understandably, and Will picked her up. He slid into the passenger seat, allowing the dog to perch on his lap.

"Let's check out Main Street." He pointed.

"I didn't drive you here to help you steal a dog."

"I'm not stealing a dog."

"Sure looks like you're stealing a dog."

"I'm taking care of the dog for a friend."

"Okay, but if you get arrested . . ."

"It'll be fine. Let's see if we can find her owner at Mazie Ray Days."

They couldn't get very close, because the streets were clogged with incoming and outgoing vehicles.

"Holy Toledo," Charlie said, observing the chaos from behind his steering wheel.

Will had to agree. It looked like a horror movie. People were scattered everywhere, lying on sidewalks, moaning, some clinging to buildings as if the ground were moving. Others just sat there. Not everyone was suffering. There were plenty of people assisting.

The unaffected people seemed to fall into two camps. Ones who were trying to help, and ones who were trying to get out of town as quickly as possible, adults holding their children's hands, some running with kids in their arms, moving toward a field where cars had been parked, everyone having expected a more pleasant outcome hours ago.

But really, he had to kind of agree with the protestors from earlier. Was death a good reason to hold an event? Especially now, with the more recent murder? Seemed pretty tone deaf, and a good time to give it all up and maybe just hold something to celebrate the town. Mixed up in all the terror of the day's new tragedy, along with a chance of a rising death count, were emergency vehicles, fire trucks, ambulances, police cars moving slowly forward, lights flashing but mainly silent, with the occasional single squelch when someone was in the way.

"Just pull over and wait," Will said.

"Not gonna wait. I'm getting out of this town. I should have listened to those idiots at the bar."

"I'll just be a minute."

"I'm leaving."

Afraid Charlie might take off with Dorothy, Will got out and grabbed Dorothy's leash, the dog jumping to the ground behind him. With Dorothy in tow, he sidestepped through the crowd. As he got deeper, he could see there was some semblance of organization. There were several people in orange glow vests wearing latex gloves, carrying black trash bags, picking up paper plates with slices of pie and melted vanilla ice cream. Dorothy moved to sniff one of the white blobs and Will pulled her back.

"Yeah, keep your dog away," a woman in a vest said. "We don't know if it's the pie or the ice cream."

"I'm gonna go with the pie."

There were cots set up under a canvas tent—a temporary field hospital. Good idea.

"Is that Murphy?" Will asked aloud, to nobody in particular.

A big guy in jeans and a T-shirt seemed to be giving directions to arriving emergency vehicles.

"Yeah."

The unexpected answer came from a woman walking past him holding several IV bags. "Nobody knew what to do, and somebody got the idea to let him out. Figured he'd run, but he's gotten things a little under control." She looked at Will. "Oh, you're the journalist." She seemed disgusted to find herself talking to him. Then she glanced over her shoulder, toward Murphy. "Personally, I'm okay with him. I'm not even sure he did it."

Will mentioned Imogene's DNA.

She shrugged. "Doesn't mean anything. People have sex. Innocent until proven guilty."

"What's going on with the IV bags?"

"It's the best way to treat ethylene glycol poisoning."

"Antifreeze."

"Yep. We started taking people to nearby hospitals. But then, since there are so many in trouble, Marshal Murphy decided it would be easier to bring treatment here unless someone was in crisis."

It made sense. Not Murphy, but the rest of it. "Have you seen Olivia Welles, or a red Cadillac?"

"No, sorry."

She continued on her way.

Will found someone at the VFW hall who told him Olivia had gone running to her car. "She's a main suspect," the woman said.

"What about the actual pie maker? Ava Ray?"

"She'd never do anything like that."

"Right."

Since Olivia wasn't at the motel, and it didn't look like she was in town, he decided the next place to look was the Ray farm, home of delicious poison pies.

With the pup tucked under his arm like a football, he returned to the dusty car, surprised that Charlie was still there. But when the old man saw him coming, he put the car in reverse.

"Hey!" Will ran after him.

The car stopped. The man put it in first gear.

Will opened the door and jumped in as tires spun and the car roared away.

"I figured you could drive faster if you wanted to," he told the guy.

"I just agreed to take you to town," the man said. "Now I'm involved in a dog heist."

"Just one more place," Will said. "It's only about five miles from here. Promise."

"Getting out of here is the best idea I've heard yet." He headed out of town toward the highway that would take them to the Ray farm.

39

Five minutes after not dying in the well, Olivia sloshed across a field to the driveway and farmhouse, leaving a trail of fetid water behind, her cutoffs and T-shirt heavy and sticking to her skin, her boots squishing and squeaking. But she only had one real thing on her mind: Where was the baby?

Ava's car was gone.

No surprise there.

The surprise was Bonnie. Ava had run off without her, leaving her free to enjoy the day. Or that's what it looked like, because Bonnie was dancing around in the front yard, eyes closed, arms raised, body swaying gently, her feet bare, enjoying the grass, as she seemed to be listening to some song only she could hear. Like some LSD-tripping Woodstock hippie from the sixties.

As Olivia got closer, she heard Bonnie humming, as if crooning and comforting herself.

The subtext of the scene: *Everything is going to be okay.*

But probably not, because it had never been okay, and Ava had just tried to kill her, and she was probably the one who'd tried to poison the entire town of Finney even though she'd blamed it on Bonnie. Someone threw excrement in her face, and that was it. Payback time.

Earlier, Olivia had marveled at the woman's grace under fire. What a fool she'd been two hours ago. In truth, Ava had been furious and had immediately hatched a plan to get as many people back as she could.

Olivia stepped closer, and still Bonnie was unaware of her presence. Olivia spoke her name and had to repeat it several times before Bonnie opened her eyes and quit dancing.

"Oh my," Bonnie said, finally seeing Olivia. "You look terrible." She staggered close, reached out. Olivia recoiled, caught herself, stopped, and let Bonnie gently stroke the side of her face. "You're hurt," Bonnie said. "Bleeding. And you're all wet."

At this point, anything that wasn't her death seemed like a win. And yet Olivia glanced down, saw the gash on her arm and another on her leg. A shiver went through her even though the temperature was close to ninety.

"And your poor hands too," Bonnie said. "All scraped. And those nails." She made a *tsk-tsk* sound as she shook her head. "So much dirt in those wounds. That's not good. They could become infected. We need to get you cleaned up." She reached out again.

With a hand that was caked in dried blood.

And now Olivia saw that both of Bonnie's hands were covered in blood. She felt a sob deep inside her belly but was able to stop it from escaping. "Where's the baby?" Olivia asked, trying to keep the terror from her voice. The sun was so bright. The sun shouldn't be so bright. All happy and shining and fake. So many lies here. So much evil.

"What baby?" Bonnie asked, her voice vague.

Olivia jerked her hand free of Bonnie's. "*Your* baby."

Bonnie spread her feet wide as if to catch her balance. Then she smiled, leaned forward, and put a finger to her lips. "Shhh. That's a secret."

"Tell me the secret."

She shook her head.

Olivia was done treading lightly. "Bonnie, where's the baby?" she asked, her voice stern, like a parent's. Or an older sibling. Meant to be obeyed.

"Safe. She's safe."

"What about the blood on your hands? Look at me. Listen to me. Where did the blood come from?"

"The baby is safe. The baby is hidden. Just like the other one."

"Hidden from whom?"

"My mom."

Maybe all the deaths *were* Ava. If so, poor Bonnie. Poor, poor Bonnie. Olivia thought about yesterday (Was that just yesterday?), when Bonnie had run from the house with her child. Had she been trying to save her?

"I'm not Ava," Olivia said.

Or was Bonnie's mind just blown? Had she killed her own children thinking she was saving them?

"I can see that."

"I wouldn't hurt your child. I want to help your baby. Maybe she's hungry. Maybe she needs to nurse."

"I wonder . . ."

Olivia didn't have her phone. It was in the well, probably shattered anyway. And a call to 911 would do nothing right now, when all available were occupied with the fallen in town.

"Let's go get her." Olivia knew the child was probably dead, knew it was probably too late, but they had to find her, regardless. "You trust me, remember?"

It was so hard to make the shift from Bonnie being the sister of Olivia's best friend to actually being Olivia's sister, flesh and blood. Which meant the baby was Olivia's niece. "You called me. Remember?"

"Oh yeah . . ." Her gaze wandered, then settled. She patted the octopus tattoo on Olivia's arm, appearing bemused and confused by it. But also fascinated, like someone who was high.

"You trusted me and wanted me to help you," Olivia said. "And the baby. That's why I'm here. Let's help the baby. Where did you leave the baby? I'll find her. You don't have to go." In case the child was dead, and she was afraid to see her. "Just tell me and I'll find her."

Bonnie frowned. She swayed.

Olivia grabbed her, helping to steady her.

Bonnie wiped the back of her hand across her brow and looked around. "It's so pretty here, isn't it? Don't you think so?"

"The baby. Where is the baby?"

"I don't remember."

"Think. Focus."

It seemed like she was trying. How much of her confusion was drug related? Had Ava been giving her more than what was prescribed? It seemed that way. She'd been flaky in jail, but she was off the charts now.

"I don't know. The medicine makes me forget. I think that's supposed to be good, right?"

"Okay, let's go in the house. See if she's in there."

"No, no, no!"

That made it seem likely.

Olivia heard a sound and looked up. In a bedroom window was a splayed hand against the glass. Behind it, a woman's bloody face.

Could this place get any worse?

"A car." Bonnie pointed and Olivia looked.

A large brown sedan was barreling up the road, the engine roaring. It barely slowed as it turned onto the dirt lane that led to the farmhouse. It lurched to a stop, dust flying. Engine was cut, passenger door creaked open, and Will LaFever stepped out.

"Oh my God, Will." Olivia was surprised to find just how glad she was to see him, but when she was surrounded by evil, creepy people, he seemed like the very best human in the world.

And it kept getting better. He had Dorothy with him.

Pulling Will behind her on the leash, the dog raced to Olivia, furiously wagging her tail, then ran to Bonnie and back to Olivia, unable to contain her excitement at seeing not one but two of her people.

"Wow," Will said, staring at Olivia. "You look like shit. Like impressively bad."

"Thanks." There was so much going on she'd almost forgotten about her adventure. "I was in a well."

"You fell?"

"Pushed."

He glanced at Bonnie. Olivia shook her head, and mouthed, *Ava.*
Will nodded and mouthed, *That bitch.*

"You look good though too," he added as if by afterthought.

The driver's door opened and a bent guy in a battered hat got out,
shuffled forward, then leaned against a front fender of his ancient car,
both hands on the curve of his wooden cane.

"That yer dog?" he shouted, his voice surprisingly strong given his
overall fragile appearance. Heroes came in many packages.

"Um." Olivia glanced at Bonnie. "Maybe. Bonnie here is the real owner."

"Okay. Just wanted to make sure this boy wasn't a dog thief."

Boy.

Will shrugged.

Unlike her, he was in pretty good shape considering his day, beginning with the parade followed by a bus ride and a day of travel. She
glanced at the old guy with the ancient car. And making new friends.

"I thought you were heading back to California," she said to Will.

"I was waiting for the airport shuttle, and people around me started
talking about what was happening in Finney. I was afraid you might
have been poisoned too."

"My loathing of apple pie saved me."

"I caught a ride. Charlie here was the only person willing to drive
into the unknown. Of course I paid him."

"Nobody rides for free!" Charlie shouted.

Dorothy lost interest in the two females and began sniffing the
grass, tugging Will away, moving with purpose across the lawn. Olivia
caught up to them. "Give me the leash."

Will handed it to her.

Dorothy continued to tug. Olivia unsnapped her restraint and let
her go.

The dog ran for the adjoining cornfield and vanished.

40

Corn was noisy. That was something Olivia hadn't known. But it made sense now that she was deep in the field. The leaves rustled and snapped. And they were sharp. And a lot taller than they looked from the road. She was wading through plants that were several feet above her head. It was easy to imagine a person being able to get lost for hours. Or days.

The ground under her feet was uneven, with a trough between the rows, and even though Kansas was experiencing a drought, the ground was damp, possibly from the massive amount of humidity being put off by so much green. Or maybe the field had been watered recently. She knew nothing about such things, and as far as she could remember, this was her first time in such a field. It was nothing like she'd expected.

She'd lost track of Dorothy long ago, but if she paused to listen, she could hear the dog moving. At one point, the sound stopped completely. Olivia called and whistled—and finally heard Dorothy coming toward her. She burst through cornstalks and shot straight for Olivia, racing down the furrow. But she didn't hang around long. She whimpered, wagged her tail, turned, and took off again.

Olivia hurried after her, the giant green leaves cutting her arms, adding to the lacerations from the well.

Dorothy shifted direction.

Olivia abandoned the easier path and squeezed between stalks of corn, the tassels dropping yellow pollen on her. She thought she'd lost

Dorothy again, when she spotted her far in the distance, facing away from Olivia.

Olivia ran again.

The dog bounded toward her for a few feet, then circled back.

And then Olivia saw it.

A baby seat, the hard plastic kind with a handle, had been placed between two rows of corn.

It was dark in the corn, yet a shaft of light fell on something metallic.

The distance from her to the carrier was maybe thirty feet. Olivia had no awareness of traversing that space. Suddenly she was just there, close enough to recognize Bonnie's state-fair necklace draped over the curved top of the white seat. She touched her own around her neck and her heart lurched.

The white handle of the carrier was bloody.

Olivia was afraid to look, knowing what she would most likely find, but she moved closer and forced herself to do what had to be done. With her heart slamming in her chest, she peered inside.

And there was the baby, completely still, leaving Olivia to fear the worst.

Dorothy barked and came closer.

She squeezed past Olivia's bare leg and pressed her nose against the baby's face.

The infant's arms jerked in a startled response, eyes opened, and she began to cry.

Olivia pulled in a shocked breath, then let out a matching sob of her own. She wanted to drop to the ground. She wanted to hug Dorothy. But the child, the child.

"Good girl, good girl," Olivia said to both of them.

She bent and carefully scooped the baby from the seat and cradled her in her arms. Olivia was aware of her own damp clothing, but at this point she couldn't worry about getting the baby wet. She unwrapped the blanket and checked the child's legs and arms and face and torso. No injuries. The blood wasn't hers.

Thank goodness.

The baby was wailing even louder now, scared of the stranger. The crying was a good sound, a great sound, and Dorothy seemed to agree because she was dancing at Olivia's feet.

Olivia heard a rustle and crashing of cornstalks, then Will burst into the little cleared area.

"I heard a baby crying." He looked at the bundle in Olivia's arms. "Oh my God."

"She's alive," Olivia said, tears in her eyes.

"Did Bonnie abandon her out here?"

"I think she was hiding her from Ava. She might have saved the child's life."

"But not if she'd never been found."

"Exactly." Had Bonnie done the same with the other children? Hidden them from Ava? Had she put Henry in the well to hide him? That seemed a little much, but with this bunch, who knew? The thought caused a fresh sob to catch in Olivia's throat.

Will picked up the carrier. "Let's get out of this swamp." They began walking back toward the farmhouse, single file, Dorothy at their heels. Olivia covered the baby with the blanket, shielding her as best she could from the leaves. Once they stepped out of the field, Bonnie ran to them.

"Is my baby okay?"

"She's fine," Olivia said. But she was not turning the child over to Bonnie. Instead, she handed her to Will and pulled Bonnie into her arms.

Sisters. Yes, hard to believe, but they were sisters. Together, they cried. And once the tears subsided, Olivia rubbed Bonnie's back and hugged her tighter. "You did the right thing." She looked across at Will, who was standing there both baffled and relieved.

"There's somebody up there," the man with the car said, pointing toward the house with his cane.

They looked at the second-story window. In all the baby drama, Olivia had forgotten about Clara, the person who was supposed to have been watching Bonnie.

"I hope she's okay," Bonnie said. "I didn't mean to hit her so hard."

"Well, she's not dead," Will observed. "So that's a win."

"I just wanted to get the baby to a safe place," Bonnie said.

Wouldn't call the middle of a cornfield safe, Olivia thought, but it really had been the only choice the poor girl had.

"I'll check on the ghost." Will started to move toward the house, then stopped and seemed to freeze. Everybody else heard it too. A sound, a distant boom, coming from what seemed miles away. Then the ground under them shook.

"Is this an earthquake?" Will asked.

"Over there." The old man pointed with his cane again, this time toward the far horizon. "Explosion."

They all turned to look, heads moving in unison, like sunflowers following the sun. It was a plume of black smoke.

41

Forty minutes earlier

Hands gripping the side of the well, Ava watched to make sure Olivia didn't resurface. When she was confident the girl was dead, she ran back to the farmhouse and her car. As she was opening the door, a movement across the yard stopped her.

Bonnie was emerging from a nearby field of corn. She had blood on her face and hands and, in true Bonnie fashion, was staggering and gazing at nothing.

Ava considered not leaving, weighing the pros and cons. Bonnie had helped load the pies. She very well could have tried to poison the town. And she might have killed Olivia too, pushed her in the well. Yes, that could work.

Ava also knew how easy it was to trick people, to fool people. She could start over somewhere else. Maybe a quaint little coastal town, where she'd open a bakery. She'd been squirreling away money for a long time. She liked the idea of a clean slate. Maybe she'd even meet a guy, get remarried, quit killing people.

Nah.

Ugh. Bonnie spotted her and was running toward the car, looking like some girl in a tragic historical and hysterical novel.

Ava got inside quick, closed the door, and started the engine. She put the car in reverse, turned, then slammed it into drive.

Tires spun, tearing up the grass. Bonnie screamed something and threw her the finger, a finger that changed into a pretend gun as she made a shooting motion at the getaway car. The girl really was a piece of work.

Having Bonnie demonstrating such disrespect gave new conviction to Ava's plan to just be done with them all. Bonnie, the pie factory, the town.

They'd miss her. They'd miss her story, the train wreck, the pies, Mazie Ray Days—all of it would no longer exist once she left. They'd miss her after she was gone.

But it was nice to be missed. Nicer than being hated and not missed.

She went flying down the lane.

In the rearview mirror, she saw Bonnie running after her. Then the girl stopped to stand and watch her go until she was obliterated by road dust.

Ava had a full tank of gas. It would be dark before she had to fill up. But she just couldn't stop herself. There was one more thing she wanted to do. Something she'd fantasized about doing for a while now.

She headed for the tracks. It wasn't that far out of the way. She could take back roads to the highway, then head southeast.

When she reached the death memorial, she pulled off the two-lane and down the steep incline to the small parking area with benches. Cut the engine and got out. She grabbed the white spray paint and walked to the granite monument.

She'd commissioned it with money donated by people in town.

She shook the paint can, popped off the top, and began writing.

The switch of long ago truly hadn't been Ava's idea. It had been Harold Welles's. He'd done it for his wife.

"She needs something to live for," he'd said.

And he'd also known Ava and her husband didn't have insurance or money. Dirt poor, they were.

"The child is going to need a lot of surgeries you won't be able to afford."

And so she'd agreed. And like people said about juicy gossip, she'd had no problem cultivating it once the seed was planted.

She'd always felt invisible in Finney. Just the wife of her then undead husband. Many people didn't even know her first name. Just Mrs. Ray. It was horrible to spend most of your adult life never being accepted by your own neighbors and your own community. Knowing she could live there forty years and she'd never be a part of it.

It weighed on her. It dug at her. It ate at her even when she told herself she didn't care what those people thought about her. Didn't care if she was never a part of any inner circle. If she was never a part of their lives. Never able to wear that aura that told people you were one of them.

But she *did* care.

It shouldn't have mattered. She'd always known it shouldn't have mattered, but humans wanted to be accepted by their own kind, by the people who shopped at the same stores, took their kids to the same schools. Whose husbands tilled the same fields. So what she discovered after the wreck was that there was a way to get in. And that way was sympathy. People rallied around, and they dropped the invisible wall that had been there. They welcomed her with open arms.

Once her child was "dead," people looked her in the eye, touched her arm in a gentle way, smiled at her. Gave her money for the monument. Invited her to silly things women did, like groups for sharing recipes. She and one of her pies had been featured at a farm-wife night, and everybody had raved. Many said she should sell her pies. They were *that* good.

That's when she got the idea to blackmail Mr. Welles. By then he was living in California, and it seemed the injured girl was on the mend, although still requiring surgeries. Ava even met him at a café in Colorado. A lonely spot partway between Kansas and California. He'd had the girl with him. Ava hadn't expected that, but she'd given her the stuffed animal she'd been saving for her. There hadn't been a flicker of recognition in the kid's eyes. That had bugged her a little. You'd think a kid would know her own mother, even on some cellular level. But the girl had taken the octopus and hidden behind her father's chair.

He'd passed Ava a thick envelope of bills, and that's how she'd started her business.

Once the local interest in her seemed to wane, she'd gotten the idea for Mazie Ray Days and the parade. And she began employing women in the town. They were grateful to her for giving them jobs, for helping to keep food on their tables. Suddenly she was more than a part of the inner circle; she was *queen* of the inner circle.

Then Bonnie started having babies. The first child's death was possibly an accident. Ava had never been sure. Maybe Bonnie was guilty. But it had recharged public sympathy for Ava and had reminded her of how much she thrived on that kind of attention, that kind of respect. And yes, even pity. When the attention began to fade again, she got the idea to do away with the second one.

It made sense. It was justified. Bonnie was a horrible mother. That was the truth of it. She really should have died that day of the train crash. Conrad was an even worse dad. The two of them should never have had kids at all. Their offspring were brats, embarrassing to take anywhere. The last straw with the third child had been when the boy dropped his pants in the middle of the sidewalk on Main Street and told a group of women to look at his worm.

Premeditated, but the train wreck hadn't been.

Ava guessed that's what you called it when you actually thought about doing something beforehand. When she rolled it back through her brain, it reminded her of one of those choose-your-own-adventure books. Where she started wondering what would happen if she did this. Or this. Or this. She'd liked the idea of just stopping the car on the tracks and walking away.

Like a dramatic movie.

It all made sense. It had been an awful day. At the fair in Kansas City, she didn't win a blue ribbon. She didn't even win a pale-green one, which was seventh place. Something shady about that. Like the judge had been slipped some money. It happened, especially at the state-fair level. And not going home with a blue ribbon for the pathetic half-eaten pie riding in the trunk wasn't even the worst of it. A couple of women from church came up and told her they were sorry about the divorce. And when Ava told them she didn't know what they were talking about, they got flustered and started spewing garbage about how Mack was leaving her for Florence Welles. The very person she was on the trip with. The mother of her daughter's best friend.

Oh, she'd had her suspicions. She'd even had her suspicions about their daughter. People were always commenting how the two girls could be twins. Like was the Welles child really her husband's kid?

So when she reached the spot with those famous railroad tracks that had killed so many people, and she heard that train coming, she wondered what would happen if she let it hit the car.

Her husband had liked to tell her she hadn't been right in the head since giving birth to Mazie. Doctors called it postpartum depression, and Ava was on medication, but nothing had helped. Her life sucked. She felt trapped. Medication wasn't going to change that. But because of the cushion it seemed to create, it made it easier for her to stop the car on the tracks and walk away. Because nothing seemed real. Everything was just her looking through a thick cloud at a world that felt fake.

And she had to be honest. Once it was done, she started to believe her own story and wonder if she hadn't been able to get the car started. If she'd flooded it, killed the engine by accident. If she'd tried to get the girls out, and then ended up saving her own life at the last second.

Sometimes she thought that was the way it really happened. And yet sometimes she enjoyed thinking she'd done it herself, on purpose.

She put the cap back on the spray paint, tossed the can in her trunk, slammed the lid, got back in the car.

The monument was in a low area, and she had to gun the engine to make it up the steep and short incline to the blacktop road. Once she was at the crest, the highest point, she paused the car long enough to look behind her to check out her work on the monument. She'd added the name Olivia Welles.

She laughed about that. Tossed back her head and laughed, then stepped on the accelerator. The car bucked forward, heading for the tracks, then came to a jarring stop, so abruptly it threw her forward against the steering wheel. She'd approached from an angle, and the tires seemed to be stuck. Maybe caught on the nearest metal railing.

She heard a train whistle. She turned her head and saw that single round light coming straight for her. The wooden safety arm came down and slammed against the top of her car so hard the vehicle rocked.

She put the car in reverse. Nothing. Forward. Nothing.

The safety arm kept lifting and dropping, smacking against the car roof as Ava watched the train barreling down on her at a high rate of speed, the horn bellowing in one long alert. Like that other time.

Everything went slow and fast.

She grabbed the door handle, tried to open the door, but the car was still running, and the door wouldn't open. Stupid safety features.

The train made impact.

She screamed.

Her last thought was hoping she'd at least poisoned the woman who'd thrown the pig shit at her.

Then the car, with its full tank of gas, exploded, sending flames high into the air.

42

They turned in the Cadillac at the airport.

The rental agent walked around the car, inspecting it, taking photos of the graffiti Olivia might or might not end up having to pay for. Then she and Will pulled their suitcases behind them into the building, Dorothy on the leash. She was small enough—about fifteen pounds—to travel in a carrier under the seat.

Automatic doors opened, then closed behind them. The two travelers stopped to look at each other. The end of a really weird adventure.

"It's been fun," Will said. "Well, except for Imogene getting killed. And the town getting poisoned. And you getting shoved in a well. And Ava exploding."

"Yeah, it kind of was," Olivia said. And it seemed like everybody had recovered from the poisoning, with hopefully no long-term damage. "I've never been crazy about pie, but this kind of sealed the deal."

"I get it. Look, I have a confession to make," Will said. "You were right. I did set my car on fire."

Olivia shrugged; it was pretty much old news.

"It was so stupid. I don't do things like that. It's not me."

"It definitely made me not trust you."

"Understandable. I had the idea that I needed to do things to drive the story. Make it bigger."

"I think it was pretty big already."

"But people like fires and explosions."

"You got one of those anyway."

Their seats weren't together on their flight bound for LA.

Dorothy was fine, although she got restless upon takeoff, possibly due to ear pain. Olivia removed her from the carrier and held her, sticking her back in the soft-sided case whenever the flight attendant passed. But Olivia eventually quit, and nobody said anything. The guy in the seat beside her occasionally gave the dog a smile, but for the most part he minded his own business.

Olivia had a window seat. She always got a window seat. Will was somewhere closer to the front of the plane. He preferred the aisle.

As the plane circled to begin the descent into LAX, Olivia saw the sun sparkling off waves in the ocean. She thought she recognized some of the skyscrapers in downtown LA, and she spotted the Hollywood sign. Her heart swelled. That was followed by a quick sinking of her stomach. Her surgery was very soon.

She planned to keep in touch with Bonnie. Discuss the sister thing eventually. And to be honest, she still wasn't positive it had just been Ava. But at least the baby was safe and under the care of the Kansas version of Child Protective Services.

There would be court hearings.

Someone had asked Olivia if she'd think about taking Calliope. At first her answer had been, *Hell no*. But then she began to give it more consideration. She hadn't mentioned the surgery to the child welfare bunch. She'd see what happened, see if she still existed in a week, then figure it out.

Ava had died in the explosion. *Gone where the goblins go.* But there were people in Finney who still rabidly defended her. One woman claimed Ava had been mistreated by her husband. Not only was he abusive, he'd been having an affair with Florence Welles. All hearsay, but it could very well be true. It would explain some things.

There were several offshoots to the Munchausen-by-proxy diagnosis. Olivia figured Ava would fall somewhere under that umbrella. Maybe at first she'd killed for the hell of it. But then, when the losses had gotten her attention and sympathy, she didn't want it to stop, so she started killing her grandchildren.

The plane landed. The pilot thanked the travelers for flying with them, announcing that it was a pleasant eighty degrees and hazy.

Passengers unfastened metal seat belts, and Olivia turned on her phone. A message from Ezra told her he'd be circling in his car, looking for her curbside. It would be good to see him again.

They disembarked. Will was off the plane before her, standing near the gate, waiting for them. Dorothy acted as if she hadn't seen him in years, jumping and wagging her tail. The humans laughed.

At the luggage carousel, they collected their suitcases, then moved away from the mob of people still waiting for theirs. In a more private area, Olivia passed Dorothy's leash to Will. He'd agreed to take care of her until Olivia recovered from surgery. If she didn't wake up or if she fell into a coma, she hoped he'd keep her for good. She hadn't mentioned that to him.

She bent and gave Dorothy a big petting, straightened, and put out both arms and hugged Will. They'd been an odd team, but she'd work with him again if the circumstance ever arose.

Feeling close to tears, she broke away. "Goodbye."

She'd offered to have Ezra drop him off, but the traffic between Will's location and hers could be bad this time of day or any time of day, so he was taking a cab. He and Dorothy moved to the public transport area, vanishing into the crowd. Olivia walked to the curbside pickup and departure.

It only took a few minutes for Ezra to pull up in his car. He jumped out, came around, and this time, unlike when he'd dropped her off, gave her a big hug, then pressed a bouquet of daisies into her hands. The hug was nice. So were the flowers.

"I missed you," he said. "Seemed weird here with you gone for so long."

"Less than two weeks."

"That's what I'm saying. A long time."

She'd forgotten what a feast he was for the eyes. Tall and thin, medium-tone dark skin, the most amazing Afro, and the most infectious smile. He smelled a little like weed, either from the few plants LA County allowed residents to grow or from smoking.

He glanced around and asked, "Where's the pup? I was looking forward to meeting the pup."

"Will is taking care of her for now."

"And Will. We talked on the phone a few times. I wanted to meet him."

"Hopefully that can happen. Maybe dinner at my place."

His face grew solemn as he took in the subtext of her words. *If the surgery goes okay.*

Then they were in his car, tunes blaring, windows down, heading toward her home in the Venice neighborhood of LA.

"I love it here," she said. That realization surprised her, because LA was a giant pain in the ass.

He nodded in approval. "I was afraid you might want to stay in Kansas."

"I did for about five minutes." She hadn't shared a lot of what had happened yet. "I have so much to tell you."

At home she went through her mail, where she found a priority package from Maureen. Inside, was a note.

After we talked the other day, I decided to go through some of your father's things. I've been putting it off, unable to even open his office door. I'm sorry, because I found this envelope with your name on it. I'm overnighting it to you at your home address. I have no idea

what it contains, but maybe it will help answer some of your questions.
Love, Maureen

Olivia put the note aside and pulled a long business envelope from the mailer. Her name was written across it. She slid a finger under the sealed edge, found and unfolded a letter. It was handwritten in her father's strong cursive style, yet with a bit of a tremble and hesitation, possibly due to his age and loss of fine motor skills, or nervousness about revealing a lie he'd carried with him for so long. As Olivia read his words, she could almost hear his voice in her head, and for a moment she was overcome with a deep sense of loss. Even knowing what she now knew, she missed him terribly. He was her father.

My dearest girl,
First of all, I want you to know that I love you. By the time you read this, you might already know everything I'm going to tell you, but you deserve to hear the full and true story from me.
I'd like to think my rash decision that night of the train wreck was heroic and unselfish, done for you and not me, but I think it was more about me, at least at the time. Although in the end, the lie we created allowed you to have your face and body restored as much as it could be. The alternative, Mack and Ava, with no insurance and no way to pay for your many surgeries, would have left you with a short life of misery and pain. I'd like to feel I spared you that, and I think I did. And I'd like to think your life with me was happy, at least for the most part. But everybody deserves the truth of who they are and where they came from, and the truth is that I was just your plain average coward with this part of your story.
I was never sure about the train accident. My wife, the one who died, and Ava's husband were having an affair. I

often wonder if Ava found out. Maybe there was an argument. Maybe Ava was distracted while driving. Maybe it was intentional. I don't think we'll ever know. And I'm sorry you and I lost contact over the years. I think I just couldn't face any of it anymore. But I do love you, and I hope you'll forgive me and maybe even understand my motives just a little. People are complex, and even now when I think about it all, I'm confused. I want you to have a good life, a full life, so please do that. You are smart and you are beautiful, and you are kind and fair, with a big heart. Somehow, you rose above the nonsense and became a better person than all of us. I'm proud of you. I've always been proud of you.

And I've always wanted to believe that there are no 100% evil people, that we are made up of layers and layers, and have many facets. But after all of this, I've felt a shift in my generosity toward those people who commit horrendous acts of violence and murder. I suspect Ava is evil through and through. I know she's your biological mother, but what happened, me taking you, making you my child, accidentally removed you from her presence, the presence of utter evil. Don't ever visit her. Don't ever try to see her or communicate with her. If you do, your life will be in danger. Of that I'm certain. And the girl, Bonnie, is just as bad as Ava, maybe worse. Don't trust her. Don't believe anything she says.

Olivia sat there a long time, holding the piece of paper in her hands. Then she folded it and closed her eyes. If she'd read the letter before going to Kansas, she would have thought her father had lost his mind. But now she knew otherwise. If anything, his warning wasn't strong enough. And what about Bonnie? She wished he'd gone into some detail because she still had no proof of anything. And he might have gotten all of his information from Ava, an untrustworthy source.

She slid the letter back in the envelope, knowing she'd pull it out and read it many times.

The next day she updated her will, most everything going to Ezra other than a generous donation to her local dog rescue. Got her affairs in order, as they said. She wrote a few letters to people who'd meant something to her. She left the packet of everything on her desk for Ezra to find, next to the flowers he'd given her at the airport.

She'd lied to him about the date of her surgery. She just didn't want to face anybody and didn't want them to know how risky it was, thinking Ezra, especially, might try to talk her out of it. So the next morning she took a cab to the hospital, and a few hours later she was wheeled into surgery. As she drifted into unconsciousness, she thought about how maybe none of her life had been real. Maybe she would wake up a child in Kansas. Or maybe she wouldn't wake up at all.

43

Her first awareness of maybe being alive was a pulsing roar. In the depths of her mind, she pictured a tornado swirling outside her bedroom window, and she imagined herself in a house flying through the air.

"I'm glad you're awake," Ezra said.

He was standing near her bed. He had a small beard that she didn't remember. It looked good though. And was that gray in his hair?

"I wanted to tell you about a case you might be interested in. In Kansas. A woman who might be killing her own kids."

No, no, no.

She closed her eyes, but had she ever really opened them? She felt herself falling away, heard people shouting for a crash cart, then oblivion again.

There was an odd sense of time, but not like time in the real world. She felt the earth turning, the sun rising and setting, remembered fields of corn and giant white wind turbines. Lies had been told, and she'd made a new friend. She had a sister and another dead mother. Life, death, were certainly strange. At one point, she felt something warm and wet on her face and heard a soft whimper.

This time she opened her eyes to what seemed like the for-real world. The brightness of the room almost blinded her. Someone noticed her blinking and shut off the lights. It must have been another dream because Will LaFever was standing in the hazy hospital room. And he was holding Dorothy.

"I snuck her in," he said with a smile.

And then she realized it had been Dorothy's nose she'd felt against her face.

She asked how long she'd been out and how the surgery had gone. Her voice was a rasp, and she briefly put a hand to her throat, questioning with her eyes.

"They recently removed the breathing tube." That came from Ezra, who was there too. He picked up her hand. "Squeeze my fingers three times if you have all your marbles."

She squeezed three times even though she wasn't fully convinced of her mental state.

"You had us scared," Ezra said, glancing at Will. "You've been out for a few days. The surgery went well, but you had a lot of swelling. They lowered your body temperature and induced a coma until it went down. And we've just been waiting."

It seemed she'd finally gotten that coma. "I had a new dream," she said. "A different dream. And you were both in it."

They looked at each other and smiled. Will put Dorothy down on the bed, and she curled up next to Olivia. "I dreamed we were in Kansas, and someone tried to poison an entire town. Isn't that bonkers?"

"Oh, that really happened," Will said.

"And I dreamed my father switched me with his own dead daughter."

"That happened too."

"And did Ava explode in a car-train collision? And were parts of her found stuck to a stop sign?"

"Not sure about the stop sign, but she's gone," Ezra said. "Very gone. But here's the big news. You have officially earned more dead cred."

"How many times did I die?"

"Twice."

Okay. She wouldn't count the well, because she hadn't flatlined. "So now I have seven."

"I have some catching up to do."

Will looked from one to the other. "What are you guys talking about?"

"How many times we've died." Olivia smiled; she wasn't sure why, after such a dark conversation, but she did.

"We're going to go now and let you rest," Ezra said.

Will picked up Dorothy, tucked her into his baggy shirt, which she now guessed he'd worn just for that purpose, and they left. And she slept a healing sleep.

A week later she was home, in bed, taking it easy. Flowers and plants were still coming, some, surprisingly, from people in Finney, but also from Coco and others Olivia had worked with in the past. The good news was that Olivia's surgery had gone better than anticipated. The plate had been removed and replaced with something that would no longer set off metal detectors, and hopefully no longer give her headaches. Her surgeon even told her she might regain some of her old memories because the plate had been pressing against an area of the brain that stored long-term memory.

She'd had a few flashes of things that might or might not have been recollections of the past. They'd been like photographs that were there and gone before she could fully grasp what she'd seen.

Conrad Murphy was in jail, had confessed to killing Imogene, and would certainly go to prison, if not worse, but he was awaiting trial. Bonnie's baby was still in foster care in Kansas. And even though Olivia's surgery had gone well, her recovery was expected to be long. She got dizzy and weak, and exhaustion would come out of nowhere, washing over her several times a day. She was in no shape to take on an infant, although she'd agreed to start the application process to become Calliope's legal guardian.

Bonnie was still being evaluated. But, with her history, even though she'd most likely been trying to save her own child, it was risky and hard to say what the future held. Very sad if Bonnie had never harmed any of her children, but she'd harmed Clara, and it was possible her first child had died due to negligence.

Olivia didn't know if she'd ever go back to Kansas. She felt a little sick when she thought about it, but the old compulsion was still there. With Olivia's prodding, Will had decided to work on his story and had even mentioned the possibility of returning to Kansas to do more research. She might go with him. And see the baby. Maybe even see Bonnie and relate the story of their relationship in person.

44

Two weeks later

Mornings were hard. Really hard.

Hard to get out of bed. Hard to make it downstairs.

In her cozy kitchen, Olivia turned on the flame under the kettle with a click and whoosh of ignited gas. She was reaching for the tea tin when her phone alerted her to a FaceTime call. She checked the screen.

Bonnie.

The tin slipped from her fingers and hit the floor.

She hadn't talked to Bonnie since Ava's death. But here she was, smiling sweetly at her. It looked like she was calling from the kitchen of her farmhouse. Seeing her there made Olivia reach for a chair and sit down. She still needed to explain how they were related, but she didn't know if she had the energy to deal with such a heavy and emotional conversation right now. Just getting through the day was still a struggle. And she couldn't quit thinking about her father's warning.

Bonnie asked about her surgery, and they talked about baby Calliope.

"I'm being evaluated by a psychologist, and I met with the court system," Bonnie said. "I hope they let me see my baby soon! I'm still pumping my breast milk and freezing it. I took some to the foster family, but they wouldn't let me see her." She made a sad face, then asked about Dorothy, who was still at Will's but might be coming to Olivia's soon. Will had brought her over a couple of times, and she seemed to approve of the place.

"She's a good dog and is being well taken care of," Olivia said.

She noticed Bonnie was still wearing the state-fair necklace. She reached for her own, then recalled she hadn't put it back on after her surgery. Maybe she wouldn't. She had two now. The one she'd gotten off eBay and the one she'd taken from the morgue.

And then the weirdest string of images flashed through her head.

The three girls (she planned to keep thinking of herself as one of "the girls") were standing next to a machine where they'd bought the necklaces. Bonnie was there, screaming and stomping her feet, a real spoiled brat, demanding a necklace of her own.

"We don't have enough money," had been the friends' explanation. But in truth, Mazie and Olivia hadn't wanted her to have one. The necklaces had been for them, for their special friendship.

"Where did you say you got your necklace?" Olivia asked now.

Bonnie touched the chain at her throat. It was shiny and new and looked like it might have been replaced at some point. "At the fair. All three of us bought one."

If anybody knew about the unreliability of memory, it was Olivia. Not only in her own life, but in her job as a detective, she'd been involved in a few cases of false memory. Kids were especially bad when it came to the accuracy of recall.

Even though she wasn't 100 percent certain, she pushed her narrative. "We only bought two." She stated it as if it were the truth. And it very well could have been.

"No, it was three."

But Bonnie was acting uncharacteristically nervous, fingering the medallion as if it were a talisman and might bring her luck. Or save her from a lie.

It was risky, because Olivia's flash of memory or vision or whatever it was might not be real, but she planned to vocalize how she suspected the night of the accident had played out.

"After the wreck," Olivia said, "when we were unconscious and injured, probably hanging upside down from seat belts—at least that's what I've always heard—I think you took one of the necklaces because you didn't get one at the fair."

Bonnie made a face of mock surprise and pretend outrage. Then she puffed up, became defensive. "So what if I did?"

Her reaction didn't prove anything more sinister, and it certainly was no proof of Bonnie harming her own children, but it said a lot about her character. Because what kind of person stole a necklace from a dying sister or friend?

"And you put it on," Olivia said. "Funny to think about how it scarred you." Olivia felt the side of her own face, in the spot where Bonnie had been burned.

Bonnie mirrored the motion, touching her cheek lightly, then seemed to realize the seriousness of the accusation. She dropped her hand.

In that moment of clarity, Olivia knew she must never let Bonnie visit Calliope unless there was a layer of plexiglass between them. It was too risky. If they were allowed in the same room, Olivia could imagine Bonnie playing the heartbroken-mother card, crying, asking to hold the infant. Then . . . Well, Olivia didn't want to think too much on how fast Bonnie could kill a helpless child. But right now, with Ava dead after trying to poison the whole town, any previous suspicion had shifted away from Bonnie, and people in town were sympathizing with her once more. She was a victim like everybody else. Or so the new narrative went.

"Mom always talked about you," Bonnie said. "About how you were her smart daughter." This was delivered with an obvious amount of sibling jealousy.

So Bonnie knew about the switch. It sounded like she'd always known. Olivia thought back to the initial phone call and the haunting words Bonnie had spoken that day.

You did die.

The comment had seemed nothing but a fanciful reference to the beginning of Olivia's deaths. Now she saw it for the revelation it was. The truth hidden in plain sight. But why had Bonnie reached out to her in the first place? Had she hoped Olivia could prove Ava guilty? Or had Olivia been a lifelong curiosity?

"I was the dumb one," Bonnie said. "Ava was proud of how she'd pulled it all off and saved you. But you know what? I always wished you'd died that night." She let out a mean little snort. "With you out there in the world, living a great life . . . Well, I couldn't compete with that. I was never good enough. My kids were never good enough. My husband was never good enough. And you never even knew the pain you caused me! The hurt. I think that bothered me as much as anything. That you didn't even know or care."

Enough of poor, poor sociopathic Bonnie. "Did you kill Henry?"

"It was Ava! She hated my kids! They weren't good enough for her."

"What about the other two? Did you kill them?"

She didn't say anything.

"What about the antifreeze?" As planned, the other children had been exhumed. Antifreeze had been found in both of them. Three for three.

"I just did what Ava told me to do," Bonnie said. "Like a good daughter."

It wasn't a confession, but maybe it was enough to get a search warrant with the right judge.

"You have to help me get her back," Bonnie said.

That must have been why she'd called.

"Come on, Mazie. We're sisters. Blood."

"I won't help you. And don't call me Mazie. I'm Olivia Welles." She refused to be stripped of the only identity she'd ever known.

The angel face changed. It became harsh lines, the circle on her cheek an angry red, her lips pulled back from gritted teeth. "You bitch!"

"Ah, there's the Bonnie I was looking for."

The teakettle began to whistle.

"Goodbye. I'll be in touch." *Or not.* Using her thumb, Olivia ended FaceTime. Then she called Coco Sandoval with her new suspicions.

Three hours after calling Olivia, Bonnie heard tires on gravel, followed by a knock. She opened the farmhouse door to find a cluster of uniformed state and local officers, one of the locals being Darlene, Conrad's sometimes partner. Was that a smirk on her face? Sure looked like it. A woman Bonnie had never seen before held up an official-looking paper. "We have a warrant to search your property."

45

Two months later

Olivia stood on Venice Beach facing the setting sun, one foot in the sand, one foot on her knee, hands high, palms together as she attempted the tree pose. She wobbled a little, then caught herself. Held the pose. She was still healing, and she'd been told it could take a year or two until she was back to 100 percent.

"Dorothy is better at beach yoga than we are." Will was trying to talk while wobbling even more than Olivia. They were side by side, Dorothy chilling behind them on a blanket after working off some zoomies in the packed sand.

The humans were both barefoot, dressed in T-shirts and loose pants. Olivia's hair was coming in dark brown and straight, now about an inch long, much of her head covered with the white beanie Ezra had given her. Life was moving slowly, and that was fine. She'd read some of Will's true-crime story—he was about one-third of the way done—and it was good. She was proud of him.

And then there was the baby.

Olivia hadn't wanted her to stay in foster care, but an unexpected ally had appeared in the whole dilemma—Maureen. She and the girls, adults now, had come to see Olivia, and Maureen had voiced interest in caring for the child, maybe even adopting her. Calliope was with her now, in Northern California, and Olivia planned to visit soon.

Poor kid. A blood test had found antifreeze in her system too, and a search of Bonnie's home had resulted in a refrigerator full of evidence. Breast milk laced with ethylene glycol. Could there be anything less maternal? And now Bonnie was in prison awaiting trial. It was interesting to think that if she'd never called Olivia to begin with, she might have gotten away with killing her final child. She might have had more children, with Conrad or someone else, and continued killing. A Ray family tradition.

Olivia and Will did a few more easy upright poses, then settled on the blanket with Dorothy, near a mysterious picnic basket Will had brought. Will opened two beers, passed one to Olivia, then both leaned back on their elbows to watch the sun finish sinking into the ocean.

"Dying seven times is enough," he said out of nowhere, but with a concern that had obviously been on his mind. "It's plenty. Nobody needs to die more than seven times. Promise me you'll stop dying."

She'd been surprised by how much of a mother hen he'd been throughout her recovery. Both he and Ezra had hovered over her, run errands, cooked, driven her to and from doctor appointments. She didn't know what she'd do without them. "Okay. Just for you."

"Good. Oh, I almost forgot." He reached into the picnic basket. Like a magician, he pulled out a pumpkin pie in a shallow metal pan. *Ta-da!* He removed the cellophane, all of this activity being viewed with intensity by Dorothy. She wasn't extremely food motivated, but she had certain things she liked.

Will handed Olivia a real fork, not a plastic one. "I know you don't like pie. I thought maybe the crust could be part of the problem, so I made this one with graham crackers. Oh wait. Hold this." He passed the entire dessert to her. Then, as if by more magic, he plucked a can of whipped cream from the basket, pulled off the red cap, shook the can, and, moving his hand in a circle, shot a massive amount on the top of the pie. Done with that, he added a glob to his finger and presented it to Dorothy.

She licked off the cream with enthusiasm.

Then he dug out a fork for himself.

"Go ahead," he said. "Take the first bite."

She tried to remember if she'd ever eaten pumpkin pie. Not that she could recall, but it didn't cause the same aversion as apple.

"Go on. Try it."

"Why is this so important to you?"

"I guess I want to get you over the pie thing. I want us to enjoy pie together." He laughed at that revelation.

"Okay, here goes." She loaded the fork and raised it to her face, closed her eyes, put the bite in her mouth, waited to be grossed out.

It wasn't bad.

They both stuck forks in the pie. Together, they ate several more bites, then Will asked, "So what do you think?"

"I'm surprised. I thought I'd hate it, but I like it. A lot more than I expected." Realizing the double meaning of her words, and that they could apply to the way she felt about him, she smiled and winked.

He laughed, getting it.

For the first time, Olivia felt like this might be her real world, and Will, as annoying and imperfect as he was, might end up being a life-long friend. To paraphrase *The Wizard of Oz*, it wasn't the journey but the interesting people you met along the way.

ABOUT THE AUTHOR

Photo © 2018 Martha Weir

Anne Frasier is the *New York Times*, #1 Amazon Charts, and *USA Today* bestselling author of the Detective Jude Fontaine Mysteries, the Elise Sandburg series, and the Inland Empire novels. With more than a million copies sold, her award-winning books span the genres of suspense, mystery, thriller, romantic suspense, paranormal, and memoir. *The Body Reader* received the 2017 Thriller Award for Best Original Paperback Novel from International Thriller Writers. Other honors include a RITA for Romantic Suspense and a Daphne du Maurier Award for Paranormal Romantic Mystery/Suspense. Her thrillers have hit the *USA Today* bestseller list and have been featured in the Mystery Guild, the Literary Guild, and as Book of the Month. Her memoir, *The Orchard*, was an *O, The Oprah Magazine* Fall Pick; a One Book, One Community read; and one of the Librarians' Best Books of 2011. Visit her website at www.annefrasier.com.